AF251699

Archangel Crusader

Vijaya Schartz

BLUE
PLANET
BOOKS

Glendale, Arizona
www.blueplanetbooks.net

BLUE
PLANET
BOOKS

Glendale, Arizona

www.blueplanetbooks.net

This is a work of fiction. The characters, incidents, and dialogues are products of the author's imagination and are not to be construed as real. Any resemblance to actual events or persons, living or dead, is entirely coincidental.

If you purchased this book without a cover, you should be aware that this book is stolen property. It was reported as "unsold and destroyed" to the publisher, and neither the author nor the publisher has received any payment for this "stripped book."

BLUE PLANET BOOKS Inc.
4619 W. McRae Way
Glendale, Arizona, 85308
(623) 780-0053

ISBN   1-930501-02-1

First Edition
Printed in the USA - 2000

Only during the tenth century
did illustrators start representing
angels with wings…
In truth, they never had any…

*To all the Archangels
who made this book possible,
To the unsung heroes
of my everyday life,*

*To my husband, Dan,
with love and gratitude,*

And to Michael...

PROLOGUE

Navajo reservation
Thirty-four years ago

Behind the blue Ouachita Mountains, the sunset bathed the reservation in cool shadows. Sitting cross-legged on the ground of the sacred cave, the one with sienna drawings of coyotes and rattlesnakes on the walls, Maria faced the warm circle of rocks. The light of the flames caressed the copper skin of her bare breasts and her flowing black hair as she swayed to the rhythm of her monotone chant. Tonight, the young girl braved the spirits alone with only White Eagle's talisman for protection. The arrowhead on a leather thong around her neck prevented evil intrusion from the Great Snake. Hopefully, the Great Spirit would grant her secret wish.

After sprinkling dry cedar twigs among the embers of the central fire, Maria poured water from a calabash onto the fiery rocks. Steam hissed and bil-

Vijaya Schartz

lowed, filling the cave. Mellowed by the peyote pipe, Maria surveyed the clouds that changed shape and color with the incantation. She expected a vision.

There, yes, there... A gentle spirit had come. His blue radiance filled her with serene rapture, as she felt enveloped by the song of angels. When the vapors condensed, Maria welcomed the loving presence and closed her eyes, heavy with peaceful oblivion... Losing track of the ritual, she surrendered to the blue light, sinking deeper into nothingness, well being, love... Ever so gratefully...

Archangel ⚔ Crusader

CHAPTER ONE

Philadelphia, present day

"Eh Blondie, two more pitchers!" a tall customer yelled over the music, slurring the words, while the three heavyweights at his table nodded approval.

At the bar, Michael Tanner nursed his bourbon, observing the room through the smoke. "You have to be bad just to have a good time," blared the country song in the background, though he could hardly hear the lyrics above the din. The young waitress in cut-off jeans and western boots smiled at him and he smiled back. Michael knew her by sight only. The girl was new, just a kid. In a few years, his own daughter would be old enough to wait tables. A frightening thought.

"Coming right up!" The girl loaded the tray and wove her way around the tables, straight and sassy, flaunting firm breasts through a white peasant blouse.

The big man watched her every move. Hold-

Vijaya Schartz

ing the tray high above her head, she pushed the ashtray aside, but he seized her wrist and pinned it to the table. "I bet you don't wear a bra under that flimsy shirt," he snarled.

The young girl blushed. "Let me do my job." She struggled to free her hand while balancing the heavy tray on the other.

Michael didn't like the big Yankee who'd sneered at his southern drawl earlier. He couldn't let that cur bother an innocent girl, so he started toward the table.

"You can't fight me, Blondie!" The man leered. "Don't look for the bouncer, he went to take a leak. Why don't you show us your tits?" The Yankee grabbed her waist.

The girl dropped the tray with a cry. It crashed to the floor, glass and beer scattering the sawdust on the concrete. The man's paw on the girl's breast closed and ripped her blouse. She screamed.

Michael pushed himself between the girl and the man. "You need a lesson in good manners!"

"No ignorant Southerner will teach me anything!" The Yankee aimed a fist at Michael's face.

Michael stepped aside, avoiding the impact. When three heavyweights joined the fight, the bouncer tried to intervene, only to find himself buried in chaos. A punch missed Michael's left ear. Applying a ju-jitsu move, he sent his opponent to the floor, into broken glass, sawdust, ashtrays, and cigarette butts. The bartender reached for the phone while the waitress, disheveled, rather nude and pale in her torn blouse and cutoffs, cowered against the bar, protecting her small breasts.

Archangel ✠ Crusader

Through the orange light, a booted foot flew to Michael's face. He caught it in mid air. A sharp twist to the right and his opponent's shoulder smashed a table, breaking it in two. A beer bottle sailed through thick haze and shattered on the heavy wall mirror, cracking it.

The kaleidoscope of jeans, cowboy hats, silver buckles, spurs, back kicks, sweat, and blood, made Michael's adrenalin pump faster. He felt happy as a fish in cool water among the toppled tables and chairs, in the smell of whisky and stale cigar. Although past thirty, tonight he felt eighteen, as wild and passionate as ever.

When Michael leapt onto the bar to get a better view, his long hair caught the breeze from the ceiling fan. A smoky reflection in the cracked mirror revealed his tall stature, chestnut hair, good shoulders, strong jaw, high cheekbones, and strikingly blue eyes... A hard body from packing lumber and driving nails all day.

His balance, he'd acquired from walking on catwalks, scaffolding and ladders, and a few beers and bourbon on the rocks didn't upset his timing by much. That son-of-a-bitch stepfather, who taught him martial arts as a kid, would be proud.

There was the muscular Yankee. Michael jumped down and headed in that direction. Blocking a strike, he dodged a chair, kicked another out of the way then leapt over a table. The man had cleaned up one side of the room and stood, waiting.

Michael felt the Indian half of his blood stir. He feinted to the right then threw a left punch to the chin. The target moved just in time to avoid the blow and

Vijaya Schartz

sneered back. Mad as hell, Michael nevertheless controlled his anger. He turned as if to walk away. Another feint. In a blur, he kicked high and hard, left heel connecting with the man's face. A jawbone cracked. The Yankee tumbled down and slid all the way back through the open front door.

The lights went out. A cold draft chilled the place as an eerie silence fell. Michael stopped moving and listened. Darkness hovered like a disquieting presence. A shadow reflected in the mirror, and his heart stopped for a second. When he looked around, dim light returned and the bar came back to life. Michael tasted blood. It was dribbling from his brow, although he felt no pain and did not remember being hit. Front row, an oblivious drunk stared through the smoke screen in a daze.

A siren sounded in the distance. Michael had to get out before the police arrived. He could ill-afford getting caught, even in a simple brawl. Too many similar incidents already tainted his record. Who'd take care of his family if he went to jail? He headed for the restrooms, discreetly exiting through the back door. He needed a drink.

Ignoring the nip in the air, Michael ran up the dark alley and headed for the white Ford van with ladders and lumber on top. Sirens blaring, a flashing red and blue motorcycle entered the passageway.

"Damn cop!" At the brink of panic, Michael heard a loud whisper.

"To your left!"

To the left, he glimpsed a narrow opening between two buildings. Michael dove into it and flattened himself against the wall, hardly daring to

breathe. Sweat chilled his hands. The police motorcycle drove by without slowing down. Michael let out
a sigh of relief.

A strange music startled him. He turned to
meet blinding blue light... Blinking, Michael protected
his eyes with one hand while his vision adjusted. In
the blue halo, he faintly distinguished a frail silhouette. His jaw fell open.

"What the hell?" Michael scratched his head.
The blue being was gone, but a voice echoed in Michael's mind: *Do not thank me, Son.* No one stood
there. He stared at an empty spot.

It took Michael a few seconds to realize, or
rather to doubt what he'd just seen. Or had it happened at all? Although sober now, he felt hesitant to
take the wheel.

Maybe he should see a shrink. What if Dave
was right and all these years of carousing finally
caught up with him? But hell, if you let go of booze
and women, what would be left in life?

Listening for any sign of pursuit, Michael
reached the white van. The Ford Econoline fit his
needs. He'd just had the wrinkles ironed out of it, and
the new white paint made it look clean. He stepped
inside through the sliding door.

Michael rummaged in the tool chest and caressed the steel barrel of a sawed-off shotgun. He
picked up an empty can of Pepsi, crushed the flimsy
aluminum with one hand then threw it in the recycle
cardboard box in the back. Since Veronica still
worked the graveyard shift, he felt in no hurry to get
back to a lonely bed.

When Michael turned on the ignition, the radio
blasted loud country rock. He winced, lowered the

Vijaya Schartz

volume and turned the dial until he heard Bruce Springsteen. On the drive home, the empty streets of Northeast Philly glided past the windows. Letting a patrol car slide by quietly, Michael slowed down to resume speed on Roosevelt Boulevard. All the lights switched to green on the main artery.

"*Michael, stop*!" a voice blared in his mind.

Startled, he jammed the brakes and smoked the screeching tires. A front tire blew up.

Out of the darkness, a black Mercedes crossed the intersection in front of him, against the light, without even slowing down. The ruthless vehicle with dark windows, all lights off, vanished silently into the night.

"Holy shit!" That was close... Michael hadn't seen it coming. What madness was this? Why did he slam on the brakes? Thank God he did. His heart thumped, and sweat streamed down his back as he looked around, shaking. Michael stepped out of the van to check the damage. "Damn!" The flat was beyond repair.

Frustrated, Michael threw the keys on the ground and ran sweaty fingers through his hair. Of course, he had no spare. Since the nail in the Lumberyard yesterday, there had been no time to get it fixed. Dejected, Michael sat on the curb, feeling the chill from the concrete crawling through his jeans.

A cold mist started to fall, forming halos around the yellow mercury lights. Michael shoved his hand in the pockets of the sheepskin vest. In the haze, he caught a glimpse of a blue light, a frail silhouette. He rose and called out. "Eh! You! Yes, you!"

Archangel ⚔ Crusader

The blue opalescence was floating away and Michael had to break into a run, trying to catch up with it. The fog thickened. Michael stopped and, except for the pastel glow of the nearest streetlight, he could not see a thing. As silence enveloped him, he wondered whether to pursue the elusive light or return to the van, although he wasn't sure in what direction that might be anymore. The gray blanket had become quite opaque.

Blue brightness caught Michael's eye deep in the cloudy veil. Was it coming back? Yes, that was the light, with someone inside... Not quite human in shape, bluish, with a big head and huge dark eyes. A luminous aura surrounded him while celestial music permeated the air.

Michael felt cold. A sense of dread seized him when he realized the precariousness of the situation. If this were not a hallucination, he could be in danger. Assuming a defensive stance, Michael let his childhood ju-jitsu training take over. The being looked small and moved gracefully. Michael felt he could take him if necessary.

Through the fog, the blue man advanced at a slow, even pace. The sheer intensity in the big dark eyes made Michael forget to breathe. He gasped then steeled himself for the impending assault. A surge of adrenalin coursed along his spine, prickling the base of his skull. Was this an alien? He'd heard stories but never believed them. Would he be abducted?

The being raised one arm. When a strange vibration like the sound of many distressed cries assaulted his eardrums, Michael panicked and

Vijaya Schartz

launched himself onto his attacker but hit an invisible wall and fell down. Scared as hell, wondering what struck him, Michael picked himself up and tried again. This time, however, he felt as powerless as if restrained by a straitjacket.

Paralyzed, Michael couldn't move a muscle or even speak. Sweat rolled down his forehead. He felt like a sitting duck. A metallic taste lingered in his mouth. Reacting to the determination in the alien's bearing, Michael stared back, hid his fear, and waited for some kind of explanation. He refused to give in to intimidation.

When the disturbing sound amplified, Michael clenched his jaw, eyes closed against the sensory aggression. Images surged unbidden on the screen of his mind. In the blink of an eye, he relived a fight on the reservation when he had enjoyed using his superior training against some Indian brothers. They called him the white man because of his looks. Few of them knew he had Navajo blood.

Michael saw the loathsome stepfather of his abused childhood, felt the hurt from the beatings, the anger, the frustration, the desire to kill the tyrant. How he loved and hated his pretty Indian mother, Maria, a slut who let it all happen. Falling to his knees, unable to control the tidal wave of repressed memories, Michael felt warm tears stream down his face.

The blue one had not moved. Standing in the powerful light, he just stared, expressionless, like a machine performing a duty. Michael felt the vibration change. Immediately the pain subsided, replaced by a feeling of well being, love, and compassion.

Archangel Crusader

Pure soprano voices sang in a chorus. Michael saw himself very young, his mother demonstrating how to throw knives and hatchets. His daughter, as a toddler, innocent and trusting, laughed happily in his arms. His young brother, smiled with understanding. Veronica looked upon him with love in her eyes, no obstacle breaking the harmony.

The visions stopped abruptly. Michael felt emotionally and physically drained while the voice in his mind spoke again. The thin blue lips did not make any words, but the message came loud and clear:

"In a short time, you have become a man, my son, albeit an imperfect one. Should you want to claim your birthright, I would gladly welcome you among us. I hold the answers to all your questions. I can help you. I also need your help to influence your people. Should you choose to join us, however, you will have to change."

The short silence that followed felt like an eternity. The strange being observed Michael still bent with exhaustion, then went on.

"Already your neural pathways are opening to allow access to your paranormal abilities. Soon, you may have total recall, see the past, the present and alternate universes. You may heal diseases, perform miracles, speak foreign languages. You will read other's minds, anticipate their moves, influence objects and people by thought to a great degree.

There is danger in what I offer, but if you do not accept your destiny, billions may die in the struggle that will surely come. With my help, you can fulfill the prophecy and change the course of events.

Vijaya Schartz

There is little time left and much to do to prepare. You can reach me anytime you choose. I will await your answer."

The communication ended abruptly. When the light disappeared, the blue being vanished and the fog dissipated. By the time Michael realized he had survived the ordeal, he could see Roosevelt Avenue. The white van waited only a few yards away. The air had cleared, crisp again, without any trace of mist.

CHAPTER TWO

Shaking his head, Michael tried to make sense of the incident but couldn't. He picked up the keys and looked around. Nothing moved. No one stood anywhere near or far. Curiously, the damaged tire looked inflated, intact, and firm against the pressure of his boot, so he climbed in and turned on the ignition. His overactive imagination had probably made it all up.

Never would he touch a drink again. Michael had a hard time separating illusion from real life. His brain did not function right anymore and the hallucinations and nightmares were becoming worse. Something else puzzled him... The blue stranger had worn no clothes at all!

During the drive home, he tried to erase the incident from his mind. It hadn't happened. It couldn't have. The blue light, however, felt somehow familiar. It brought back unsettling memories.

Vijaya Schartz

Fifteen years ago, his newborn son and teenage wife had died during birthing. He'd been mad, blaming the Almighty. It wasn't fair. They were innocent. He remembered lying in bed, wide-awake with anger, when a blue light blinded him, and he levitated. While he lay, paralyzed in mid air, a voice had boomed. *"No, Michael. It is not my doing."*

Had the voice come from inside or outside Michael's mind? Had he been scared? No. Thinking back, he'd been irate, helpless, manipulated by forces he could not explain. He'd felt uncomfortable. Most of all, he disliked not being in control.

Michael parked the van in the back of the rowhouse, stepped out, and opened the door silently, careful not to wake up Jennifer. The child always seemed aware of his slightest move as if she read his mind. He pushed open her bedroom door on the second floor and walked to the bed. Jennifer slept snugly with Shadow, the huge black and white cat. The feline raised its head at Michael's familiar step.

"Sleep tight, angel." Michael kissed his finger, touched his daughter's forehead then left the room.

How many times did he tell her not to sleep with the damn cat? But the truth be told, he understood her need for comfort.

The quiet house smelled of freshly baked apple bread, a new recipe Veronica favored these days. It was her place. He counted on her to help raise Jennifer, soon to become a beautiful teenager. Michael did not keep his hopes too high, however. Women had come and gone in his life, and Veronica, although he loved her deeply, may be no exception. He could see signs of fatigue in the fabric of their relationship and wondered if his life would ever change.

Archangel Crusader

The next afternoon, back from finishing a re-modeling job, Michael dropped the blue beer cooler on the beige carpet. Making a face, he removed the dirty band from his soaked forehead then shook his long hair, streaked by the sun with light golden tones. "Honey, I'm home!"

Veronica, tall, lithe, auburn hair neatly pulled in a bun, came down the stairs and flashed a hurried smile. "Oh, hi, honey. I was just leaving." She gave him a quick kiss and checked the pink uniform in the full length mirror by the front door. "There's food in the Fridge. Are you hungry?"

"Hardly... I'm thirsty, though."

"I'd better hurry." As she gave him another peck on the lips, Michael tried to seize her waist, but she retreated. Green eyes sparkling, she said, "That'll have to wait. Work first, then play. Okay?" She blew a kiss and turned to leave, but she faced him again, serious this time. "You look strange to-night. Anything wrong?"

"No, I'm fine. A little tired, that's all... Run off or you'll be late."

Veronica only smiled.

Forcing a grin, Michael scratched his head. His timing always stunk. He watched the door close then sunk heavily onto the blue velvet sofa. Big hands explored the cushions. "Where's the damned thing? Jennifer! What did you do with the remote?" He found it and winced. It stuck to his fingers.

"Hi, Dad, I thought I heard you." Jennifer came down the stairs bare-footed in a white T-shirt

Vijaya Schartz

and purple shorts showing lanky legs. Her big green eyes lit up in a candid smile.

"You watched TV again instead of doing your homework! You can't fool me, kid." Michael tried to look stern but couldn't. Hell, how often did he do what he was supposed to? "Tell you what, I'll forgive you if you get me a cold beer..." As she stared but didn't move, he added, "What are you waiting for?"

Jennifer scurried to the kitchen while Michael turned on the news. When the refrigerator door opened with a thud, she called from the kitchen. "Can I have the last piece of cake? There's just a little bit left."

"Uh? Oh hell, why not. Go for it, kid." If he could have his beer despite the harm it did to his brain, she could have chocolate cake.

Jennifer returned from the kitchen, a plate in one hand and a can of Coors Lite in the other.

Michael took the beer and popped the tab. He'd sworn never to drink again, so he'd only have one. "How was school today?"

"Boring." Jennifer licked her fingers.

"Oh, I wish I had a boring day at school." He looked at her plate. "Holy Moses! Are you going to eat all that? I thought you said a small piece?"

"I can eat it all." No doubt she could when it came to chocolate.

He gulped half the beer. "Give me a bite."

"I thought you didn't like chocolate!"

"Goes well with beer." He took a forkful. "Umm! Good stuff... Can I have another little piece before you finish it off?" He smiled mischievously before taking a huge bite.

"Dad! That's a big piece!" But she laughed. He liked that about Jennifer. She held no grudges.

He chewed with exaggerated gusto. "What can I say, I have a big mouth. And since you're up, go get me another beer." He turned his attention to the television screen and switched the channel. One more beer couldn't hurt.

Jennifer came back and handed him the beer. "Can I sit in your lap, Dad?"

"You're getting a little heavy for that, kid, but how can I resist those beautiful eyes?" He treated her like a woman, always had. It made her feel important. That way she didn't resent his girlfriends as much. There had been so many before Veronica since his teenage wife and son died. Jennifer's mother had been one of them...

Jennifer jumped on his lap and spilled the beer.

"Goddamn, girl! You have been doing that since you were four!" He brushed the wet couch. Was she doing it on purpose? She knew he always kept his beer on the right side. Even as a toddler, she would come straight at him and spill it. "Go get me another one."

Jennifer hurried to the kitchen and back, handing him another can with an unsteady hand. "I'm sorry Dad. I didn't do it on purpose, I swear."

"Yeah, yeah, I know. Come give me a hug." He kissed her on the forehead. "You know, if you become as pretty as your mom, with these big green eyes, I'm going to have to lock you up, or make you wear braces or something, before you turn thirteen."

" Was she pretty, my mom? Why don't we have any pictures of her?"

Vijaya Schartz

"Good question. I think Krystal burned them."

"I never liked Krystal, and she sure didn't like me."

"You never liked any of the women I brought home."

"Veronica's okay... Do you think Penny is in heaven?"

Michael braced himself. Why did kids always have to bring up painful memories? Little Penny... Krystal's daughter, not his but close enough. He couldn't stand children's suffering. "I'm sure she is up there, Jen. Why do you ask?"

"Kids at school... They say heaven doesn't exist." There was a short silence. "Penny would be eleven now... Why did she call you Dad? You were not her dad."

Michael smiled sadly. "No, but I was there for her, so I was kind of her dad since he wasn't around. I always wondered, were you jealous of Penny?"

"A little bit, I guess." She closed her eyes, as if with guilt. "She always got everything she wanted."

"That's true... But since she had cystic fibrosis, we knew she was going to die, so we tried to make her happy."

"I know... She really loved you. Just before she died, you were the only one she wanted to see... Why?"

"She knew I loved her too. She wanted me to die with her so she would not be alone up there."

"Is that why you tried to kill yourself, Dad?"

"I don't know, love... I really don't know." Why did kids ask the darnest questions? "But I know that if I'm here today, it's because of you. You're what's keeping me alive, like a guardian angel."

Archangel Crusader

Shadow the cat appeared in the hallway and jumped in his lap. Michael petted the big furry head.

"Are you going out tonight, Dad?"

Michael recognized the emotional blackmail. "I don't know. Maybe. Anyway, it's your bedtime."

"Dad?"

"What is it?"

"My mother... You told me I looked like her... I know she was doing drugs and stuff, but you told me that when I was old enough to understand, I could see her. I think I'm old enough now. I would really like to see her."

Michael wasn't ready for the anger that swirled in his chest. He thought he'd dealt with it long ago, but he still resented the runaway junkie. "Damn! Girl, you never make it easy for your old dad, do you? I don't even know if she wants to see you..." Hell, he didn't know if she was still alive.

Jennifer frowned as if the thought of rejection had never occurred to her.

Michael forced a reassuring smile. "But you're right. Even though I still want you to be my little girl, you're probably responsible enough now." Jennifer was growing fast. "I'll tell you what. We'll make a deal. I'll call Dave and find out where she lives and how she's doing, if that's so important to you."

Jennifer broke into a radiant smile. "Oh, Dad... I thought you'd never let me see her. I always wonder about her. Thank you, Dad. I love you." She threw herself in his arms, scaring the cat away.

"Wait a minute... I make no promises...but if she's clean, I let you see her."

"That's all I ask, Dad." There were tears in her eyes when Jennifer turned and started up the stairs.

Vijaya Schartz

"Sweet dreams, honey. I love you," he called to her retreating back.

"I never dream."

"Sure you do, you just don't remember."

"I love you too, Dad." Jennifer disappeared up the stairs.

Now she wanted to see her mother, as if his life wasn't complicated enough! How long could he keep his family together without losing his mind? Deciding he had better stop drinking for the night, Michael went straight to bed and promptly fell asleep.

CHAPTER THREE

The crimson glow of the dying star bloodied the devastated landscape of the red planet. Underground, in the circular sanctum at the heart of the secret city, green flames crackled on the sacred stone in the center of the checkered floor while the smoke released a bittersweet scent.

In a quiet shuffle, hooded silhouettes in long silver capes filed in orderly ranks along the smooth white wall to their appointed places in the temple. In unison they struck an eerie tune, high-pitched and punctuated by hisses, rattles, shushes, and clucks.

As the vibration of the shrill notes intensified, hollow claps paced the harmony of the chorus with dry consonance. In alien words, the chant spoke of Krastinios, son of Lufriec, who would soon fulfill the prophecy and open a new world for his people. An electronic gong

Vijaya Schartz

reverberated, changing the tone of the unfamiliar music.

Meanwhile, in a thick rain forest of Central America, concealed by the vines invading every crack of the venerable stones, the ruins of a long lost Mayan city stood among the songs of multicolored birds. There, lurked a threatening presence.

Oblivious to the tropical stench of rotting vegetation, scaly patches of brown and black slithered up the collapsed steps of the truncated pyramid. The huge anaconda flicked its purple tongue and climbed with purpose, answering the call of the strange symphony. When it reached the sacrificial stone stained with ancient blood, the snake coiled up at its center, basking in a pool of sunlight. Content, the reptile then veiled its eyes.

When the vibration escalated in intensity, the birds stopped singing. A chilly wind rose, blowing the vegetation away from the gigantic Mayan sculptures. Stone statues of plumed serpent-gods decorated the corners of the temple.

While the alien chant gathered power, the anaconda smiled in its sleep. Black strands of hair unfolded, smoothed, lengthened and straightened at the head of the sleeping snake. As if obeying the same tide, the green forest cover receded further, revealing more and more of the Mayan architecture.

The creature on the top platform uncoiled and thickened, changing shape. Ex-

tremities grew where there were none before. More swelling and bulging of skin and muscles occurred. Slowly, a roundish head formed under the length of jet hair. Protrusions and depressions appeared under the skin, sculpting brows, eye sockets, nose, lips, chin. Bones strengthened and lengthened. Hands and fingers grew out of human limbs. The scaly skin smoothed and warmed, taking on a healthy, tan glow.

For a moment, a beautiful male body lay there, naked and clean. All the vegetation vacated the stone structure, and the man now lay peacefully in the morning sun while the chant praised the birth of Krastinios. As the man turned in his sleep, for an instant the reptile lingered, but it was only an image, a lifelike tattoo occupying the whole back and muscular shoulders of the stranger. The snake still breathed under the human skin.

The naked man seemed to revel in the alien chant, as if it gave him pleasure. When he sat up, luminous brown eyes opened to the morning light, and graceful hands felt the tight skin of his face. As the man looked down, a black garb of supple leather dressed his body.

Krastinios tied the long shiny hair neatly into a ponytail, sprang up, looked at his hands with wonder, flexed long fingers, stretched lithe muscles, and smiled with satisfaction. He then started the descent of the pyramid's ninety-one steps with the easy grace of a jaguar, a voluptuous bounce in his stride.

Vijaya Schartz

The alien chant stopped abruptly.

On the red planet, the ritual ended. In perfect order, the sect members shuffled out of the temple. The green flame in the center took the shape of a small reptile, which slithered silently away on the smooth checkered floor. The last silver-clad silhouette turned for a final look, pushing back the hood from his head. Huge, menacing eyes peered out of the alien face of a scaly reptile, straight into Michael's soul.

Michael screamed. The draft from the open window cooled his sweat.

"Wake-up, honey, it's only a nightmare." Veronica's gentle fingers stroked his hair.

He jumped. "What? Oh boy! You scared me. Something terrible is happening."

"You were having a dream. It's over now. You're all right," she said as if trying to calm a child.

"No, it wasn't a dream. It was real. I was there..." Michael shuddered at the memory. "I could smell the stench, feel the breeze, the unnatural cold. I was there, and that monster marked me. I can feel it. Something evil was born before my eyes, and it's after me."

"Tell me about it."

"I'm not good at talking."

"You're better than you think, if you'd only try."

"But this is insane... I must be going crazy. It doesn't make any sense. How could you understand?"

"You underestimate the capacity of love, Michael. I bet I can understand anything. Try me, really... Try me once, please." Veronica flashed him the expectant eyes he never could resist.

In the faint light of daybreak, Michael propped himself up on a pillow and painfully proceeded to tell Veronica about the hallucinations and dreams of the past few days. While she listened quietly, he recounted everything as he remembered it, describing every detail, including the proposition of helping the blue being. When he was finished, a pale sun shone through the open window.

"Do you think I'm crazy?" Michael concluded.

After a long silence, Veronica's analytical mind took over. "Either you're hallucinating, and that's scary enough, but there probably is some available therapy... Or else, this is really happening. What a frightening thought! I know you wouldn't lie about something like that. But imagine for a moment that this is for real... What will you do? That blue being wants you to help..."

"No way... What could I possibly do?"

"You are very resourceful." She sat up straight.

With the morning light playing in her hair, Veronica mentioned their plans to escape an eventual disaster, the survival packs in the garage, the motorcycle ride across the country to the log cabin in Oregon, how they would find water, grow food, watch out for each other.

"I wish it was that simple." Michael scratched his head. "But this would take someone who can deal with the political crap, someone with connections

Vijaya Schartz

in high places, someone with a good reputation, a clean police record. Not me!"

"What about the powers they told you about? Wouldn't they make almost anything possible?"

"Look what it did for Christ... His miracles took him straight to the cross. Thanks but no thanks. Besides, I would have to shape up, change my ways. You know how hard I tried... I never could."

"Maybe all you need is a cause. You always dreamed of becoming a hero. This could be your chance."

"I couldn't do it even if I wanted to, not alone, and I'd never ask for help. Me, make a contribution to the world? What a joke! I don't even like most of the people in it. Besides, since it's confession time, I'm scared." Michael paused for a second and looked at his girlfriend for reassurance.

Veronica touched his shoulder. "I've never seen you scared before, but I'm here, and I love you."

"I know..." Michael couldn't shake the dream. "I don't like that pretty boy born of a snake, not a bit. Krastinios... The name sounds familiar. And the snake-monster with the silver cape... Lufriec, that's it, his name was Lufriec! If that creature exists, I'd rather not face him. He gives me the creeps. I'll never forget those eyes, that scaly face and forked tongue as long as I live." Michael felt better now that he'd admitted to his fear.

Veronica stroked his hair gently. "Gee... He must be something. Still, if my life depended on it, I would rather have you in charge than a stranger." As Michael fell silent, she went on. "Now, I understand why you want Jennifer to meet her mother so soon.

You believe that if the world comes to an end, she may not get another chance. I love your generosity under all that gutsy pride." She smiled warmly.

Michael reached for Veronica and drew her close. They always slept in the nude. As he felt her warm skin under the sheet, she smiled, green eyes glittering in the ray of sunshine sweeping the bed. Whether or not she believed his story did not matter right now. She trusted him and Michael felt stronger for it.

His desire hardened when Veronica caressed his hair, locking his head in a long, soft kiss. Michael's hands traveled along the smooth back, firm buttocks, and long, shapely thighs. The perfume released by the heat made his pulse race. The strength of his grip extracted a soft moan then one calloused hand probed the secret moist place between her thighs, the other fondling hard nipples.

"Oh yes..." she whispered urgently, "Now... Please..."

"Please what? You've got to tell me or you get nothing," Michael teased.

Veronica reached for his aching member and firmly pulled it to herself, wrapping her legs around his waist. Michael groaned feeling hot silky moisture surround his hard extremity, delighting in the musky scent.

"You're cheating," he protested, all the while driving hard into her.

"Whoever told you that life was fair?" Veronica retorted. But she stopped talking, her small cries turning into groans that could be heard half a block away.

Vijaya Schartz

Michael enjoyed feeling her pleasure. He held out as long as he could but finally succumbed to bliss. In a mighty roar, he collapsed on her bosom, sweaty and exhausted, smiling contentedly.

Veronica laughed in a broken voice. "I hope the neighbors have their windows closed."

"If not, I hope they enjoyed it." Michael laughed.

"I like it when we talk openly." Veronica sounded serious. "So often I feel that you're pushing me away... It hurts. I wish we could always feel as we do now, without hurting each other."

"Yeah, I know what you mean... I feel good, too. Maybe we should trust each other a little more." Michael tried to make it sound light, but he meant every word. "Maybe I could change a little, surprise you, make you proud of me."

"I would like that." Veronica's clear smile warmed up the whole room.

"I promise to give it my best shot." He kissed her forehead, hoping he didn't lie.

"I love you, Michael Tanner," she whispered softly.

"I don't know what I would do without you." He embraced her, answering her pleading green eyes. "Let me make love to you again, without rushing it this time..."

* * *

That afternoon, driving home on Verree Road, Michael felt sick. The dark stranger from his nightmare had haunted him all day, a malevolent smile on his face. Now, something felt very wrong.

As he neared Red Lion Road, the traffic slowed to a crawl. Police cars and ambulances rushed to the intersection. From a distance, it looked like an awful mess. Michael stopped the van by the curb and, since there was no way through, stepped out and walked to the scene of the accident.

Several cars had careened off the road, but it appeared that the main collision involved a red Miata and a black Mercedes with tinted windows. Michael winced at the small convertible. Veronica drove one just like it. But it couldn't be... Veronica never had an accident. She was so careful.

Michael edged closer, heart pounding. It almost looked like her car. The black Mercedes also stirred up a vague uneasiness. His heart skipped when he recognized the little blue Smurfs dangling from the rear view mirror of the Miata through the gaping windshield. There was fresh blood on the empty seat. The black Mercedes looked intact. God, he hoped Veronica was all right!

Controlling his aversion for the police, Michael approached a blue uniform, "Officer! The woman in the red car... Is she okay? Where is she?"

"Are you a relative?"

"Sort of... She's my girlfriend. How is she?" Why didn't the officer tell him? It couldn't be that bad... He couldn't stand it if she died. The thought brought a wave of nausea.

"Come this way." The policeman led him off to the side. "They took her to Albert Einstein Medical Center...unconscious. Alive, but it didn't look good... She took the full impact... Go to the hospital, I won't bother you now. Just stop by the precinct later, we may need some information."

Vijaya Schartz

"What happened?" A creepy feeling told Michael this was not an ordinary accident.

"The black vehicle crossed against the light full speed... No one saw the driver... No license plates, no fingerprints... Quite unusual... Strange accident."

Now, Michael recognized the Mercedes. This couldn't be happening! He couldn't lose the woman he loved. "I've got to go."

"I understand. Good luck." The officer nodded a dismissal.

As he started back to the van, Michael saw a familiar figure in the crowd, dressed in black leather, smiling. Immediately, his body stiffened. The long black hair, the handsome face, it was Krastinios, the man born of a snake.

"You, mother-fucker!" Pressure tightened Michael's brain in a vice. He flinched, brought a hand to his eyes.

A voice blared in his head. "*I warn you, Earthling. Do not contact the Blue Angel, or I will kill you, too.*" The man of his nightmare smiled, looking him straight in the eyes, then simply vanished.

Kill? Surely, Veronica wasn't dead. "What are you? Did you do this?" But Michael talked to empty air. "I'll get you for this!" he muttered in a dangerous whisper. Retrieving the van, he turned the vehicle around and sped to the emergency room, cursing the traffic.

Too late... Veronica was no more, said the physician in blue scrubs. She had died of massive hemorrhage, the surgeon explained, as if the technical details made any difference.

Like an automaton, Michael identified the mutilated body lying, abandoned, under the white sheet of a gurney in the cold emergency unit. So this was all that remained of the beautiful woman he loved. Where had the laughter and the happiness gone? Michael felt cheated. The medical staff left the room to give him privacy. He drew the sheet over her bloody face and held her inert hand as if to comfort her. "We were good together... Don't worry, honey, you'll be all right. Just wait for me up there, will you? I'll be gentle telling Jennifer." He closed his eyes, remembering her smiling face this very morning, with clear eyes dancing with life.

Inside him, a deep void, a numb, empty hole... Never again would he hear the comforting voice, feel the satiny skin... Never again would she run fingers through his hair... Never again... Michael wanted to howl like a wounded beast. So many innocent people had died around him, his first-born son, his teenage wife, Krystal's little girl, now Veronica. Why was life so unfair?

What about Jennifer? She remained his only anchor in life. Would she have to die, too?

Michael wondered if he would survive the unbearable pain. He could not fathom the loss. Veronica... All the love he'd felt for her and never expressed. Michael realized how much she had meant to him. If only he could tell her now... At least apologize for being such a jerk sometimes. She would probably forgive... He would do anything to make things right again, to tell her one more time that he loved her.

Michael wiped a tear and collected himself. He squeezed Veronica's hand, knowing she wouldn't approve, but he had to do this. "I promise you,

Vijaya Schartz

honey, on Jennifer's life and mine, that I will exact revenge. I will kill the bastard who did this to you. Over
your cold body, I swear it. Never let me forget it."

CHAPTER FOUR

"Hi Dave, it's me." Michael hoped that calling his younger brother would help. They had shared rough times over the years.

"Mike? Something wrong?" Concern colored Dave's thick speech.

"That obvious?" Michael felt his voice tremble.

"Well, it's three in the morning and you sound awful."

"It's Veronica, a car accident. She died at the hospital." Michael's grip strengthened on the glass of bourbon, threatening to break it.

"What? My God, Mike! How are you holding up?"

"Not good. It's hard... The hardest thing since Krystal's kid died three years ago." Michael struggled not to cry.

"Mike, talk to me, brother, I don't want you to do anything crazy like last time... We love you. The

Vijaya Schartz

world wouldn't be the same without you. Think of Jennifer. She needs you badly."

"I know... Don't worry. I won't try that again. It didn't work last time either." The smiling picture of Veronica looked straight into his soul from the bottle of Jack Daniels he had propped it against.

"I know your relationship was not perfect, but you loved Veronica very much, I know that."

"Yeah, I miss her... She changed my life forever. I'll never be the same again. What am I going to do without her?" Michael toyed with a birthday card on the desk, with Veronica's writing on it. "When I think that just this morning... we opened up, finally. She seemed to understand me. We were so happy, as if we made our peace just before... Then Zap! Bizarre accident, too. Sometimes I think I'm going crazy. I've got to tell someone about this."

"Of course, Mike. I'm really sorry. Tell me everything..."

Michael retold the events of the past few days, his nightmares and pseudo-hallucinations. As usual, Dave listened patiently. Michael could not have wished for a more attentive brother. Nevertheless, Dave's final advice did not match Veronica's vote of confidence.

"I think you should try to forget about the whole thing. What you need is a vacation. Why don't you come here for a while, with Jennifer? You haven't been in your hometown in twenty years. You could help me build my house, just like old times. Becky and the kid would love to have your company."

"Come on, Dave. Did you hear my story? Are you deaf or what?" Michael's voice rose several decibels. The anger withheld so far needed to erupt now. He could not control it anymore. Standing up suddenly, he knocked the chair down. The receiver in one hand and the glass in the other, Michael paced up and down the living room like a caged beast. "I said I have to find out what happened to her. Do you understand?"

"Yes Mike, I'm sorry. I think I understand." Dave always apologized. Michael didn't like that.

"I know the black leather guy wants to get to me. If the son of a bitch killed her, he'll pay for it, I swear." Michael kicked the wall with a boot, leaving a dent. Still not relieved, he sent the empty glass crashing against the kitchen tile. "I know he did it! And he'll kill me too if I don't stop him. Mark my words."

"Calm down now... Don't do anything rash. You know where it led you before. You don't want to find yourself in jail, do you? You're paranoid, man. Are you taking your pills?"

"Not for ages... That stuff makes me feel dead inside." Michael didn't like to be reminded.

"I was afraid of that. You should take them, you know. That mood disorder of yours is quite serious... Anyway, it's none of my business."

"Damn right! None of your goddamn business." Michael drank a gulp of scotch straight from the bottle and slammed it back unsteadily on the coffee table. He felt so vulnerable as he stared at Veronica's photograph. "She just happened to be in the way, man... She believed in me, thought I could help the blue bastard. She wanted me to do it. I owe her... Someone will pay for this."

Vijaya Schartz

"Maybe when you go to the police they'll volunteer some information," Dave ventured timidly.

"Me? To the police? You're dreaming." Michael took another gulp of Jack Daniels. "I jumped bail on two DUIs. I'm not taking any chances."

"Well, anyway... My offer still stands. You're welcome here anytime. How's Jennifer taking it?"

"She cried a little. I told her Veronica went to heaven with Penny. Kids take it a lot better than we do sometimes. When little Penny died, Jennifer didn't even cry. Of course she was prepared then. But this!" Michael paused, a painful knot contracting his throat. "I don't understand this. It's so... unexpected." He sighed but did not feel any better for it. Then, his powerful shoulders heaved out of control, and he broke into wretched sobs.

Dave's voice came to him, soft and warm. "It's all right, brother, it's all right to cry. You're entitled. Maybe it'll make you feel better."

Good old Dave always took anything Michael threw at him and never complained. After a while, wiping his face with one sleeve to clear the pain, Michael added, "There's something else... Do you know whatever happened to Jennifer's mother?"

"Tori? Last time I heard, she married a Frenchman and went to live in Paris. I could ask her mother."

"Thanks, I'd appreciate that. Did she kick the habit?"

"I heard she was clean when she got married."

"Good! Jennifer really wants to meet her. I can't say 'no' forever. Sooner or later, it'll happen. Maybe this is a good time for her to visit Europe."

Archangel Crusader

"She's a little young, don't you think, to travel alone?"

"She can handle it."

"Are you going to be all right, Mike? Call me anytime... I wish I was there with you."

When Michael finally hung up, thoughts of his childhood with Dave brought up tough memories. So much hurt, so much pain, what for? Sometimes he wished he had killed his stepfather when he'd had a chance that day, long ago, when they were chopping wood in the forest. The son-of-a-bitch had ducked the ax flying at his face. Too bad, that good-for-nothing did not deserve to live.

* * *

Two days later, Veronica in full makeup looked serene and beautiful as usual, lying in the expensive casket her parents had chosen. Tender pink roses and pure white carnations filled the cold room with fragrance and softness. Muted, pointless conversations buzzing in his ears, Michael felt awkward, even after a few beers. He never liked social gatherings while Veronica enjoyed them.

Michael was glad for Bill's presence and conversation. The big man in his fifties had been his friend and working partner for the past two years. Michael trusted Bill's pale eyes. The weathered face and receding hair had lived through many experiences. It showed in the way Bill always understood, whether it pertained to work or personal matters.

Except for Bill and Jennifer, Michael did not care for anyone here, mainly acquaintances of Veron-

Vijaya Schartz

ica's mother and a few co-workers from the hospital. Lying there in state, Veronica held the center of attention one last time. *Where are you my love... Oh, how I miss you.* For an instant, he saw the shadow of a smile on the cool red lips, but no, although the body rested here, Veronica was gone...forever.

As Michael stared wordlessly at the loved made-up face, Veronica's mother, impeccable and disdainful despite her red eyes and silk handkerchief, crossed the room, supported by a few friends. When she saw him, she approached as if to give him a hug. Michael stepped back instinctively.

"Thanks for arranging all this," he said, a little more bravado in his voice than he intended. "I know she likes it."

"Yes, she enjoyed parties. Where is Jennifer?"

"Somewhere around the chocolate cake, I think."

"I should have known. Dear child... Oh hi, Bill, it's nice to see you. Michael, I want you to know that although Veronica is gone," she dabbed at her eyes with a handkerchief, "you and Jennifer will always be welcome in our home."

The sweet words stung Michael like poison. This was the very woman who had tried to steer Veronica away from him, undermining the relationship with her venomous tongue.

"Save your breath, woman. It's no secret you never liked me, or anyone for that matter. You never understood why your daughter loved me, and to tell the truth I don't either. But Jen and I won't stay around much longer. Have no fear." Michael's tone, louder than intended, made some heads turn.

"We'll miss you both," said the older woman, obviously containing a smile of relief.

"You may miss Jennifer, but I don't believe you'll miss me much Ma'am. And I won't miss you either." Michael felt Bill's restraining hand on his arm.

"Well... I have to see to my other guests... Good luck to you, Michael, and to Jennifer." She might as well have said, good riddance. Never one angry word. The hatred was all in the nuances.

"Thanks anyway, we might need luck sometime soon."

As Veronica's mother retreated, surrounded by her faithful friends, Michael's gaze wandered past the heads of the guests across the room, focusing on a particularly tall and handsome back in fine black leather, harboring a dark ponytail. The man turned around, flashed an engaging smile then raised his glass in a cheery toast.

This was too much. Michael pounded his glass on the nearest table. As he stared at the stranger, unblinking, the blood drained from his face. "Asshole from hell," he whispered dangerously, "How dare you?"

Outwardly calm and resolute Michael cut his way through the small groups in the direction of Krastinios. In his chest, however, the very name sent red-hot flames fueling a hatred worse than any he had ever known for his stepfather. Hands clenching as he traversed the distance, Michael was aware of Bill following him with difficulty, but the man in black quickly headed for the door.

Michael followed the stranger outside. By the busy street, Krastinios waited in the shade, sitting

Vijaya Schartz

with nonchalance on the railing separating the front garden from the public sidewalk, legs dangling in the air. An arrogant smile lingered on his face.

"So, Tanner, did you make up your mind yet?" came the suave question.

"What? You bloody killer! I'll erase that smile from your pretty face. Fight me if you are a man."

"Sorry. I may look like a man, but you and I know I am not. Besides, I wouldn't derive pleasure from fighting a lowly Earthling. Where would be the challenge? If and when we do fight, I intend to have my fun, too."

Like a mad bull, Michael rushed him and tumbled against a nearby tree. Krastinios had suddenly vanished to reappear ten feet behind Michael, laughing this time.

"Do not make a foolish choice, Tanner." The threatening words sounded as musical as ever. "Do not come after me. You have too much to lose... I understand you have a lovely daughter. You would not want anything bad to happen to her, too?"

"You stay away from my daughter! I'll find you. I'll kill you, wherever and whoever you are." Michael shouted now. Passers-by looked at him as they would a rabid dog, giving him a wide berth. When he realized that he threatened empty air, Michael stopped, suddenly self-conscious.

Bill, who had witnessed the end of the exchange, approached him, a little pale. "Who was that?"

"Did you see him?"

"Of course I saw him. Where did he go? Do you know this guy?"

"That, my friend, was not a hallucination. He's the one who killed Veronica. If it takes me a lifetime, I'll find a way to destroy him, even if it's the last thing I do. I wish I could crush him with my sledge hammer." Michael sounded hysterical even to himself.

"Slow down, man... Don't get so worked up, it's bad for you." Bill pressed him on the shoulder comfortingly.

Jennifer walked out the door toward them. "Dad? Are you okay? Are we going home now?"

"Yes, Honey. I guess it's time to go home." Then to Bill, in a firmer voice he said, "I'll call you in the morning. Thanks again for coming today."

Michael encircled Jennifer's shoulder protectively as they walked to the van, then he opened the passenger door. "Whatever happens, always remember that I love you, pumpkin."

"I know, Dad." Jennifer smiled, framed in the door like a Mona Lisa, saying, "I love you, too."

From a distance, Krastinios observed the scene, and smiled.

Vijaya Schartz

CHAPTER FIVE

That night, after Jennifer had gone to sleep, Michael lay on the familiar couch of the living room, a glass of Jack Daniels close at hand, unable to erase the smiling face of Krastinios from his mind. The threat, the dangerous power emanating from this abject character frightened him. Michael needed to protect his daughter, but what could he do against such evil? Maybe he'd find some clue in the events of the past few days.

Concentrating, he realized he could remember with surprising clarity each and every word spoken or telepathically imprinted on his mind in the past few days. The blue being had mentioned psychic powers and expected an answer... Krastinios alluded to a choice, calling the apparition a Blue Angel.

Veronica had been right. Michael had not hallucinated. For the first time, he realized that all these occurrences connected with reality. Something be-yond human comprehension affected his life. Could this Blue Angel who seemed to know so much pro-vide the answers? And how to make contact?

Since the strange being had emphasized mind communication, Michael would try that first. Relaxing on the couch, he noticed the peace and quiet of the living room, the purring of Shadow dozing on the white Afghan. As soon as he visualized the stranger, Michael felt a response: a slight tremor of the mind and a vaguely familiar voice, warm and comforting.

"*Do you have any questions, Michael? Would you like to come to us?*" uttered the melodious con-tralto in his brain.

As he remembered with apprehension the painful incident in the parking lot, Michael strength-ened his resolve. "I guess I've got to."

Fingers tingled first, followed by toes, arms and legs. The pleasurable sensation slowly spread to Michael's body, all the way to the heart. Warm and secure, Michael wished he had known these feelings as a little boy, when love was frigid and hard as a fist. Such a shame he didn't have a father to love and pro-tect him then.

Soon, the familiar surroundings faded and dis-appeared as Michael levitated. Eyes half-closed, he floated in a bright cloud. When the sensation stopped, a soothing light surrounded him, cool and energizing.

Adjusting to the blue glow, Michael's gaze caught a slight movement. The radiant being stood there, small, obviously naked, obviously male. Smooth skin the shade of the deepest sky stretched on a thin body. In an elongated head with no hair or

Vijaya Schartz

ears, huge almond-shaped eyes shone dark blue over high cheekbones. An indefinable smile brushed the thin lips under a very small nose, while a turquoise aura bathed everything around him.

"Welcome, Michael," said the Blue Angel in a melodic tone, "My name is Amrah. I will answer your questions and help you if you wish."

Still tingling, nerve endings alive with energy, Michael, despite his curiosity, could not help but relax into the seat. No fear spoiled the moment and he felt good. In his amazement, he forgot the questions he had meant to ask. "Am I dreaming?" he mused aloud.

"No," answered Amrah. "You are fully awake, here among us."

"What's this place?" Michael noticed the strangeness of it and the bizarre aspect of its inhabitants. It smelled of fresh flowers but there weren't any, only smooth curved surfaces lit in pastel colors.

"Our traveling home away from home," came the nostalgic reply.

A vivid picture formed in Michael's mind: a small orb of opaque material suspended in black space, behind the moon. In the background, a blue planet, quite familiar in every respect.

"A spaceship? Are you serious?" Michael reclined in the seat.

"Quite serious."

"Excuse me for doubting, but with all the satellites and telescopes we have up there, how come no one noticed?"

"Maybe someone did and neglected to report. Maybe your technology cannot detect us, but most likely the moon provides adequate shadowing."

Archangel Crusader

"But... Who are you people? Or are you people at all?"

"Beings... Other beings, somewhat like you, somewhat different."

"Different all right, I'd say!"

Michael thought he saw the shadow of an amused smile on the friendly face. Other beings walked around, all five feet tall, bluish, hairless and naked, male and female, some more alien than others and some, like Amrah, quite human in proportions. They went about in quiet harmony, performing tasks Michael did not understand. He then realized that he sat comfortably in nothing... No chair. When he felt for a seat under him, he only touched his jeans.

"What kind of technology is this? No control panels, no computers?" His voice trailed when he realized he had spoken aloud.

"We use the energy of the mind." The being still stood in front of him, his colorful skin vibrant in the light.

"Who are you? Or should I say, what are you?" Mesmerized, Michael couldn't help but stare at the naked aliens who seemed undisturbed by his presence.

"We call ourselves Blue Angels, but we've been called deities, demigods, heroes, aliens, even gods, depending on where and when. "

Did he imply aliens were the old gods? As preposterous as it sounded, Michael felt in no position to contest.

"Actually, we carry the same genes. Don't you think my features resemble yours a little?" That fleeting smile again.

Vijaya Schartz

Michael wiped a sweaty palm on his jeans. "What do you want from me?"

"Our Seers predict the near extinction of mankind at the hand of an alien invader. Although they did not specify which race would storm your planet, they hinted at an ancient evil. Man needs to evolve fast. We came to help humanity prepare."

"But what does this have to do with me?" Michael asked in earnest. "I don't even understand most of that stuff."

Amrah looked amused. "I guess I owe you an explanation."

"I would appreciate that very much, yes sir." *Who the hell does this freak think he is?* The thought escaped Michael unbidden.

"Freak? How ironic..." Amrah chuckled and waved away the comment. "Did you ever wonder why you always felt different from your brothers, different from your friends, estranged from society? People either love you or hate you on sight."

Michael tried to refrain from thinking since the alien obviously read his thoughts. He wondered how the Blue Angel could do that. Sometimes Michael had mind contacts with Jennifer, but it had never happened with a stranger before. "Yeah..." he answered. "I don't know why, but I always felt that way. I'm a rebel, they tell me. I never conform to the rules... Only trust my instinct."

"Then think back, Michael. Think of when you were just a baby, warm, safe, happy. Do you remember that time?"

"Not really. Just a feeling of well being. It did not last long, though."

"Wasn't your mother sweet and loving? Then something happened, and everything changed... "

"That's for sure... So what?" Michael didn't like to talk about his wretched childhood.

"When your mother was but a virgin, alone, yearning for love and understanding, she had a dream."

"That two-faced, cheating Indian bitch?" Michael stood up, disturbed by the thought, then felt he should be sitting but did not know where since there was no chair.

"Anywhere you choose to sit, lie, or climb, support will materialize." Amrah's eyes blinked slowly. "Remember, we use the power of the mind."

Hesitantly, Michael felt around with one hand: Nothing. He tentatively sat and found comfortable support meeting his very shape. To cover his confusion, he urged the alien, "You were saying?"

"Your mother invoked the Great Spirit of her ancestors and came to me in a trance. I welcomed and comforted her. When she asked for a special son, someone different and valuable, someone to give her life meaning and worth, I gladly obliged. That night, you were conceived."

"Are you saying you slept with my mother?" Michael couldn't stand the picture forming in his mind. "This is outrageous! You can't possibly be my father!" He refrained from standing up again.

The alien smiled at Michael's plight. "You are free to doubt or free to believe."

"How do you expect me to believe that?" The challenge in Michael's voice seemed to desecrate the peaceful place.

Vijaya Schartz

"I know this is very sudden, Michael, but you will understand, in time."

"Just what I need!" Michael felt ready to explode. "So now I'm a frigging alien?"

"You are physically human, Michael, but you also are a child of mine." Somehow, the alien voice had a soothing effect.

"Great! And all that because my mother couldn't keep from fooling around, even in her sleep..."

"She was pure then, Michael, ignorant about men. Can't you understand?"

"No. What do you mean, she didn't know she was having sex?"

"Not in her waking state, but I brought her peace and happiness, at least for a while. As long as I stayed close, I sustained Maria's precarious balance through her dreams. When I had to leave, for reasons beyond my control, she resented me, then you. Then she married." The alien eyes clouded in shades of gray, and the voice softened even more. "I have not contacted her since."

"Yeah, she resented me all right." Painful remembrance assailed Michael. "She resented everybody... She made our life a living nightmare, with the help of that sick bastard." The memory still stung.

"I watched you from afar but could not intervene. Those trying times forged your character."

"What character? I'll tell you what that bitch and her husband made me: a warped soul who'd rather hate than love and sooner hit than talk. I can't trust anybody, not even myself. I couldn't keep my word if my life depended on it. That's what I have to thank them for."

"Yes... Nevertheless, I expected you would come."

Was that a pulse Michael detected under the supple skin of the chest? "Do you even hear what I'm saying?" But how could Amrah possibly understand?

"I heard you perfectly. But now is the time for you to learn of your destiny and fulfill it." The even tone could be aggravating too.

"Wait a minute. I agreed to nothing. I'm not the hero type."

"You will be, my son, in time... You were born for this. You cannot ignore your very nature. Deep down inside you always knew it, as Veronica sensed it too."

"Veronica? My God, of course, you know about her, too. Do you know the bastard who killed her?"

"Killed her?" Amrah looked surprised. "Did she not die in a car accident?"

"But who drove the black car? That raven? What's his name... Krastinios?"

"What?" Obvious concern creased the alien face. "What name did you say?" Amrah seemed lost in a complex net of unpleasant thoughts. "Krastinios? Are you sure?" The hairless eyebrows knitted, as in worry.

"That's the name he imprinted on my mind. That's the name I heard in my dream. Why? You know him?"

"No." The blue gaze looked far away. "Just old stories about an extinct race."

"If the son of a bitch killed Veronica, and somehow I know he did, I'll smash his arrogant smile... I'll kill him, I swear." Michael wiped the sweat from his forehead.

"I'm afraid it will not be that easy. By the way, those are harsh words for an avatar." Humor danced in the wide, dark eyes.

"What's that?"

"An avatar? A great soul reincarnated to guide the world through critical times."

"Me, a great soul?" Michael burst out in laughter, but Amrah didn't seem to share his mirth. "Come now, who'll believe that?"

"Everyone in my part of the Galaxy does, Son!"

"Like hell!" Michael wasn't about to be seduced by flattery. "What do you know about Krastinios?"

The Blue Angel looked uncomfortable. "Only a long forgotten legend, and a dark prediction no one believes anymore... How did you learn about him?"

"A vivid nightmare...it's rather complicated."

"Then allow me, Son." The alien brought his delicate fingers to both of Michael's temples.

"What are you doing?"

"Reading the dream from your mind. May I?" Amrah stared past Michael, eyes deep and shiny, his face a mask of serenity.

Far from resisting, Michael enjoyed the warm touch of the long-fingered hands. The subtle contact, although foreign, caused no discomfort. The tender presence in his mind assured him that all would be right. A little shy at first, Michael finally surrendered to the pleasurable experience.

After a few seconds, the soothing voice resumed. "Do you feel all right, Son? That was not too bad, was it?" Amrah withdrew his probing mind from Michael's thoughts.

"How did you do that? Can you teach me? It felt great! Did you recognize that bastard?"

"Yes indeed, and I learned everything else about you, even a few suppressed memories."

"Damn you!" Prompted by the violation, Michael stood up, threatening. "I never gave you the right to all my memories, you goddamn freak! So, now you think you know me... But you don't!"

Michael felt cheated, buried in humiliation. This alien knew too much about him, now. All the slip-ups, mistakes, degrading bouts of alcoholism... Even the shameful abuse Michael had been subjected to as a child. Head down, he paced the perimeter of the ovoid chamber.

"Deep inside you wanted me to, Michael. You carry too much pain and hatred, but this is the fate of your race." Amrah's tone neither condemned nor judged.

Nothing Michael could do after the fact. Actually, he was glad someone knew, even a Blue Angel, whatever that was. He didn't have to carry the burden alone anymore. Controlling his conflicting emotions, he changed the subject. "What can you tell me about Krastinios?"

"He did kill Veronica and now wants Jennifer. Just as I feared, he will do anything to hurt and weaken you. Ultimately, he seeks to destroy you, and his powers are far greater than yours at this point."

Michael pivoted to face Amrah squarely. "What powers? What exactly can he do? I need to

Vijaya Schartz

know how dangerous he is, if I am to protect Jennifer."

The alien eyes looked straight through him. "I do not want to scare you, but to become his match, you would need the full might of a trained avatar."

"Trained?" Michael didn't like the sound of that. "What kind of training?"

"Once your powers awaken, you need to learn how to use and control them. You also need the wisdom to apply them with discrimination."

Michael sat down again. This time he did not even look down, not caring whether he sat or fell. He slumped and sighed heavily. "If I want to avenge Veronica's death and get that bastard, I guess I don't have much of a choice, do I?"

"No," Amrah answered matter-of-factly. "You never had one. Your motives may change, but you cannot escape fate."

Michael snorted. He'd never believed in fate, but if the Blue Angel could help him beat Krastinios, there was nothing to lose. "Let's say I accept this job, hypothetically of course... What comes next?"

"I will start your education immediately."

"Hold your horses! How long does this take?"

"It depends mostly on your willingness and flexibility, but time is irrelevant. It can be warped."

"Really?" Michael paused, intrigued by the concept. "What about Jennifer?"

The big eyes veiled briefly. "She does not need to know yet."

For some reason, Michael didn't like hiding the danger from Jennifer, something he'd never done. "You're very sure of yourself, aren't you? You can do things that I don't understand, but why should I trust you?"

"I would not harm my son or my granddaughter, Michael. You are both very dear to me."

Michael melted inside at the thought of family. The grief at the loss of his newborn son long ago and the joy at being a father again with Jennifer made him ache to believe. Could this alien father feel as much love for him as he felt for Jen? Sudden doubt made him hesitate. "What if I change my mind halfway through?"

"That is your privilege, of course. You are free to recant at any time, but I do not believe you will."

Now was the time to think straight. Michael wanted to crush Krastinios so bad he could taste it. There was no denying the compulsion. If it took becoming an avatar, taught and trained by this alien, that's what he would have to do. Besides, the wise blue goat might be good company for a while.

Painstakingly, Michael formulated the words, first in his mind, then aloud. "Well, I'm willing to give it a try." That was it. He'd said it. "Fair enough?" He immediately rose to depart.

"Your decision makes me glad, Michael. You will enjoy being an avatar, I promise you."

"We'll see about that. How do I get back home?" Michael detected a chuckle from his alleged father.

"Lesson number one: How to get back home, which is the same as how to get here, or anywhere for that matter." Amrah's voice took on a particular rhythm, a ring that made it unforgettable.

"Visualize the place where you want to be.

Vijaya Schartz

Draw a perfect image of the place in your mind with all the minute details. Picture your body in the scene in a specific location and position. Relax... Then will your spirit into the picture of your body."

"Just like that? Sounds simple enough. You think I can do it?"

"I know you can."

Michael envisioned in every detail the familiar living room with its blue drapes and blue velvet couch, the coffee table, the cat, the end table with the glass of Jack Daniels, and pictured himself lying on the couch. Then, just as Amrah had suggested, Michael easily slid into his visualized body.

After a second or two of feeling confused, he shook his head and looked around. This was really his place with everything as he'd left it. Shadow the cat awoke when Michael moved. The Timex had stopped ticking. Michael set the useless watch on the coffee table and ambled to the kitchen. His stomach felt empty.

According to the clock on the stove, four hours had passed... Then again, Michael could have slept and dreamed. But no... He wanted to believe it was all true, for nothing made sense otherwise.

* * *

"So, you really want to see your mother?" Michael asked Jennifer two days later, picking up on her thoughts.

The excitement in the girl's eyes made Michael

feel like a hero. She grinned. "Yes... I guess... If that's all right with you."

"Well, Tori lives in Paris, and I think it's okay for you to see her. She married a rich Frenchman and doesn't do drugs anymore." In truth, Dave had made the arrangements. Michael had refused to talk to Tori, still angry at her walking out on him and Jennifer ten years ago.

"Paris, France? That's far away, Dad!"

"Not as far as that, just on the other side of the ocean. Would you like to go there for a few months?"

Jennifer stared at Michael in shock. "That's a long time." She hesitated. "Are you coming with me?"

"As much as I'd love to, I can't. I have work to do here. But don't let that stop you, kid. It's your call."

"I don't know, Dad... Will you be okay by yourself?"

"Don't worry about me, kid. I'll be all right. Besides, I won't be by myself, I'll be helping Dave build his house."

"Oh yeah, I forgot about that... Still... Are you sure?" Timid hope shone in Jennifer's green eyes as the beginning of a smile dimpled the corners of her mouth.

"Yes, I'm sure. Is that a deal?" Michael forced some enthusiasm into his voice.

"Oh, Dad! I'm going to see my mother?" Jennifer's voice reflected the eagerness in her face. She grinned, blushing with barely contained excitement. When she jumped onto his lap and held him in a bear

Vijaya Schartz

hug, Michael thought nothing in the world was more precious than the love of his beautiful little girl.

Archangel Crusader

CHAPTER SIX

The phone rang, echoing eerily in the house. Michael stared at it then picked it up. "Yo!" Silence settled over the line, and the sound of the ocean.

"Hello! Is this Michael Tanner's residence?" A pretty feminine voice flowed over the expanse.

"Yes, this is he." Memories of his boisterous youth flooded back... Savage motorcycle rides, beautiful girls, wild addictions... It was such a long time ago. "Who is this?" he asked, although he already knew.

"Hi, Michael. This is Tori. It's been such a long time. Dave gave me your number. How've you been?" The voice sounded eager and bubbly, just as he remembered.

"Fine." Cold silence. "Thanks for buying Jennifer's ticket." Tori had insisted on it.

"Don't mention it. It's the least I can do." Short pause. "My God, it's been ten years. It feels like yesterday. I can't believe I have a daughter that old, but I'm sure glad you're letting her come see me. I've

Vijaya Schartz

thought of her often these past years. Not knowing where she was...that was the hardest thing... I wondered if she knew about me. What is she like? What does she look like? This is so exciting. I can't wait to meet her. Do you think she'll like me?"

Repressed feelings rushed to the surface so fast, Michael couldn't think of what to say next. Vent his anger? Forgive? Make peace?

As he kept silent, she went on, "Will you ever forgive me? Can we be friends again?"

"I don't know." The words stuck in his throat. "After what you did, it's hard. I know you wanted an abortion, but walking out of the hospital, leaving a baby like that between life and death? Letting Jennifer grow-up without a mother, at the hands of other women..."

Tori didn't talk right away. "Dave told me about Veronica's accident... I'm very sorry."

Hard to imagine this was the same woman. She sounded soft and caring. Michael did not know what to say anymore.

"I want to apologize for what happened ten years ago," Tori went on. "I was young, scared, not myself. I hurt many good people then. I will never forgive myself for abandoning my baby. You called her Jennifer? That's a pretty name. I wanted to call her Sativa after the marijuana plant, but I knew you didn't approve... I didn't understand then. I do now."

"Well... She's definitely your daughter. You'll understand when you see her."

"Thank you. You know, I'm a different person now... After rehab, I decided to settle down. I went back to school, got married." She sounded mature.

"Yes, I heard." Michael cursed the intense emotions that prevented him from finding the right words.

"I don't ride motorcycles anymore." He could see her smile in his mind. "But I still think about it once in a while. I'm not nearly as wild as I used to be."

Hearing the sincerity in her voice, Michael warmed up. "Neither am I, although I'd like to believe it sometimes... I still have the Harley, though. I ride it once in a while."

"My irresponsible ways caused so much loneliness and despair... Finally, I found real love, and Jean-Marc has been great. So supportive... I feel lucky to have escaped with my life and my mind. Now I feel clean, happy. I've been given another chance."

"I'm glad. You sound great!" The words came unbidden, and to his surprise, Michael realized that he still cared about her.

"And here you offer me my long lost daughter. She's very important to me now. Knowing her will make me feel whole again. It's kind of you, giving me a second chance after what I did."

It took Michael a few seconds to sort through the erratic flow of mixed emotions. "I was waiting on the sidelines, waiting for you to straighten up, and for Jennifer to be old enough to understand." He paused. "She's a tough little lady. I think you'll like her. I love her very much... She's been an anchor in my life for the past ten years. I've known some hard times, too... You know my problem. I've been pretty good recently, though."

Vijaya Schartz

Suddenly, Michael felt Jennifer's presence. How long had she been standing there? The girl had guessed who was calling and she could hardly contain her exhilaration.   She looked ready to burst. It made Michael grin. "There's someone here who's dying to talk to you, Tori. Are you ready for this?"

"Oh my God! Jennifer is there? Yes, yes of course.   What do I tell her?"   Tori's precipitated speech betrayed traces of panic.

Michael handed the receiver to Jennifer. "Would you like to say something to your mother, Jen?"

The girl's eyes opened wide.   "So, it is my mother? What do I say?"

"Whatever you want, you always know what to say when you talk to your friends, same thing." He smiled at her confusion.

"Hello... Yeah, this is Jennifer." Michael observed a little tension around his daughter's mouth at first.   Suddenly, the green eyes smiled, and the child's face filled with pleasure as she listened. When Jennifer turned to look at her father, her eyes said, "Incredible, I do have a mother."

Michael gently probed into his daughter's thoughts, like Amrah had been teaching him for the past few days. He could read happiness and gratitude.   The quality of their psychic contacts had improved greatly. Michael now felt comfortable with the idea of parting from her since he could contact her mind and respond at the slightest threat. Soon, Amrah promised, Michael could do wondrous things, even materialize anywhere, if needed, to help or protect his daughter.

Archangel Crusader

Voluble as ever, Jennifer spoke gaily of new clothes, hairstyles, and fun things to do with her newly found mother.

Michael confirmed the flight number and arrival time with Tori who would meet Jennifer at the airport in Paris. He worried about the little girl traveling by herself, but it was for the best. Paris was a good place to hide her from Krastinios.

* * *

Philadelphia International Airport resembled any other, but Michael had never been there. He checked in Jennifer's bag, had her passport approved, then found the boarding gate to the Continental flight. It was crowded. European businessmen with dark suits and attaché-cases, nice-smelling ladies, and skinny young men in casual attire spoke a foreign language he assumed was French.

After father and daughter waited at the gate a short time, a blonde flight attendant met them and introduced herself. The young woman flashed a friendly smile accentuated by red lipstick, assuring Michael his daughter would be in good hands, cared for, watched over, and delivered safely into her mother's custody as soon as they arrived.

"Well, kid, this is it." Michael found it hard to speak. "You have a good time with your mother. And remember, anything goes wrong, anything at all, you can contact me the way we practiced, okay? You have my mobile phone number. You'll be fine." As he uttered the words, Michael realized it was himself he tried to reassure.

Vijaya Schartz

He picked Jennifer up in a hug. "I love you, Jen," he said softly.

"I love you too, Dad."

The child's eyes glistened as Michael lowered her to eye level. "Send me some postcards at Dave's address." He cleared his throat.

Jennifer nodded as he set her on her feet. "Bye, Dad." She gave him another hug and a kiss on the cheek.

"Say hi to your mother for me, will you? Bye, kid." Michael straightened up, gave the hand-carry to the blonde attendant and braced himself to watch his daughter leave.

Jennifer looked back once, attempted a smile and waved, then walked away chatting with the friendly flight attendant. Michael could tell from the bounce in his daughter's step that she had already left, set on the adventure ahead. Would she miss him?   Michael would miss her, but above all he wanted her safe and happy.

Glued to the glass, Michael watched the big plane taxi up to the runway. When the jet stopped at the far end, a black limousine escorted by a motorcade appeared on the field. A maintenance truck followed, with rolling stairs in tow. The cortege headed straight for the waiting plane. Someone boarded the aircraft at the last minute. Probably some diplomat, or a CIA big wig. Obviously someone with connections.

Michael shuddered.   Some people held a frightening amount of power. Finally, he watched the takeoff, but after the plane disappeared in the sky, Michael felt uncomfortable. He already missed Jennifer as he walked slowly toward the exit, clearing his mind for the task ahead.

* * *

Jennifer relished the window seat. After the pilot apologized for the delay, she observed the VIP boarding. All this fuss for one passenger? Finally, the plane took off over the roof of the terminal and the parking lot. The plane veered then flew over the Naval Base and the Delaware River. Soon, according to the map, they would cross the ocean. Not much to see there.

Jennifer had brought a book, *The Abandoned*, a story about a little boy who became a cat. She had read it before, but it was easier the second time. She also really enjoyed the story. Mostly, Jennifer cherished it as a gift from Veronica. She missed the lovely woman and felt a little lost without Shadow. The cat had been like a sibling to her. She felt utterly alone as she dutifully chewed on the piece of gum offered by the flight attendant.

Jennifer had flown before with her dad, a long time ago, on a glider. She remembered only vaguely the sound of the wind in the light canvas. This was different. She could hardly hear the engine but felt the dull vibration.

This, she thought, was real flying. Comfort and luxury... She wished her school friends could see her now. The plane flew over sparse cotton clouds that cast shadows on the green landscape below. After the seat-belt sign went off, some passengers started to move around. The seat next to Jenni-

Vijaya Schartz

fer remained empty. No one to talk to. This would make for a very long flight.

At the end of the aisle, the blond flight attendant smiled to a nice-looking fellow, pointing to the empty seat beside Jennifer. The man thanked her. Gracefully, he closed the distance, dark velvet eyes and irresistible smile on Jennifer all the time.

"Good morning, Miss," the stranger said in a most charming tone.

"I know who you are," Jennifer exclaimed in recognition. "I saw you getting on the plane at the last minute. Good thing we waited for you."

"You are absolutely right, Miss, and I apologize for the inconvenience." The smile broadened. "I understand that this seat is not taken. Do you mind very much if I keep you company for the duration? The man next to me snores and I do not care much for it. What do you say?"

Impressed by his good manners, Jennifer thought he would be fun to talk to. "You can sit here. I know what you mean... I think snoring is so disgraceful." The little girl whispered the last words in confidence, thrilled for the company. Besides, the stranger looked real cool, with a black ponytail, dressed in black leather. Wearing a gold chain and a small diamond in his ear, he resembled a character from a TV show.

"What an elegant dress," The man remarked politely.

Jennifer could tell he knew about fashion.

"I love this red on you, it brings out your green eyes. Did you buy it in Paris?"

"No," Jennifer answered truthfully. "Veronica bought it for me at Northeast Mall, with her credit card. It was on sale."

"I see, very interesting. A good bargain I bet."

"I think so," the child replied seriously.

"I am awfully sorry. We have not been properly introduced. My name is so complicated, call me Mr. K. Glad to meet you. And what might your name be?" Mr. K smiled again, and Jennifer thought he was just darling.

"I'm Jennifer. Nice to meet you, too. Do you play chess? I brought my set."

"I'd love to play a game with you. Are you good at it?" Mr. K inquired.

"Not as good as my dad, but I have to warn you, I won the school championship."

"Oh, I see... Then I'd better watch myself."

Mr. K laughed, and Jennifer grinned with delight. This would be a great adventure. She had already made a wonderful friend, someone she could trust like a father and love like a friend.

Vijaya Schartz

CHAPTER SEVEN

Michael sat comfortably in his favorite armchair and visualized the spaceship as he had seen it before, the blue reflective wall surfaces, vacant floor, soft light and serene atmosphere. Picturing himself standing in front of Amrah, he entered his own projection. A subtle change in the air, in the soft light, and Amrah greeted Michael cheerfully.

"You show unusual promise, my son. Even for an avatar you learn fast. It pleases me immensely." Warmth transformed the strange features.

Michael smiled. "I came to learn. Please teach me."

Over the past days, Michael had learned to tell time by trusting his inside clock, on any world, in any part of any galaxy. He could now effortlessly read simple minds but still struggled with closed or hostile characters. He excelled at mind-speaking, however, and could hear or be heard almost without restriction, and across great distances.

Archangel Crusader

Next came telekinesis, the art of moving objects by the power of thought. The first attempts, however, proved disappointing.

"Do not force it," Amrah repeated for the tenth time.

"Damn!" came the frustrated reply.

The dark beads of blue oil had not moved in the pink liquid where they floated. Michael's strong will surpassed his willingness to conform to the teachings. Wrestling with stubbornness, it took him hours of concentration to let go of the strain, relax, and trust his natural ability. Only then did Michael get the dark blue beads to float easily in predetermined patterns. From then on, he made astonishing progress.

After Michael had mastered the art of moving heavier objects without strain or struggle, Amrah asked him, "How would you like to pilot this ship?"

"Me?"

"You have learned much since your first lesson. Just think for a moment. You now trust and respect wisdom. You gained self-discipline. You flow with the energy rather than struggle against it. I think you are ready for a little reward."

"No shit, it's about time. What do I do?" Michael exulted.

"The same thing you did with smaller objects. This craft is no different. Visualize it in its entirety."

Eyes closed, Michael visualized the ship, with which he had become familiar. From the outside, it looked like a dark orb with no color of its own, mimicking the surrounding shades like a chameleon. A permanent mental shield made it invisible for whomever did not specifically look for it.

Vijaya Schartz

"I've got it visualized... What do I do now?" Michael couldn't keep the excitement from his voice. He felt like a happy kid.

"Would you like to take it to Venus?" Amrah offered.

"Venus? Why not? Where's that?"

"It is the closest planet. Tap your universal memory and visualize the solar system."

"All right, I see it now. Venus... How long would it take?"

"Time is irrelevant. When would you like to get there?"

"I don't know... Tomorrow? Today? How about yesterday, can I get there yesterday?"

"You could, but you never know how your presence may affect the past. It could mean disaster for present and future, so we avoid it as much as possible."

"Whoa!" Michael almost let go of the ship, thrilled by the discovery. "I'm beginning to like this stuff." Amrah had never talked about moving through time before.

"You just have to be very specific. Be precise about the place and circumstances. Visualize..." Amrah suggested.

Michael pictured the exact place then mentally brought the vessel to the coordinates. A slight shimmer blurring the outlines was all he perceived in the mental picture.

When Michael opened his eyes again, everything on deck looked the same, except for the planet seen through the convex, transparent bulkhead. Instead of the dark craters of Earth's familiar moon, the crew now gazed upon the soft, blue and orange light of a celestial body covered with thick, sulfurous clouds.

"Just like that, I can really fly this thing?" He stared at Venus with wonder.

"You can do anything your mind can conceive, Son. If you do not restrict yourself, you can do anything at all."

"I understand I have different genes, but could anyone else do it?"

"They would have to work harder and may not achieve the same level, but yes, anyone on your planet has this potential. I included it in the genetic blueprint. Unfortunately, unused skills tend to wither over the millennia."

On Amrah's ship, time flowed at a different pace. Never needing sleep there, Michael studied for what seemed like days on end while, in his world, mere hours had passed. Often, he thought of Veronica. He missed her. She had filled his life in subtle ways, unobtrusive, efficient, omnipresent. With only the ever-roaming cat, the house felt empty. Sometimes he missed her companionship and sound advice, other times her wholesome cooking. Most of all, he ached for the womanly ways and the comfort of her slender body.

For the first time in his life, Michael had a deep sense of worthiness that enabled him to face the truth at any given time. Not that anyone would believe the story if he told it. Nevertheless, a newly discovered self-esteem along with new powers transformed his

Vijaya Schartz

view on life. Michael trained for a job he scarcely believed he could do, but it served his double goal to avenge Veronica's death and protect Jennifer.

Michael had never liked philosophy or history, but Amrah's version wasn't taught in any public school.

"This planet was visited many times by different intergalactic species, " Amrah declared during a lesson. "The various races on Earth did not result from climatic conditions or obscure laws of evolution over millions of years on this planet alone. Beings came from far galaxies, other universes."

"What do you mean?"

"At one time, a dark-skinned race from Sirius, a planet of Alpha Centauri, colonized and ruled the continent you know as Africa. Later, when their culture dwindled, other visitors with yellow skin colonized the Asian continent. A blue race had already almost disappeared from the Middle East at the time of Christ."

"Hot damn! I never heard that before." Michael exclaimed in awe.

"Some white galactic colonists grew in number and evolved separately to high levels of technology on a continent now under the ice of the Antarctic. The Greek mythology recounts the exploits of the crew of an intergalactic vessel marooned on a Mediterranean island. The red skin of the Aztecs, Incas, and American Indians bears witness to a race that landed on the ancient continent of Lemuria, now lying under the Pacific Ocean."

"So, when did you come for the first time?"

"We established our first headquarters in Assyria, where we gave life to Adam and Eve."

"You created man?"

"Not exactly. We adapted the species."

"Fascinating! So what's their real story?"

"They were our first experiment. We brought a human specimen especially engineered for life on this planet. Since we only had a male, we cloned a female from one of his ribs, modifying the genetic pattern to accommodate the female organs. They were destined to mix with the other existing races, blending and widening the genetic pool of Earth's particular species. At first, except for the fact that they had no past, no racial memories and no knowledge, just an intelligence, things looked very good."

"But something went wrong?" Curiosity got the most of Michael.

"No, everything went too well. Let me explain."

As Amrah closed his eyes, images formed in Michael's mind: a luxuriant oasis in the desert, cool and refreshing fountains, marble pools bubbling with soft water, dark green vegetation alive with birds' songs. Imposing stone pyramids stood under the deep blue sky of ancient Persia. The exotic flowers smelled intoxicating. Naked humanoids of luminescent blue came and went in the shade of tall cedar trees. Adam and Eve, fair of complexion, perfect in their human shape, played and laughed, enjoying a carefree life of idleness.

In the background, Michael could hear Amrah's voice explaining further. "Unfortunately the female, Eve, became too smart. Too soon, she understood that the only difference between us and herself was the knowledge and the memories we had. So,

Vijaya Schartz

she conspired with a staff member of a different species, a Reptilian."

The alien who came into focus bore an amazing resemblance to Lufriec, the snake-creature from
Michael's nightmare of the red planet. Michael shuddered as, in the present vision, the Reptilian enticed
Eve into an intense conversation.

Amrah's voice in the background explained.
"The Reptilians had fallen from grace in the superior
council when we discovered a rebellious movement
to seize control of the Alliance. They tried to sabo-
tage the experiment and almost succeeded."

While new images appeared in Michael's mind,
Amrah's voice paused, then resumed. "Much later, a
natural cataclysm destroyed their home planet. It is
now an incandescent piece of rock. They totally disappeared as a race long ago. We believed them extinct, for we never heard of them again. Until now..."

Michael interrupted. "How did they manage a
revolt in such a paradise?"

"The reptilians spoke a seductive language.
This one had fed Eve with dreams of power and high
status. He also impregnated her with a son then convinced her that possessing our records would give
her the knowledge she lacked. So Eve persuaded
Adam to help her steal the forbidden information, po-
etically later called the fruit of the tree of knowledge.
There were no apple trees in Persia...wrong climate."

"How did you prevent them from succeeding?"
Michael asked eagerly.

"As soon as Adam and Eve breached the pro-
hibited perimeter, their heart beat, particular to your
race, was detected by our sensors and they were
caught. What were we to do?"

"So you kicked them out of Eden?" It all made sense to Michael, now.

"We had no choice. They had become a danger to themselves. Eve was obsessed with the information in our data banks. They were not ready to handle such technology. Letting them fend for themselves in the wild, away from our protective custody, would keep their mind off our own work and provide them with an opportunity to learn at their own pace."

Amrah paused again, looking at Michael intensely. "Time is an important factor when it comes to evolution. Despite the mixed blood of their son Cain, Adam and Eve started a new race and multiplied for many generations."

"When you say you colonized Earth, you mean as a race, right?" An awesome concept had just crept into Michael's mind.

"Yes, I mean us, the Blue Angels, including each member of my present crew."

"But... How long ago was this?"

"About twenty five thousand years."

"What? You're kidding me! How old are you?" Michael felt his jaw open.

"Too old to count and too young to care. Among us, age is quite irrelevant." Amrah looked as cool as ever.

"By golly... I can see that. I wish... Do you ever die? Don't you get sick? Don't you get tired of living?" The thought boggled the mind. Michael felt suddenly warm.

"Our bodies are sustained by light, channelled through our minds," Amrah continued in his melodic voice. "They do not degenerate as long as our will to

Vijaya Schartz

live remains strong. When a body gets destroyed by accident, the mind seeks a new body to give life to. We keep a few spares for that purpose."

Michael whistled softly at the staggering thought. Such possibilities... "And these bodies, do they come from... Well... You know what I mean..."

Amrah laughed lightly. "Not at all. Our embryos are grown in suspended animation until a spirit is ready to enter them. When that happens, the new body can function within a few days. Only the best specimens of our race are selected for reproduction. As you can see, we do experiment with mixing species. Personally, I am half human (or its galactic equivalent). Our breeding techniques were perfected over millennia of genetic engineering."

"I should have known... So, how come we don't live as long as you do?"

"Your spirit does. Your bodies tend to degenerate faster, so you have to get a new one more often, and when that happens, you tend to forget your previous experiences. In time, your mind will grow stronger and you will remember. Most likely, you will lengthen the lifespan of your body... If your species survives long enough, that is."

"Yeah... Right. Reincarnation... I heard that before. So time is nothing to you, is it? We live and die in the blink of an eye."

"But time is not as important as timing," Amrah explained. "Your mission, for example, comes at a very specific point in time, just as for the others before you. You could learn much from their work."

"What others before me?" Michael wondered.

"Christ, or Krishna in India, Gautama Buddha,

Archangel Crusader

Muhammad, you resemble them in more ways than you think. You started your education a little later in life, but in essence and spirit you are the same."

Michael let go of his breath in a long whistle. He never was modest, but some comparisons did scare him a little.

So, he came to learn about his predecessors, some of them still well known and revered among powerful religious groups, others totally forgotten once their mission accomplished. All had only one goal, heighten the awareness of the people of their time. Now it was Michael's turn to do the same, in a different time, with the same people. He still didn't have the faintest idea of how to go about it.

Soon, Michael came to understand the value of self-discipline and self-control. His respect for the gentle alien who claimed to be his father grew in direct proportion to his own knowledge.

"You always seem to know the right thing to say at the right time," Michael commented to Amrah.

"I do not. Before I talk, I listen to my heart. Love is a force to be reckoned with. It can make you anything you want if you use it wisely. Misguided love, however, can wreck entire worlds, my son, and it has on occasion." Amrah seemed to reflect on a faraway memory.

"My emotions are so strong they blind me sometimes. How do I know what's right and wrong? How do I persuade myself to do the right thing?" Michael looked to Amrah for answers.

"You can regulate the chemical imbalance in your brain through meditation. Drugs are obsolete in our culture. At your present stage of evolution, the mood disorder you call bipolar personality can be compensated by one hour of deep meditation each day. Your diet will change as your self-programming kicks in. It is the safest route for you."

Toward the end of Michael's training session, Amrah offered, "Would you be interested in visiting our embryonic tanks?"

"Hell, yes!" Michael had been hoping for such an opportunity.

"I was waiting for you to be ready for the shock." Amrah's thin lips stretched in a faint smile.

"Well, that didn't stop you before. You always seem full of surprises." Michael stood up to follow his alien father down the humming corridors of the spaceship.

"This is a very complex process," Amrah explained as they walked along the soft light guiding their steps. "We aim to give our bodies regenerative capabilities in order to achieve the degree of longevity we are accustomed to. Memory is very important as well. Nothing in our reproductive process is left to chance, as it happens most of the time on your planet."

"You mean not like me? You and my mother, I often wondered... It must have been rather primitive... I mean for such an evolved being as you."

"No. Not primitive at all, very loving actually. We both enjoyed it very much. We did not beget perfection, though."

Michael lifted an eyebrow, repressing a comment. "So what's the big shock?" he asked instead.

"Here, see for yourself."

A panel slid open in total silence.

Archangel Crusader

Michael stepped back, astounded. Behind the glass, in a blue light, floating in suspended animation, immodestly naked and staring back, stood a full-size replica of himself. He looked at Amrah for an explanation. When the alien offered none, Michael's initial surprise turned to righteous wrath. "What the hell do you think you are doing in here?" As much as Michael knew about his father's civilization, he was not prepared for this.

Amrah willed another panel to open.

Michael blanched when he saw, beautiful as ever, in the same naked inanimate state, the graceful body of Veronica. He ached for her so much that he could contain his fury no longer. "Is it fun to play God? Who gave you the right? Who are these people? What are they? Don't you have any respect for anything at all? I am shocked. This is so..." he felt at a loss for words.

"This, my son, is our specialty," Amrah answered undisturbed. "This is what we do best, engineer, reproduce and even create intelligent prototypes. Do you like them? I think they go well together. They may be the future Adam and Eve of the next world we decide to populate. Of course, we will need a soul to inhabit them, a spirit to match these bodies."

Amrah studied Michael's reaction then went on. "Although they look like ordinary humans, internally they represent our latest technology. They can stand repeated interstellar travel and regenerate themselves indefinitely without aging, just as we do. Their capacity for wisdom and memory is almost unlimited. As soon as they start breathing, their natu-

Vijaya Schartz

ral psychic faculties will awaken, and they will probably never have an evil thought as long as they live. I am particularly pleased with them."

While talking, Amrah walked toward more side panels that opened by themselves as he went. In tanks of assorted colors, various human, less human, and totally alien shapes floated, in different stages of growth. A soft harmonic sound seemed to nurture all these staring bodies of various species. Michael could not think of anything to say. By now he had a hard time figuring out for himself whether to be angry or flattered by the selection.

To avoid getting mad, he chose the technical approach. "So you are never really babies, you just take a body already grown and partially conditioned?"

"Yes, it is a good approximation."

"Doesn't sound like much fun, never being a kid... Don't you miss it? Don't you miss having a mother?"

"No, I do not suppose we do. Are your childhood memories so precious to you?"

"No, I couldn't say that. My childhood was mostly a nightmare, but I hope Jennifer's childhood is happy."

Amrah nodded as if he understood.

Despite their cultural disagreements, Michael had learned much from Amrah and secretly admired his wisdom. Once again, he would have to trust the gentle alien and let go of his anger. Suddenly, Michael felt the urge to go home. It was time to move on.

Amrah must have felt his impulse. "Son, it is time for you to start on your mission. I taught you as much as I could. I gave you the tools to effect changes in your human brothers' minds. In a first step, take humanity to the next level of awareness. In the process, you will develop and learn from the experience. Then, you must face Krastinios." Amrah sounded sad.

Michael felt a pang of melancholy. He would miss the long conversations, the compassion in the Blue Angel's eyes. "Can I visit once in a while?" he asked, almost shyly.

"We will see each other again, my son." Amrah's gaze burned with intensity. "In the meantime, I will lend you strength."

"Thank you, Father..." the word still felt odd in Michael's mouth. "How long have I been away?"

"Time is an illusion. When you return, only a few hours will have passed. Jennifer's plane hasn't landed in Paris, yet." The ageless head tilted with compassion. The long-fingered hand came to rest on Michael's shoulder, and the gesture more than the actual contact sent shining rays of warmth throughout his body and mind. "So long, my son." Regret shaded the musical voice. "I will be with you wherever you go."

Vijaya Schartz

CHAPTER EIGHT

When Michael returned to his living room, he was thirsty. All these exercises in teleportation, tele-kinesis, mental healing and mind reading had left him parched. It seemed like weeks since he had touched a drink. In truth, his extensive training had only taken a few days. Michael immediately went to the refrigerator for a Coors and popped the tab. Checking himself in mid movement, he emptied the can in the sink. He hated the debasing habit, mainly since he had a new purpose in life.

After throwing a few clothes and his favorite hatchet in the saddlebags of his motorcycle, Michael slipped a knife in his boot. He'd traded his fun for an Uzi and packed that, too, then he called Shadow. The big cat came to him in the garage. Michael picked it up and tucked the feline inside his leather jacket, straddled the motorcycle and took off. He first stopped at Bill's place.

Archangel Crusader

His good friend and long-time work partner had agreed to take care of things during Michael's absence, including baby-sitting Jennifer's cat. He apparently even enjoyed this addition to his household.

After goodbyes and last recommendations to Bill, Michael mounted the Harley and turned on the ignition. He felt lighthearted and almost happy to be off. No more daily responsibilities. "Krastinios, here I come!"

The superb machine slowly wove its way in and out of traffic as Michael freed his mind to fully enjoy the moment. With Jennifer safe on her way to France, he could relax and concentrate on his mission. Although he felt guilty about it, for the first time in ten years Michael savored his freedom. The little girl had filled his life. Raising her had been fun most of the time, even when it meant changing diapers and feeding the baby on a construction site while his crew wondered about his sanity. Although Michael already missed her, Jennifer's absence would make his task easier.

If Amrah had guessed right, Krastinios would soon show himself. This time, however, Michael would be ready for the confrontation. His powers, exceptional from the start, were developing fast. To speed up the process, he must renounce his favorite red meat. His temper might still flare once in a while, but with time his willpower would increase. Daily meditation also helped improve his concentration.

On this beautiful spring day, cruising with a warm breeze bathing his face, relishing the smell of freshly cut grass in the park, Michael basked in freedom. He could not help thinking about how good he

Vijaya Schartz

must look perched on that beautiful piece of black, shiny steel, long hair flying in the wind, the sun reflecting on his sunglasses.

Veronica would have teased him and Michael would have liked the compliment. Veronica... So much had happened in a few days. She seemed far away now, almost like a dream. Michael cherished her memory. Would he finally become the man she wanted him to be? If she could see him now... Then he realized she probably could and the thought comforted him.

Briefly going over the maps earlier, Michael had memorized the road to the capital city. He could sit back and enjoy the ride. He knew where to find the help he needed. On his way south to Dave's house in Little Rock, he would stop to visit Debbie, Dave's sister-in-law. She lived in Washington, D.C. Michael had not seen Debbie since last Christmas when they had gathered at her house for the holidays. Dave and his wife had also attended the family gathering, still childless at the time, looking forward to adoption. Finally, two months ago, they'd succeeded in adopting an orphan girl a little younger than Jennifer. Now they had everything they wanted.

How Jennifer and Veronica had enjoyed the holiday...

Funny, everyone expected Debbie to die soon, not Veronica. Michael wondered whether Debbie was still on chemotherapy. Divorced with two sons in college living with their father, she knew how to fight. Debbie loved life with a passion. She battled poverty, injustice, the disease that plagued her, although she knew her life would end soon. Each day constituted a victory over the disease that steadily ate her insides. The cancer slowly spread despite all known therapies. Ahead of her lay only pain followed by death.

Michael remembered a picture on the front page of the *Philadelphia Inquirer* earlier this year. Debbie had led a demonstration in front of the White House. The black and white photograph accentuated the black rings under Debbie's eyes, the tired look, but also the fire still burning inside... A remarkable soul... Knowing she could not escape fate, Debbie was trying to help those who could still be saved, the needy children of her world.

When Michael had called her this morning, Debbie had sounded happier than usual, delighted at the prospect of seeing him soon. Somehow he hoped she would listen to his story. As a lobbyist, Debbie had many connections in Washington and could help Michael implement his plan.

There was so much to do. Where to start? Veronica always said, "Just start, then it will come to you, you'll know what to do next." Michael would do just that: start with Debbie and go from there.

As he reached the outskirts of the city, Michael felt good about himself and in no hurry. Wouldn't it be the perfect time to show off someplace? As he recognized Tiffany's from a distance, Michael remembered the girls he used to talk to and decided to pay them a visit.

He would just get into the cool dark cabaret for a short while, say hi, maybe have a drink, just one for old times' sake. It couldn't possibly hurt him now. Besides, he deserved it. Trusting his new powers to

Vijaya Schartz

keep him out of trouble, he parked the motorcycle and walked straight into the bar.

* * *

From the sky, Jennifer watched the city lights glow like a great beacon in the night. The red sign above her seat blinked.

"*Veuillez attacher vos ceintures pour l'atterissage*," confided a disembodied female voice through the loudspeakers.

"She said to buckle your seat belt," Krastinios translated. "That was French. We are landing soon. Do you speak any French?"

"Only a little bit. I had some in school last year, but not much... I can say '*Bonjour, comment allez-vous, je m'appelle Jennifer!*' But that's about it. I listened to the people behind us. I can't understand a word they said. I'm afraid this is going to be hard. Good thing my mother speaks English."

"Good thing indeed... If you'd like someone to talk to in English sometime, give me a call. I am staying at the Astoria Hotel, suite 666. Here is my card. You may call me anytime."

"Really?" Jennifer felt flattered. This handsome grown man genuinely enjoyed her conversation. She basked in the recognition, carefully placing the red and gold card in her purse.

Had it not been for the slight bump of the wheels on the ground, Jennifer would have missed the landing altogether. Since she would disembark last, Mr. K, *what a cool name,* gallantly offered to keep her company until she would meet her mother.

The flight attendant welcomed the delightful company as much as Jennifer did.

"You may want to brush your hair," Mr. K suggested to Jennifer. "You never get a second chance to make a first impression."

"Oh, I forgot. Thank you." She fished for the hairbrush in her purse.

"Please allow me." Krastinios took the brush from her hand and very slowly, with the gentlest touch, proceeded to untangle Jennifer's long chestnut hair.

The girl enjoyed the sensual feeling. No one had ever brushed her hair so gently. Not even Veronica.

After most of the passengers had left, several employees started checking the overhead compartments for any carry-on left behind. At last, the trio stepped off the plane.

The modern airport of Roissy en France was a huge concrete structure, brightly lit, cold and impersonal, despite the fancy windows and bright posters. It smelled of Swiss chocolate, Italian espresso, and French perfume from the duty-free shop. The monstrosity had been named Charles de Gaulle, after a famous dead general, or president, or both. Jennifer was not quite sure, but Mr. K would know. The moving sidewalks went on forever. Jennifer's excitement now turned to apprehension. On the phone, her mother had sounded nice, but still...

Through a side door, they skipped immigration with a smile and a salute from a young uniformed man. They retrieved their luggage from the carousel. Mr. K didn't have any. Jennifer found that rather cool.

Vijaya Schartz

They glided through luggage customs without being asked a single question, almost as if they had been invisible.

"Here is the arrival gate," said the pretty attendant with a pearly smile. "Your mother should be waiting for you there."

In the crowd beyond the gate, Jennifer tried hard to spot a likely mother, but she was led straight to the hospitality desk where a gentleman made an announcement in French. A tall, elegant woman, beautifully lean in her red dress came forward, chestnut hair cut short in a daring fashion. The woman's enormous green eyes met Jennifer's. She was breathtaking, made up as if out of a fashion magazine. Jennifer froze in surprise.

"Jennifer? You are so big for a ten-year-old. Let me look at you." Although she gave Jennifer a timid smile, the lady looked ready to break into tears as she embraced her, kissing both her cheeks, French style, as Mr. K had explained earlier.

Jennifer couldn't believe it. This was the mother she had wanted to know all her life. Her heart pounded in her chest. She felt giddy and smiled, unable to say a word.

"There's no mistake here, said the friendly hostess, you two look so much alike it's amazing. Madame Fontaine, I believe Jennifer had a good flight, thanks in part to this gracious passenger who insisted on seeing her safely with you."

"Why, I don't know how to thank you, sir," Tori said, her eyes still on her daughter. Tori's full height included a few inches of high heels, as Jennifer noticed when she straightened. "My name is Tori

Archangel   Crusader

Fontaine, delighted to meet you." Tori offered a handshake, and Mr. K brought her hand to his lips.

"You may call me Mr. K. All the pleasure was mine, Madame. Jennifer is delightful company indeed. I will add that she is very good at chess, and if you want my advice, never expect to win a game against her."

"He's good, too," Jennifer pointed out. "He did beat me once." She insisted on being fair.

"What does the K stand for? I'm just curious."

"A name too difficult to pronounce it right, so I only go by Mr. K."

Tori frowned slightly then her face relaxed. "Oh, anyway, my driver is waiting as we speak. Would you like a ride into the city? It's thirty miles away. I'm sure Jennifer would love to have your company a little longer. Am I right, Jennifer?" Tori's moist stare looked straight into the girl's heart.

"Yes, I would like that," Jennifer confirmed with a grin.

"I would not want to impose on your family reunion." The handsome man remained ever so polite.

Finally, it was decided that they would drop him off at his hotel, which happened to be on the way to Tori's home. Mr. K hailed a porter to carry Jennifer's luggage.

As they came out in the open, a black Mercedes pulled up, followed by a long, white limousine. Krastinios discreetly made a sign to the driver who barely acknowledged with a nod, then left. Mr. K then followed Tori and Jennifer inside the white limo. Busy studying each other, mother and daughter missed the whole exchange.

Vijaya Schartz

Tori's chauffeur closed the trunk then took the long, white car silently toward the French capital. The three passengers made small talk on the way to Paris. Even on the freeway, the long vehicle seemed out of place among all the tiny European automobiles. It was late by the time they reached the city, so the goodbyes with Mr. K were brief. He mentioned something about seeing them again sometime. Jennifer sincerely hoped that it would be the case.

Now, alone with her mother for the first time, in that huge limo cruising the streets of a foreign city, Jennifer felt lost, intimidated by this gorgeous woman who was so obviously her mother. Tori played nervously with the back of her cropped chestnut hair, smiling in a friendly way. Jennifer could see some fear, some vulnerability under the lovely façade.

Tori took her daughter's hand. "Jennifer, I have waited a long time to meet you. The last time I saw you, you were a tiny, ugly little bundle, under some Plexiglas, with needles and tubes stuck everywhere. I never held you in my arms. You were too fragile. No one knew for sure if you would survive, and it was all my fault."

A little overwhelmed by this outpouring, Jennifer listened intently, not daring to break the flow. Good thing the driver could not hear behind his dark glass panel. This would be very embarrassing.

"I was very young," Tori continued in a soft voice, "almost a child myself, unprepared for such responsibilities. It's probably hard for you to understand now, but I hope that one day you will, and I hope you will forgive me." A sob escaped Tori's throat.

"It's okay." Jennifer patted her mother's hand reassuringly. "Dad told me a little bit about it. I always knew I had a mother. I just didn't know where she was or what she looked like." No wonder her father had kept her away from Tori. The woman cried like a baby for no apparent reason. Good thing Jennifer had a good head on her shoulders. Right now, she felt the oldest of the two.

Tori dabbed at her eyes with a tissue then smiled. "Well, we almost look like sisters. Maybe I can help you become a model like me, if you like."

Stunned, Jennifer realized she'd never paid much attention to the compliments about her looks. And she certainly never believed them. Resembling her mother so much was a revelation.

"I'd like to make up for some of the hurt I caused in the past," Tori went on. "I was so removed from reality... I lived in a world of dreams and nightmares. That's what happens when you do drugs. I hope you never get into that hell. It's not worth it, believe me, I know..."

So, this was the mother Jennifer had longed to meet. How strange that she spoke to her like an adult. Of course Jennifer understood addiction. By watching her father, she had learned everything there was to know about it.

Her luminous eyes on Jennifer, Tori squeezed her daughter's hand gently. "I'm so glad to have you here. Welcome to Paris! So, what do you think so far?"

"I don't know." Jennifer hesitated. "It feels so... Different." Definitely an understatement on her part.

Vijaya Schartz

"I know. All these buildings, eight or nine stories high, huddled against each other, with no space in between, arches, Greek temples, Egyptian obelisks, Roman churches and statues. I felt that way the first time too. But in the daylight it's beautiful. I'm sure you'll like it. There is so much to see. You may have to choose what to do first." Tori took a small paper from her purse and put on a pair of elegant glasses. "Here, I made a list for you." Her gaze went down the list. "We could start with the zoo or the Eiffel Tower. I think we'll do some shopping, too. Do you like shopping?"

"I love buying clothes," Jennifer answered truthfully.

"What about museums?"

Jennifer made a sour face. "Booooring..."

"Maybe a ballet?"

"Yes!" Jennifer exulted "I would like that. But don't you have to work?"

Tori laughed. "Oh I don't work much anymore."

"Veronica worked at the hospital. She was a nurse."

"Yes, I heard... Did you like Veronica very much?"

"I guess so... She was nice to me... She was strict sometimes too, but she always gave me things. She helped with my reading and gave me books. Where do you work?"

With an amused smile, Tori looked at Jennifer, as if with new respect. "I modeled for a while for the Haute Couture... That's clothes, you know... I did a few ads for the magazines... It was fun, but very hectic, and I was away most of the time. Now, I like to be with Jean-Marc, although he does travel too."

"The Frenchman you married, is he nice?"

"He's wonderful. Jean-Marc helped me when I got off drugs. I think he will like you very much too. He's in New York on a business trip, but you'll meet him in a few days when he comes back. In the meantime, it's just you and me."

The white limo slowed down and stopped in front of an imposing building. The doors of the limousine opened automatically and they stepped out.

"How did he do that?" Jennifer asked, full of wonder.

The chauffeur winked. "A button on the dashboard." He retrieved Jennifer's luggage from the trunk then carried it through the plush lobby. Thick, red carpet, white columns, gold rims and crystal chandeliers reflected endlessly into mirrored walls.

"Here we are. I hope you like the Duplex."

Tori had sounded nervous. Once in the elevator, the driver inserted a key into a panel and pressed the top button. They rode quietly to the sound of soft classical music. The chauffeur, in navy uniform complete with cap and gloves, again winked at Jennifer who returned a timid smile. Jennifer felt better as she noticed that Tori clutched her purse compulsively. She gave her mother a candid, reassuring look.

The polished brass of the elevator doors reflected Tori and Jennifer, side by side, each wearing a bright red dress. Jennifer could now see the resemblance. Same green, lively eyes, same high cheekbones and high foreheads, same wide mouths with small dimples when they smiled, and the same

Vijaya Schartz

chestnut hair. Except that Tori's was cropped so short, almost like a boy. Jennifer took pride in her long, shiny hair.

The elevator door opened, unveiling luxuriant vegetation. At first Jennifer thought they had stepped outside on the roof, then she noticed the glass panels framing the stars and the sky. *What a beautiful night*, she almost said aloud. She could see many small trees potted in barrels, flowerbeds, white garden furniture... The penthouse had an indoor garden, glass walls, a big terrace, and a wonderful view of the city.

"This is the orangery," said Tori, as a perfect hostess. "Jean-Marc likes to have breakfast among his citrus trees."

Jennifer had never seen a penthouse, except maybe on TV. The driver disappeared discreetly with her suitcase. Tori kicked off her shoes, inviting Jennifer to do the same. The posh, white carpet felt like grass between Jennifer's wriggling toes.

"Dad says that nothing feels better than stepping barefoot in fresh, warm cow dung. Isn't it gross? I think this carpet feels better between my toes." Jennifer dropped onto the purple sofa.

Tori laughed with good humor and asked, "Are you hungry? Thirsty? Would you care for a pastry, some ice cream, or some milk?"

"Ice cream?" echoed Jennifer.

"The best in the country, with all the fat and all the cholesterol... A real dream... Vanilla, coffee, or chocolate?"

"Chocolate," Jennifer blurted out.

"I'll have some with you," Tori declared, on her way to the refrigerator.

The kitchen looked clean and smooth, in white and natural wood colors, with thick, white rugs on the hard wood floor. When Tori pushed a button, the refrigerator door hidden in the wood paneling opened with a soft whirring sound. She lavishly scooped ice cream into crystal bowls then produced silver spoons from a drawer concealed in the wall paneling.

They enjoyed dessert in the living room, making light conversation, sitting cross-legged on the great triangular couch of purple silk. Jennifer had never seen so many strange paintings hanging from the ceiling, modern ones, set slightly away from the mauve drapes that covered the glass walls. She stared, fascinated. Each canvas had individual lighting and a dull, gray metal frame.

"The metal is pewter," Tori volunteered. "But you must be tired. Personally, I'm bushed. I'll show you to your room. I hope you like it. I decorated it myself."

They walked up a circular, open stairwell to the second level of the penthouse and entered a dream fantasy room of pink ribbons and white lace. Delicate, fluffy pillows and silky ruffles adorned an elegant brass daybed, complete with Barbie Doll and Ken reclining on the comforter.

"Oh my gosh!" The cry of delight escaped Jennifer as her heart leapt. Opposite the bed stood a small table, on which a pink-and-white marble chess set seemed to wait. Each hand-carved piece sat on its proper square, ready for a game. On both sides stood a white leather stool where Jennifer sat for a second in amazement, looking around her. "Unbelievable!"

Vijaya Schartz

Jennifer's clothes already hung in the walk-in closet. A door stood ajar, revealing an adjoining bathroom with lots of lights and mirrors. Beside a white lacquer drawer chest sat a giant TV and home entertainment center. Also, a full-size Nintendo game screen stared from under shelves of cassettes. Next to it on a white desk, a computer and a lime green telephone. The huge room opened on an outside deck.

At a loss for words, Jennifer threw herself in Tori's welcoming embrace. No one had ever spoiled her before and this was just too much. The girl cried and laughed at the same time, enjoying every bit of her incredible luck. "This is the most beautiful room I've ever seen."

"Thank you." Tori held her tight, choking on the words. "I hoped you'd like it."

"I love it. Thanks... By the way, what should I call you?" Jennifer disengaged herself when her mother finally let go.

"Whatever you like." Tori smiled as she wiped a tear. "I'm not used to being called Mom, but I don't mind at all. And if you want to call me Tori, that's fine, too."

"Maybe I can call you Tori for now. It's a nice name. I like it."

"Well, good night, big girl. My room is across the hall if you need anything. Sweet dreams... I'll see you in the morning." She gave Jennifer a last kiss on the forehead before disappearing behind the closing door.

Jennifer's excitement kept her awake a while longer. She paced the room, touching each and every thing as she undressed and got ready for bed, wondering if she were dreaming. In her excitement she jump-sat on the mattress, rolled on the fluffy comforter, checked the dress of the Barbie doll, then lay down on the soft pillows.

Before closing her eyes, she remembered her father and called him in her mind. *Dad, I'm here... It's wonderful... I'm very happy. My mother is so nice and I have a beautiful room. I hope you're okay. I love you.*

She half expected to feel the tender communication they usually had when she thought about him, but her wandering mind only encountered silence and void. Of course, they were so far apart... Must have been the distance. Jennifer felt a little sad. She would have liked to share her happiness with her father, but she wouldn't let that spoil her pleasure and went to sleep full of gratitude.

* * *

"Goddamn... Leave me alone," Michael protested, eyes still closed, to the bothersome hand that shook him roughly. As he rolled over, his head hit something hard that sent jolts of pain through his skull. "What the hell?"

"Hey man, you shouldn't stay here, it's not safe. The cops will be patrolling soon." The hoarse voice emanated from a foul-smelling mouth.

At the word "cops," Michael opened one eye to see a grubby-looking fellow and a Shopright cart stacked with black garbage bags full of dubious contents. Michael's head hurt worse than it ever had. A timid dawn paled the chilly sky. He almost envied the

Vijaya Schartz

homeless man his pitiful coat. "What the hell am I doing here?" He sat up, instantly wide awake, regretting the sudden move.

"Eh, man, you shouldn't stay here!" the wretched being insisted.

"Get your hands off me, you filthy bum."

"Asshole," the vagrant mumbled. "That'll teach me to help a stupid drunk..." He walked away, slowly pushing his creaking cart. Michael wondered how the man stole it since they were so efficiently guarded behind steel rails at the supermarket.

While sitting in the gutter, aching from every bone, cold and sick to his stomach, a wave of self-loathing washed over Michael. How could he do this to those who counted on him? His training had not saved him after all. He still had to work at it.

Looking around, Michael realized the depth of his predicament. He couldn't manage on his own. Veronica could have helped. She was the only one strong enough who cared about him. How he hated her for abandoning him to an impossible task.

Veronica... Never to see her again... Never to feel her soft skin, never to kiss her smile, never to see the trust in her eyes. Silent tears ran down his cheeks. Michael was mad at the world, mad at Veronica, mad at himself. Once again, he had betrayed his promise. But above all he felt dejected and alone. And here, he was supposed to be this knight in shining armor who should save the world from evil and abuse. What a frigging joke. Michael couldn't even escape self-destruction.

At the sound of an engine in the distance, he collected himself enough to hide behind a concrete trash enclosure. The police car drove by at an even, slow pace as dawn intensified in the east. Traffic would resume soon.

Michael checked himself out for physical damage. Although he couldn't remember, he must have been in a fight because he felt beat up. His wallet was missing... Fortunately he had stashed most of his money inside his belt and still wore it. Michael smelled booze as he rubbed the heavy stubble on his chin. Dammit, he had to stop screwing up. He'd worked too hard to lose everything now. *This is the very last time I fall,* he promised himself.

Remembering his training Michael cleared his head to assess the minor injuries. He couldn't. His brain hurt. The alcohol had muddied his mind. He tried again, wincing at the pain in his head as he willed his neural pathways to open. Finally, after a painful struggle, something popped in his brain, allowing him to relax and empty his mind. Only then could he concentrate enough to mentally heal his injuries.

Michael then set out to retrieve the motorcycle and found it in the parking lot. As the morning sun cast peach rays on the nearby roofs, he resolved to pick up the pieces of his life where he had left them the day before and go on to Washington.

While he left the outskirts of Philadelphia behind him, old memories surfaced. His half brothers, all six of them, most of them in jail or not much better off. Only Dave had succeeded in leading a normal life, maybe because Michael had taken him away in time.

Vijaya Schartz

His stepfather had taught the boys to fight and forced them to learn fast. As a child, Michael, not as big or as strong as his half brothers, had to fend for himself, sometimes just to get his share of supper. The tyrant would organize games for them, tournaments where they fought each other in single combat. He demanded perfect technique, each blow applied full force. First blood was only the beginning. No whimpering. No giving up. If the boys didn't fight well enough, punishment would follow. Many cold, moonless nights Michael had spent in the chicken shed as a child... Many hungry days he cried secretly. Many pails of coal he heaved from the pit before dawn...

Upon reaching a fork in the road, Michael entered the freeway and soon rode through open country. He loved the smell of the fields in the spring. The miles went by with ease. Stopping at a trucker's rest stop to freshen up, he called Debbie at the office to let her know he was on his way. She suggested they have dinner with Walter, her newfound love. Michael smiled at the idea that she would seek his approval, feeling happy for her. Maybe she would not spend the last months or years of her life alone after all.

CHAPTER NINE

On this fine sunny day in late June, in Washington, D.C., Debbie's thoughts rumbled happily. She had looked in the mirror and liked what she saw. Big brown eyes consumed her thin face, but the new makeup worked wonders. The shadows had fled to the far recesses of her mind and, for a short while, Debbie felt as free and healthy as any beautiful woman in love had the right to feel. She would have lunch with Walter on the set, right after the news.

Walter differed from most news reporters Debbie had encountered. He did not seek stardom, and his honesty seemed complete. His search for the truth included compassion and understanding. Walter's coverage of Debbie's "Plea for the Children" event had been extremely well presented and, unlike some other reports, Walter's had been intelligent, articulate, and favorable in its objectivity. In the few weeks she had known him, they had become close.

Vijaya Schartz

It would not surprise her if they soon had a more intimate relationship.

To tell the truth, Debbie had fallen in love, and she suspected Walter had too. Nothing had been said yet, but their conversations, purely professional in the beginning, had become more and more personal. The friendship had evolved into a stronger bond. Debbie wanted it, hoped for it. She fully enjoyed this sweetest time of love, when you know, and yet you fear that you may be wrong. The only shadow on the horizon was death itself, but she wouldn't tell Walter about it, not yet, not ever if she could help it. She didn't want pity but a real chance at love and life before the inevitable.

In a state of excitement, Debbie reached Studio Five, fresh and flushed by her brisk walk and the expectation of what this day would bring. Doing so much for others, she never thought much about herself. To do so brought a strange and delightful new feeling.

The small coffee shop of Studio Five, crowded at this time of day, smelled of freshly baked lasagna. Debbie spotted Walter first. As soon as he saw her, he waved from his booth on the far side. A smile brightened his clear blue eyes as they held her exclusively. Debbie rejoiced at the delight in his square face.

Walter, usually serious or concerned in front of the cameras, looked cheerful now, almost boyish despite his obvious maturity. He wore his legendary blue suit. As Debbie reached the table and held out her hand, Walter stood up and took it in both of his. He kissed her fingers with a fervor that made her tingle all over. "And how is my favorite lobbyist today?" Walter's suave voice sent a shiver up Debbie's back, her scalp prickled, and her cheeks felt hot. What a wonderful feeling.

They talked with animation over chicken Parmesan and wine, laughing and smiling a lot. Debbie caught Walter looking at her surreptitiously, but then again, she did the same. While pondering their chances at a successful relationship, she outwardly discussed the filming of the next special report on the needy children of the capital.

"This is how it could start," Walter offered, slicing his chicken. "A few blocks from the White House, people sleep on the sidewalk, on benches. Poverty strikes at the heart of the nation. We roll the camera on the needy, then we show the white tents erected in the public parks throughout the city, providing meals and clothing for the destitute." He ate a bite.

"Good." Debbie dabbed at her chin with a napkin. "But you should also mention the insufficient shelters, whole families paying the price of cold, political games. I would like the emphasis on the children, young children, babies. They are the ones I'm most concerned about at this point, the innocent victims."

"You love those children, don't you?" Walter smiled, all indulgence. "You protect their rights with great conviction."

"I do my best to restore human kindness to this world," Debbie said, embarrassed by the compliment.

"I know, applying your own weight against the odds, fighting to make a difference. I watched the videotapes of your speeches from our archives...

Vijaya Schartz

Your conviction can be quite inspiring, even for a professional like me..."

After lunch, Debbie took a cab back to her office on Pennsylvania Avenue. She wondered about Michael's call, he had talked in riddles. Tonight's dinner would certainly prove interesting.

Debbie always enjoyed the long conversations with Michael. Each time he visited, they spent hours sharing views on life, philosophy, politics, or how to raise chickens. They did not agree on everything but usually ended up very close in their opinions, sometimes after much debate. That was the fun part of it. They both enjoyed spirited discussions.

It might be awkward to explain to Walter that this man, who was not exactly family, would stay at her house for a while. Nevertheless, Debbie wasn't about to compromise. She never had and probably never would. Michael was a friend and family-in-law. Case closed.

That afternoon, when she pulled into the driveway of her suburban home, Debbie noticed the black Harley-Davidson and could not help but smile at the similarity between the machine and the man. Wild, handsome shiny steel, with raw power and reckless instincts.

Debbie found Michael on the back patio, playing with her new German shepherd. So much for a watch-dog. Through the open sliding door, the smell of blooming roses filled the living room, mixing with the scent of Michael's aftershave. From the stereo, an unfamiliar radio station broadcast country rock, something she hadn't listen to in many years. Michael really looked like a cowboy, with long jeans and boots. Debbie knew he never wore a hat, but he was true country all the same. So was she, inside, despite her many years in Washington. Michael reminded her of her roots... Arkansas seemed so far away.

"Did I leave the patio door unlocked?" Debbie inquired as a greeting.

"I guess so," Michael lied. "It's so good to see you."

They hugged, giving each other much-needed comfort.

* * *

"I'll get the door," Michael told Debbie as she pulled off her apron and ran into the powder room. They had prepared dinner together. One more thing they had in common, they both enjoyed cooking.

The solid oak door opened to reveal a bunch of red carnations hiding a blue blazer and a smiling Walter. The grin dropped an inch and froze for a second while the two men took each other's measure. Walter, shorter and older than Michael, stared with frank blue eyes.

"Hi! Walter, I presume. Please, come in. Debbie will be right back." Michael liked Walter's strong handshake. A slight mind probe confirmed the favorable impression as he closed the door and hushed Walter into the living room.

"These need some water," said the older man, a little uneasy.

"Here." Michael took a tall crystal vase from a Chinese buffet and handed it to Walter with a smile. "The kitchen is that way. Would you like a drink?"

Vijaya Schartz

"Thanks, Maybe a glass of wine." Walter disappeared into the kitchen. Sounds of running water, big splash... "Shit!"

Michael ran into the kitchen to find Walter on all four, trying to mop a huge spill on the floor with paper towels.

"Hey man, let me do this. Don't be so nervous... She's crazy about you." Thinking this would be as good a time as any to test Walter's view on the paranormal, Michael snapped his fingers, making the spill reabsorb and disappear, but not as fast as he expected. The flowers jumped into the vase full of water, paper and ties vanishing from view into the garbage can.

"What in heaven?" Walter stared and followed Michael who took the flowers to the dining room table.

By that time Debbie appeared, smoothing her white summer dress, smelling good, with a fresh coat of lipstick, distracting Walter from asking any questions, although he looked in Michael's direction, puzzled. Debbie made the introductions then served a delicious tomato-tarragon-chicken dinner with French ratatouille. Michel refused the wine. Toward the end of dinner, the conversation turned to more serious matters. The time had come for Michael to find out if his plan could work.

He had the best possible audience. These two influential friends could mean success or failure. Michael had to win them over to his cause. Since ethics forbade coercion, however, he would let his friends make up their own mind. He'd have to trust in their good will.

"So, are you going to tell us what brought you to the capital?" Debbie asked, as if on cue, producing caramel custard cups on a tray with a pot of fresh coffee.

"I thought you'd never ask." Michael collected his thoughts, reclining slightly in his chair.

"As much as we like each other's company and conversation, I know that you didn't come just to visit with me." Debbie sat, looked for a cigarette, then stopped herself and served coffee.

Michael smiled with sympathy. He knew what she was going through. Addiction made a powerful contender. He felt appalled at his own conduct of the day before.

"I can't tell you everything yet," Michael started, alert and a little nervous. "But I'll tell you this: I had some kind of revelation... Don't ask me how or what... I want to start a consciousness movement. A planetary quest to elevate the ecological and spiritual awareness of the people of America first, then of the whole planet. I'd like to call it the Earth Crusade. What I need is some exposure, maybe TV coverage."

"Don't you think the world has enough gurus and TV preachers?" Walter vehemently stirred sugar in his cup. "They made a bad reputation for themselves over the years."

"I'm not asking for financial support," Michael explained, ignoring his coffee. "My purpose is just to make people aware."

"Something like the Hunger Project in the eighties?" Debbie suggested, seemingly more open to the idea.

"Yeah... An appeal to the masses to support whatever organizations are already in place and func-

Vijaya Schartz

tioning. Everything from ecology to anti-racism and charity, including anti-violence, the study and development of psychic abilities, UFO research..."

"That's quite a spectrum!" Walter interjected. "How do you expect people to take you seriously if you spread yourself so thin?" He unbuttoned his blazer and sat back, crossing both hands on his stomach. "Besides, some of these issues are very iffy. UFO research? The serious viewers may take you for a flake. Even the network may object under the pressure of the Council on Foreign Relations and the Trilateral Commission. As for psychic powers, I personally think they are a hoax. I never met anyone who could prove or demonstrate them beyond the shadow of a doubt." Walter lifted an eyebrow at Michael, in challenge.

Michael had not expected him to resist so much. If the trick with the flower vase hadn't impressed him, Michael would have to resort to a more dramatic demonstration.

"I have good reason to believe in psychic faculties from first hand experience." Michael slowed his breathing, concentrating on a point low in the center of his forehead, at the level of the pineal gland. "Have you ever seen an aura? You know... The magnetic field around the body?" As four avid eyes stared in silence, Michael continued. "Watch, and tell me if you think this is a hoax."

Eyes closed, Michael heard static and felt the warmth radiating from his body. The air around him sizzled with electricity. Surprisingly, his head hurt with the effort. When he opened his eyes, the room shimmered with blue brilliance.

"Beautiful!" Debbie marveled with a bemused smile. "Did you do that? How?" Her wide, brown eyes sparkled.

"Impressive trick," Walter admitted, sipping coffee. "But this does not constitute hard evidence. Optical illusion, magnetic phenomenon... This house could be rigged. After all, David Copperfield made the statue of Liberty disappear."

Michael could see the hurt on Debbie's face. "Then what would it take to convince you?" he asked. "Materializing something where there was nothing before?   Moving objects from a distance? Walking through walls? Speaking from mind to mind?"

"Let's be reasonable here." Walter spread his hands in conciliation. "These things are scientifically impossible."

"You said it. *Scientifically*, they are, at least for now. But they can be done through other means. Let me demonstrate." Michael rose from his chair.

"You can't be serious." Impatience tinted Walter's tone.

I'm dead serious. How do you think I mopped up that spill in the kitchen earlier? Michael screamed in Walter's mind, leaving him red-faced and wondering. "You want proof?" Michael said aloud, some irritation in his voice. "Let's go to the back yard, so you cannot say that the house was rigged." He walked straight to the wall, and banged his head."

Debbie and Walter looked at each other and laughed.

"What did you do that for?" Debbie asked, still laughing. "Are you all right? I'm sorry for laughing but it was funny."

Vijaya Schartz

"I meant to go through the wall, but I don't feel quite right today." Michael rubbed his brow, wondering at his failure. The drinking of the day before must have affected his neural pathways. Also, he had lost his calm.

Still chuckling, Debbie came with a napkin dipped in cold water and dabbed at his forehead.

"Let me try again. This time, I'll concentrate better." Michael gently pushed Debbie's hand away from his face.

"This is ridiculous, Michael, don't do it," she pleaded.

"I have to convince some skeptics." After a look at Walter, Michael closed his eyes and breathed slowly, concentrating through the pain pulsing in his skull. When he felt all the molecules of his body adjust to the new vibration, Michael slowly walked through the wall and onto the patio.

Debbie and Walter stared at the wall, speechless, then used the sliding glass door to join him outside.

"My God, Michael! Is this how you got into the house this afternoon? I knew I locked the doors this morning." The German shepherd almost ran Debbie over, rushing to be petted by Michael. "I've never seen him like this with anyone before. He's supposed to be mean."

"He can be…" Michael petted the dog.

"Well... How do you explain this ability of yours?" Walter finally gave in to professional curiosity.

"It's an unbelievable story. Let's only say for now that I was born with a special gift. I always suspected it but only recently learned to use it. We all have it to some degree, though, and can develop it."

"Did you learn it on your own?" Michael could tell Debbie was hooked.

"No, I had some help" He hesitated on how much to tell them, then continued, "from my father."

"Your father? Michael, no one ever knew who your father was. Your mother even denied you ever had one. How did you find him?"

"I didn't. He found me. He was far away all this time but just came back."

"This is great news! How wonderful. I'm so happy for you. How do you feel about it? Can we meet him sometime?" Debbie bubbled over.

"Maybe, who knows... Anything is possible, but for now, I have to make a case for psychic powers, so let's just do it. Debbie, didn't you mention this afternoon you found this cherry tree too small and too far from the house for decent shade?"

Walter rubbed his chin, but Debbie seemed to enjoy the game. "Yes, I said I would have liked it right there at the south corner." She pointed, delightful in her excitement.

"Like this?" A slight flicker of magnetism, a faint rustle of leaves. Now, the cherry tree, three times its original size, stood at the southern angle of the house. Instead of blooms, it carried dark red cherries, months ahead of the season. Michael then teleported himself to a heavy bough and picked a handful of crimson fruit. "Care to try some?" He popped one in his mouth and jumped down like a cat, dropping the rest of the cherries into the hands of a wide-eyed Walter.

Vijaya Schartz

"This is too much. No one can do this." Debbie, in shock, laughed nervously. "I had no idea you could do such things. This is incredible! Someone pinch me. I must be dreaming this."

"Is there anything you cannot do?" Walter, sober and dead serious now, asked. "Do you know what this kind of power could do in the wrong hands?"

"Unfortunately, yes. I even experienced it." A shadow passed over Michael's mind. "Veronica's death was not an accident as it was made to appear. There are others with no scruples, no ethics and no conscience. I need your help to fight my battle. I want nothing for myself, I only want to make this world a better place."

"All right." Walter stuck both hands in his pockets. "I guess you made me a believer in the paranormal, but UFOs are another matter altogether. I know about the big controversy in the media about the Roswell incident and government secrets of that time, but I'm not convinced that there are aliens out there."

They all walked through the open glass door, back into the living room.

"All these things are linked," Michael continued. "You will just have to take my word for it. I can't give you any proof. Let's just say that if it weren't for a UFO, I wouldn't be here today. Literally." Michael sat in the armchair, leaving the couch for Debbie and Walter.

"Whoa! I would really like to hear about that." Debbie's enthusiastic curiosity comforted him, but it was too early to explain, yet.

"Why are you doing all this? What's in it for you?" Walter's inflection still had a ring of suspicion. He had taken Debbie's hand.

"Besides the challenge and the obvious satisfaction of doing the right thing?" Michael felt like a mischievous child. "To be perfectly honest, I'm settling a score with Veronica's killer. I would love to nail him to the wall and, given a chance, I will. But I have to warn you that if you are thinking of helping me, you are placing yourself in the path of danger. This deadly character knows no compassion, no human feelings. He's after me and will stop at nothing to see me dead. You could get hurt in the shuffle, or worse..."

Walter looked absorbed in thoughts. "I don't know... I could risk my career getting involved in this kind of venture."

Ever prudent Walter, Michael thought, but he remained silent, letting them make up their minds.

"Oh please, Walter, let's help him. You can get him on at least four different TV programs. You have friends in almost every network in the country. You know all the talk-show hosts. You could even get him some free commercial time. No matter what you think about some of the issues, it's all in the best interest of humanity." Intensely vibrant, Debbie was definitely Michael's best advocate tonight.

"Lovely Debbie," Walter started with a smile then paused. "How could I possibly decline such a passionate plea?" He brought her hand to his lips.

Michael sensed the strong currents flowing between his two friends. He could feel Debbie's hopes and Walter's sensual desire. Reading Walter's inten-

Vijaya Schartz

tions, Michael stood up and shook his hand. After kissing Debbie on the forehead, Michael thanked his friends and excused himself, discreetly retiring to a bedroom on the second floor. The incredible expense of energy needed to perform the display of psychic powers had drained him. He felt weak. Away from the energizing presence of his alien father, he needed much meditation and deep sleep to recharge.

* * *

After Michael left the room, Debbie's warm and trembling gaze fell expectantly into Walter's deep blue eyes. "Thank you, Walter," she whispered. "This means a lot to me."

"The Crusade?"

"Yes, the Earth Crusade...and also the fact that you're doing it for me. It makes me feel very happy inside... I don't know how to explain." She looked for help in his eyes, at a loss for words.

Walter took over. "What if I told you that you are so important to me, that the highlight of my day is when I see you for lunch or for dinner? What if I told you that a day without seeing your smile or touching your hand would feel like an eternity?" He had both her hands in his now. He was so close, so vulnerable, so openly inviting.

"Walter, I couldn't bear not seeing you. I need your strength, your fortitude, your conversation, the way you look at me when you think I'm not watching. I want you near me." Now that Debbie had bared her soul, was he going to hurt her?

"I know, Debbie. So do I."

Walter shifted slightly on the couch. His lips came close, almost touching. "I'm in love with you, Debbie." His sweet breath caressed her cheeks. He held her frail body against his chest.

Debbie welcomed the demanding lips that covered hers in a long, soft, endearing kiss. "Walter, I will love you like no one did before," she echoed in pure bliss, hoping this was not just a dream.

* * *

Jean-Marc Fontaine slammed down the receiver and burrowed in the breast pocket of his beige Pierre Cardin blazer for a piece of gum. He chewed it nervously, breathing fast, not even enjoying its icy taste. He could have chosen a better time to stop smoking.

Fists clenched and unclenched in the deep pockets of the creased tan pants. Facing the wide bay window of his office, Jean-Marc did not really see the view. Manhattan, from the thirty-seventh floor of the Chemitek building was still only Manhattan, just another place to work.

Jean-Marc, the French corporate director in charge of the European division, a sharp dresser in his mid thirties, wore elegant, loose-fitting clothes in a deceivingly casual way. Today, however, his nonchalant attitude gave way to explosive wrath.

As he paced back and forth, he grumbled in French, passing long, smooth fingers through light brown hair, once short but now curling in the back of the neck and around the ears. Jean-Marc pressed

Vijaya Schartz

the red button on his desk, and his assistant's head popped through the open door.

"You called me, sir?"

"Yes, Miss Goldbloom. I need your help. Come in, please. Sit down," he said with a heavy French accent.

The young woman in the navy business suit and high-heeled shoes looked tall and heavy compared to the shorter, slender Frenchman. Her subdued demeanor, however, left no doubt about who was in charge. Jet-black hair, pale skin, bright eyes, and prominent nose made her handsome rather than beautiful.

Jean-Marc Fontaine opened the manila folder with the red "confidential" stamp lying on the desk. "How long have you known about this?" He pointed a finger at three lines highlighted in bright yellow in the middle of the last page.

Miss Goldbloom, who had never seen her boss outraged before, seemed shocked at the tone and the flash of anger in his eyes. "I heard a rumor a few weeks ago, but I did not believe it... Not until I saw the report myself this morning."

Since she sounded genuinely concerned, Jean-Marc felt grateful for her feelings. At least he was not the only one appalled by the ethical violations corroborated by the American Board of Chemitek Enterprises.

"Do you have any children, Miss Goldbloom?"

When she blushed, Jean-Marc realized his mistake. "Of course not. I'm sorry... Well, I don't either... But my wife has a daughter. Do you know what this careless disposal of chemical waste can do to innocent children playing in their backyard or on the school playground, given the right atmospheric conditions?"

"I read horror stories in the paper, but as long as it cannot be definitely tied to the dumping, it's only a coincidental observation. Circumstantial evidence, though disturbing, is insufficient. The secret dumping will continue. Our CEO will make sure of that. The cost of safer disposal would be outrageous. The board did not deem the expense cost-effective." The regret in the woman's tone contrasted with her accurate account.

Deciding to trust her, Jean Marc ventured, "I need names, places, times, anything you can find out about what is going on. They won't tell me much. They know where the European Community stands on these matters, but they have no reason to suspect you. How long have you been with the company?"

"Five years, Sir." Apprehension modulated her voice.

A short silence followed, filled with the soft humming of the air-conditioning. Jean-Marc broke it first. "How would you feel about losing your job? It could happen, you know, if you are caught hacking into the company's secret files. I may not be able to save you."

His honesty seemed to touch her more than any plea. "I'll be careful." She smiled timidly, implying acceptance.

"Thank you, I knew I could count on you. How would you feel about working exclusively for me if we succeed?" Jean-Marc returned the smile.

"I would like that." Miss Goldbloom looked

Vijaya Schartz

down. "Excuse me." She pushed the blinking button on the desk phone. "Jean-Marc Fontaine's office. How may I help you?" She had regained her professional composure. "Certainly, please hold... It's your wife, long distance, on line one. I'll keep you posted." She disappeared discreetly and closed the heavy door behind her.

"Tori? *Comment vas tu, mon amour*? In English? Of course... Hi, Jennifer. Welcome to Paris. I wish I could be there with you both, but something came up. I have to stay a little longer to straighten out this mess. It may take a few more days, or a few more weeks... Jennifer's dad? Not really... His brother's farm in Arkansas? That would be central time. Give me the number just in case."

He took a fountain pen out of his pocket and wrote the number on a note pad. "Of course. I'm sure you can have fun without me for a while. I will let you know as soon as things clear up here and I can come home. In the meantime, I send you both my love. I miss you. *Je t'aime, Tori... Au revoir mon amour*."

When he hung up the phone, his features had relaxed, and a dreamy smile brushed his lips. Jean-Marc had often wished for a family. It would feel good to become a father, even for a little while.

CHAPTER   TEN

Playing with a single ice cube in a glass of Chivas Regal, Krastinios smiled to himself. He enjoyed the stare of the women here tonight, especially the blonde *femme fatale* watching him from the end of the bar. Her black velvet sheath revealed white shoulders and ample breasts...a bombshell by international standards... Krastinios looked at her once and knew exactly who she was, how he would crush her indomitable temper, and how he would dominate her and make her beg before the evening was over.

Krastinios already enjoyed Paris, the capital of innumerable pleasures and infinite possibilities. Some men stared at him too, hypnotized by his grace. An interesting thought sprouted in his mind. Why not create a new cult, a fresh supply of pleasure slaves for private orgies? But not tonight...

Krastinios made the light dance in his dark velvet eyes as a subtle smile softened his flawless features when he approached the blonde. Perfect

Vijaya Schartz

French with just a slight, indefinable accent would add to his exotic charm. "I love the lace of your black underwear, but Jean Patou is too light of a fragrance for your personality. You should wear Poison," he declared with a smile he made irresistible. Looking straight in the woman's eyes, Krastinios could read her thoughts vacillating from embarrassed to ashamed, to flattered, to angry.

The blonde's clear blue eyes glinted gray. Only for an instant, Krastinios thought she might slap him and briefly wished she would, but instead she answered with venom, "Insolent," then picked up her small black clutch. She stood, turned her back to him and left.

Krastinios did not try to stop her, rather he watched her walk sensuously away. As she reached the open doorway, he suddenly re-materialized on the other side and greeted her with the most winsome smile.

"Leaving so soon? I was hoping we might get to know each other." Reading her most intimate thoughts, Krastinios played with her feelings.

"How did you do that?" The woman touched her forehead as if she felt dizzy. "I think I had too much to drink. I'm seeing things. Please step aside." Her attempt to look offended failed. Krastinios knew she secretly enjoyed his insistence. The poor creature did not stand a chance but did not know it yet.

"I have chosen you tonight. It is a great compliment. What do you say?" He patiently waited for her response, witnessing her weighing the consequences in her mind. The husband was away on a trip... Krastinios reveled in her absolute attraction to him and already savored the young voluptuous body with generous curves in the right places. He read as well her strong-minded temper, spoiled childish habits, propensity to have things her way. Krastinios relished the prospect of breaking her. He would make her his first *Chosen.*

Many others would follow. Of course, Jennifer and her beautiful mother, too, would be his before long. Krastinios had already seduced their minds. He would shield them from any outside interference. Soon, they would no longer know the difference between right and wrong, ready for him, innocently playing into the palm of his hand.

For now, this woman would do. Krastinios delighted in manipulation. The pretty blonde did not have to answer at all. He simply took her arm then smoothly guided her toward the elevator. On the way, he materialized a bottle of champagne and a bunch of fragrant red roses.

Conveniently, the couple did not meet anyone on the way to her hotel suite, as if the omnipresent staff and guests had suddenly vanished. The blonde beauty smiled now. Her manicured hand wrapped around Krastinios' arm, she fingered the supple leather of the black jacket, bewitched enough to follow him anywhere. The woman did not question him but smiled, adoring eyes on Krastinios all the time. She did not notice how he opened the door, or that the room smelled of incense.

Krastinios hypnotized, subdued, and overcame her easily. The woman giggled and laughed then drank the champagne from a crystal glass. She moaned with anticipation while he slowly and tenderly

Vijaya Schartz

peeled off her clothes. The sweet perfume diffused stronger waves when she offered her lips. Krastinios carried her to the bed, gorgeous in her naked state, wavy blonde hair cascading down softly.

Smiling in reassurance, he took her hand, brought it up to the brass post of the bed, then bound the wrist to it with a soft leather cuff. He gently kissed the bound wrist, slid his mouth along the arm, over her generous breasts, mouth, shoulder, and along the other arm, all the way to the other wrist that he deftly bound to the opposite post in the same fashion. For an instant, a question flitted in the woman's eyes, but Krastinios erased her doubts with a languorous kiss.

Taking his time, he explored with hands and mouth the hard nipples, then, further down, her navel. The blonde beauty moaned again while his tongue invaded a moist, warm private place, but did not resist as he gently fastened her ankles apart with soft leather ties.

As the drug in the champagne wore off, the woman slowly came back to her senses, opening wide eyes as she took in the scene. Krastinios flashed her a benign smile and gently caressed the smooth skin inside her thighs. When she responded sensually, he proceeded to slowly arouse her, from hard nipples to the soft white skin under the breasts, smooth underarms, and nape of the neck. He left no sensitive zone untouched.

"We cannot make any ugly noises now, can we?" Krastinios said in a suave voice. He kissed the slightly open mouth with passion then slowly taped it shut with wide surgical tape. Seeing the fear in the woman's eyes, he whispered, "There, there, it's all right. Now we can have a good time without scaring the neighbors."

Standing up, Krastinios walked to the table and picked one of the red roses from the vase. Walking back to the bed, he produced a dagger of hard, dull silver in the shape of a serpent, the handle encrusted with gems. To test the razor-sharp edge, he sliced the rose blossom twice through the center. The scarlet petals, like tiny butterflies, flew and settled on and around the white exposed skin of the woman's body.

Krastinios then lowered himself comfortably on the bed beside her, brushed the flat of the blade against her nipples, soft belly and tender throat. He smiled at her terrified face. The smell of fear lent an edge of loving cruelty to his voice as he said, "Now, my beautiful Chosen, let me teach you what true pleasure is all about..."

* * *

The next morning, Jennifer woke up to sunlight filtering through the pink drapes of her dollhouse bedroom. Breaking the silence, a bird sang outside while the smell of fresh coffee teased the nostrils. This would be a good day, she decided.

Tossing back the covers, Jennifer jumped out of bed and opened the drapes to a breathtaking, sunny view of the city. When the sliding glass door opened easily, she slipped onto the deck surrounding most of the second floor of the glass structure. The

Vijaya Schartz

happy chatter of a sparrow attracted her attention. Perched on the branches of a potted citrus tree, it stared at her, fearlessly chirping away. Delighted, Jennifer observed it for a while, happy to be alive and wide-awake on such a beautiful day.

Barefoot, Jennifer scampered down the white-carpeted stairs to find Tori on the purple sofa, reading the newspaper.

Tori looked up with a smile. "Good morning, little girl." She took off the glasses.

"I'm ten, I'm not little anymore. Good morning anyway."

"Sorry, my mistake. Good morning, young lady."

"Now, that's more like it."

"Would you like some croissants and hot milk with a little coffee in it, French style?"

"Is it good?"

"I like it. Would you care to try it?"

"Okay." Jennifer hardly noticed the old servant in the kitchen, until the woman set breakfast in front of her.

"Where is the rest of it?" Jennifer pointed at the paper folded on the couch.

"Oh, that's all of it," Tori answered. "This is a French paper, only a few pages. Just essential news. No junk."

"Whoa, this is really small. Can you read French? What does it say?"

Tori put her glasses back on and applied herself to translate the headlines for Jennifer. Suddenly she exclaimed, "My God, someone got killed at the Astoria last night!"

"The Astoria? That's where Mr. K is staying isn't it? It wasn't him who was killed, was it?" Jennifer felt uneasy, almost a feeling of impending doom.

"No, it was a woman... Oh my, what a vicious killing! She was cut into pieces alive!... But I shouldn't tell you that, you are too young. Besides, you're having breakfast..." Tori paused. "Sorry, I did it again. No, I'm not going to treat you like a baby."

"I hope not. What did she do? Why was she killed?" In Jennifer's mind, there had to be a reason.

"I don't know, but this is something about big cities you will have to be aware of. You cannot trust strangers. You have to be very careful. Paris is a dangerous place for women and young girls."

"Do they know who killed her?" Jennifer attacked her croissant . She was hungry.

"Not yet. They say it might be the work of a cult." Tori turned the page.

"What's a cult?"

"Dangerous people doing mean, crazy things."

"What for?"

"The worst of it is, they are so twisted that they believe it's the right thing to do."

Jennifer dropped the matter. Such a heinous crime so close to someone she knew made her uncomfortable. She finished her breakfast in silence then asked, "Do they have tigers at the zoo?"

"Certainly."

"Can we go to the zoo today?"

"It's a good day for it."

"I like tigers and timber wolves. Do you think they have timber wolves?"

"I wouldn't be surprised at all if they did."

Vijaya Schartz

CHAPTER ELEVEN

"What kind of degenerate is your best friend, my dear?" Walter seethed, raging out of bounds.

Standing in the middle of the living room, Debbie could not think of anything to say. Walter had uncovered a truth she could not deny, but how to explain the unexplainable?

"According to my sources, and they are extremely reliable," Walter went on, "Michael Tanner is a despicable character, an alcoholic who jumped bail on DUI in two different states, a brawler arrested on one count of aggravated assault with intent. There are warrants for his arrest in several western states. He frequents the most dubious establishments, rubbing shoulders with go-go dancers." Walter turned away, staring through the patio doors.

Debbie had to control her outrage. Her own sister had been a topless dancer before she married Dave. "I know, but he never got a chance to even start right," Debbie pleaded. She slumped onto the sofa, feeling defeated. She should have known something had gone wrong when Walter took two days to answer her messages.

"Easy excuses. He's a mean bastard, your best friend. And you are asking me to help him get exposure for a moral crusade? What kind of joke is this? I can't believe it from you. I trusted you. In fact, I thought you could do no wrong. Please, Debbie, tell me this is a mistake... Michael was only twelve when he attempted to kill his stepfather, for heaven's sake. How trustworthy can he be?"

"Please Walter, you have to understand... His childhood was a nightmare."

Walter's face, red and congested, remained immovable. "I was raised by a very strict father myself. Nowadays, they call anything abuse. I got hit, too, when I did something wrong."

Debbie boiled inside, the sensation of heat reaching her temples. She rose and paced the room, remembering her fighting spirit. "Did your report also tell you that Michael took his ten-year-old brother, Dave, away from that tyrant. At fifteen, Michael raised his young brother, working hard to feed him, providing a roof over his head and keeping him in school. Only later did he finished his own education, attending night classes at a community college."

As Walter's stubborn expression did not change, Debbie went on. "His wife and baby died when he was a teenager. Later, when his dopey girlfriend had a sick premature baby and ran away, Michael raised Jennifer himself, and very well I might say. What he needs is love, understanding, another chance at life."

Still no reaction from Walter, but if Debbie pushed a little more, maybe he would give. "Often his extreme sensitivity pushed him to the limits," she continued. "Do you know that he raised several sick kids that weren't his own? There was a little girl with cystic fibrosis, Penny. Michael bankrupted his business paying her hospital bills. When she died, at seven, despair made him swim out to sea, hoping to join her. He was rescued unconscious by a fishing boat. His bipolar personality drives him to extremes in stressful times. But all his life he tried to help others, giving a job, sharing his place with a homeless for a while, doing free carpentry work for charities that needed it, helping his neighbors and his friends when they hit hard times." There. Debbie breathed better now.

"I didn't know that, but it doesn't change anything."

"Walter, you don't understand. Michael always had love at heart, but his stepfather beat him regularly because he was smart, sensitive, different. Michael had to fight back to protect himself and those he loved. Hatred, he learned from his stepfather who, I suspect, also abused him sexually, although Michael never told me that..."

Walter remained silent, his face an unreadable mask.

Undaunted, Debbie continued. "The mother was a pretty young thing with no skills who couldn't manage by herself. She married the wrong man then kept a cleaver under the pillow at night, just in case he would try to brutalize her, too."   Debbie could smell her own sour sweat now and hoped Walter could not.

"I'm sorry, Debbie. Lots of people who had a difficult childhood don't break the law at every turn because it's convenient. I cannot jeopardize my career by endorsing someone I don't trust, even for a good cause."   Walter turned suddenly, bumping the table, shaking the vase still containing the red carnations. "This campaign is different from simple news coverage... I would be personally involved. I just don't trust him enough. I'm not even sure I can trust you anymore. Now I wonder what else you're not telling me. Is Michael your lover? Why do you support him so unconditionally when he's on the wrong side of the law?"

Debbie could not pretend any longer a calm she did not feel. "Walter, that's enough!" she said louder than intended. "Michael and I are childhood friends. Besides, he has changed. Can't you tell that he's no longer the man you describe?"

But nothing she said could stop the flow coming from Walter's angry mouth. "This guy comes out of nowhere, shimmering, demonstrating incredible powers, but who is he inside? Who am I giving my support to? How do I know he's not going to start drinking again tomorrow and become that depraved addict, that criminal portrayed in my file? What happens when he's found out and gets arrested on the set and his crusade turns to ridicule? Debbie, you disappoint me. I thought you had higher standards."

Vijaya Schartz

"I asked you to do this for me because I know it's right. Of course, there are no guarantees, but I've known Michael as long as I can remember. We have no secrets from each other. I know his heart is good and I do trust him. Besides, I owe him too much to refuse him. He was wonderful to me when I needed him. Michael brought me back up when I was down. He understands me better than anyone else. We helped each other through thick and thin over the years and I will not let him down."

"What did he help you with?" Walter asked with vehemence. "What did you need him for?"

"I can't tell you that, not yet... But most of all, I didn't expect you to investigate him. That alone tells me that you didn't trust me in the first place." By now Debbie fumed inside. "And yes, there are things you don't know about me... Maybe you should ask your private detectives to hit their computers and start a file on me, if you haven't already."

"Well my dear, I just might take your advice. I'm a practical man who believes in facts."

"I don't have to explain myself, and I'm not going to," Debbie burst out. "I have my reasons for doing what I do, and I will tell them to whomever and whenever it goddamn well pleases me!"

"So be it! Count me out." Walter looked at her with hurt in his eyes. "Goodbye, Debbie... If you change your mind and want to see me, you know where to find me."

There was a cool draft as Walter opened the door with an angry pull. Debbie's heart shattered into sobs after he slammed it shut. He hadn't looked back.

Archangel † Crusader

* * *

The past days had been filled with preparations. One night, when Debbie came home, Michael talked on the phone while stirring gravy in a pan. "See you Monday morning at ten, thanks again." He hung up the phone, turned down the flame, then abandoned the stove to help Debbie unload the groceries. "That was Channel Three. They set up the interview for Monday morning," he announced with a smile of triumph.

"Great. Everything's going smooth so far." Debbie smiled back, going through her mail. A red invitation stood out from the junk mail and bills.

"I wonder how it got into my mailbox, there's no stamp or postmark." Debbie opened the stiff envelope. It did not have an address, much less a sender's name. She opened the thick paper with anticipation but blanched as she read.

"What is it?" Michael asked. Automatically making contact with Debbie's mind, he read through her eyes the perfectly calligraphed words.

> *"You have wandered beyond the safe path. Stop now if you value your life, for I do not. You could lose blood and soul in your very last scream. Signed K."*

"Krastinios... I knew it! The bastard must be awfully close. How does he know so much so fast?" Michael wondered aloud.

"How do you know it's him?" Debbie's words came out faint and shaken.

Vijaya Schartz

"Oh, it's him all right. He didn't deliver it personally, I would have felt him near, but he sent it, no doubt. I bet he has connections in Washington. I warned you about him."

Michael suddenly remembered the gravy on the stove. "Damn!" He ran to the kitchen and turned the wooden spoon in the pan a few times. "He's something like me, except that he uses his powers for evil. Debbie, I won't hold it against you if you don't want to go through with the Crusade." After turning off the stove, Michael tapped the spoon on the edge of the pan, wiped his hands then sat on the couch. He took Debbie's hands and looked into her eyes. "Krastinios is more dangerous than you can imagine. He means what he says. He already killed Veronica. I couldn't bear losing you, too..."

"Come on, Michael, you warned me in the beginning. I haven't come this far to stop now." Debbie's voice, though resolute, still had a ring of fear and uncertainty.

"I appreciate your courage, but you may want to think about this."

"I thought about my life a long time ago, when I learned I had cancer. I decided then that fear would never rule me, that no matter the consequences, I would do what I thought was right. And I happen to think that what you're doing is right. I only have a short time left... I might as well use it to bring hope to humanity." Tears made her eyes brighter. With her chin set, she looked like a martyr unwavering in the face of death.

Michael gathered her in his arms. "While we work together, I will not let you out of my sight. I may be able to protect you if you are close. In any case I'll feel better."

Debbie's smile illuminated her face. "I wish Walter understood me as you do," she said wistfully.

* * *

That night, in need of reassurance, Michael visited Amrah's spaceship. Away from it for several days, he realized how much he had missed his father. Amrah, even kinder than usual, seemed glad to see him.

"Father, I don't know if I can handle this job," Michael confessed with humility, an uncomfortable feeling at best.

"You can, and you will. I know it." The gentle alien shimmered in reassurance. "It will be all right. You can handle it." Amrah looked sad for a second. "My main concern is Krastinios. The extent of his abilities, his motivations, his real purpose are still a mystery. Be careful, my son. He may be more dangerous than even I can imagine."

"I'll be careful, Father. Don't worry about me," Michael said, with more bravado than he felt.

* * *

Crowds had always fascinated Michael. This particular throng rumbled deep and strong as an ocean. It had kept swelling since early morning and, from the side of the podium, Michael could watch it grow, filling up the patches of green grass still visible from the park along the avenue. Despite the presence of several groups of diverging opinions, the

Vijaya Schartz

gathering had remained peaceful so far. The cause of hungry children did not have any opponents. Everyone wanted to be part of the supporting event.

Debbie had worked on this for weeks before Michael came to the capital. She had invited leaders from all walks of life to deliver a speech for the children. Ignoring the threatening message of the night before, she arranged for Michael to talk as one of the many guest speakers. Since he did not want to give his real name, Debbie insisted that he be introduced as Crusader. Michael agreed, although he felt uncomfortable about it. The title sounded pretentious.

Since the national press monitored each and every happening in the capital, Michael knew the journalists would attend. White, blue, yellow and red Vans from CNN, NBC, and every other TV channel and radio station lined the periphery of the multitude.

When Walter had stopped helping, Debbie worked doubly hard. Thanks to the chance she gave him, Michael would monopolize the eyes and ears of the media, using the exposure for the Earth Crusade. The sooner Michael started, the sooner Krastinios would show himself. Several guests had already delivered their speech. Michael was next. When the sun hid behind small clouds, he felt a chill in the air. He had never spoken in public before.

Despite the smell of spring flowers surrounding the stage, Michael still had misgivings as he ascended the steps of the podium. When Debbie waved at him from the other side, Michael scanned the crowd for any danger to her life. He could see none. With butterflies in his stomach he started talking, surprised at the sound of his voice through the loudspeakers. No pyrotechnics or pretenses, he would just tell the truth as he felt it. As soon as he spoke, all his fears vanished and he enjoyed a deep communion with the crowd.

"Children have filled my life with laughter and tears," Michael said, recalling vivid memories. "I have known no greater joys and no greater pains than from the children I loved. Most of them need so little, just love and food. Some need a lot more care, and for others, it's already too late."

His voice choked at the memory of Penny's death, and he had to take a deep breath to clear the tears blurring his vision. "But don't let the fear of losing them stop you from adopting, loving, or helping these children. The next time you see a child in need, stop making excuses and do something about it, anything from calling the authorities to giving him a piece of fruit. There's no excuse for beating or starving a child, or standing by while such abuses happen. Today's society suffers from a common disease called indifference."

As he paused, Michael noticed the lulled silence of the crowd. Although he did not use his powers, the audience felt the strength beyond the words. But something else caught his attention, something evil gathering above. Was Krastinios trying to stop him? Michael hoped for a confrontation. Watching Debbie and the heavy cloud billowing above him, he went on.

"We can cure this indifference by simply listening to our hearts. Deep down we know what's right and wrong, and we all yearn to help. Whether it's about the children, the people of Earth or the planet

Vijaya Schartz

itself, let's make a commitment to help in any way we can. Love is contagious, too. Spread it!"

The cloud above darkened then emitted a blinding light a quarter-mile in diameter. The air threatened to explode. Michael, sweating despite the unnatural chill, concentrated his energy to spread a protective shield over the crowd, like a shimmering dome.

Frantic activity possessed the camera crew. Michael's eagle eye could see them desperately fitting filters and lenses to get the phenomenon on film as best they could. Transfixed, the silent crowd stared at the luminescence while Michael struggled to keep the evil cloud away.

Suddenly, the threat was gone. The cloud and the light dissipated and Michael relaxed. Krastinios had retreated this time. Canceling the shield, Michael ended his talk as if nothing unusual had happened. "Thank you for your attention. May your good will be rewarded in your hearts."

Dead silence. Michael could see tears rolling down young and old cheeks. The quiet crowd then started a low murmur swelling into a crescendo of voices. Frenzied effervescence surged in the area of the press. Everyone rushed to reach the stage before Michael could step down.

With tremendous authority, Michael influenced the chaos into order. He gazed in concentration into each and every camera, answering questions with purpose, monitoring the effect of his answers through the mind of his close listeners. On his far left, Michael could see Walter walking slowly toward Debbie while the crowd pressed Michael with questions.

"What was this thing? How did you do that?"

"Was this a natural phenomenon?"

"Is this a hoax?"

"What kind of power are you using?"

"Why do you think people were crying as they listened to you?"

"Is Crusader your real name? Are you hiding your real identity?"

"What's the meaning of your speech today?"

"Is this part of a new political campaign?"

Michael fed the media answers that would elicit more questions, carefully preparing a fruitful exposure. Each opportunity to talk to the public gave him one more chance to impart his urgent message to his fellow humans.

* * *

Debbie observed with interest the unfolding of the plan Michael and she had developed, amazed at the accuracy of his insight. It had really started. She could tell by the crowd swarming the stage. Michael was handling things so well...

Debbie's heart beat fast with excitement but almost stopped when she saw Walter coming toward her, looking as embarrassed as a little boy. Although glad to see him, Debbie could not help being sarcastic. "So, you finally changed your mind?"

Walter winced at the remark. "Debbie, please, I want to apologize, I'm really sorry. I had no idea... I had no right to talk to you the way I did."

"That's right, you didn't." Debbie hated herself for the harshness in her tone.

Vijaya Schartz

"But I couldn't possibly know what you were going through..." Walter looked contrite, blue eyes searching hers. "I should not have quarreled. Now that I know everything, I understand."

Walter reached for her hand but Debbie stepped back. "What are you talking about? What do you know? How do you know?"

"I have ways of finding out." Walter blushed slightly but went on. "Debbie... I called your sister in Arkansas. She told me about your condition. "

"Damn Becky and her big mouth. And damn you, too. How dare you spy on me? So you haven't changed, have you? You still don't trust me... You won't take my word for anything! You are despicable! Get out of my sight, or rather get out of my life!... The only reason you come to me now is probably that you want the exclusivity on the story. Now that Michael is news, you're interested. Is that it?"

"Debbie, you're not being fair," Walter pleaded, eyes downcast like a scolded puppy.

Debbie looked back toward Michael, still surrounded by journalists. Unable to stand Walter's narrow-mindedness any longer, she started toward the curb where the red Jeep was parked. Walter chased her across the lawn.

Suddenly, she heard Michael in her mind, a desperate command, "*Debbie, Debbie, STOP!*" Instinctively, she stopped, so abruptly that Walter ran into her. Lost for a second, Debbie wondered at the injunction when an explosion filled the air around them. A burning wind heated her cheeks. The car was engulfed in flames and smoke. Debris fell in slow motion all around the perimeter.

Archangel ⚔ Crusader

Debbie heard screams. She saw people running in every direction. The cameramen turned toward the scene. Coughing through the thickening black smoke, she heard police sirens closing, or was it the ambulance or the fire truck? Her legs buckled as strong arms seized her.

Walter's urgent voice reached her ears. "Debbie, are you all right? Debbie... Oh my God! Debbie, I love you."

Shaking uncontrollably as Walter held her tight, Debbie clung to him with the energy of despair. She did not want to die, not yet, not before enjoying his love for as long as she could. "I love you, too," she whimpered between sobs. Closing her eyes, she rested her head on Walter's shoulder then fell into a black void.

* * *

Michael rejoiced when Debbie was up and around again. Walter had raced her to the hospital after the failed attempt on her life. He now served as her chauffeur, bodyguard, and knight in shining armor. Fortunately, there had been more fear than harm.

For a whole week, Michael's picture had monopolized the news. Debbie collected as many diverse newspapers as she could find, from the *Washington Post*, the *Philadelphia Inquirer*, the *Denver Post*, and *USA Today*, to the *National Inquirer*, even the *San Francisco Chronicle*, and from as far away as the *Honolulu Advertiser*. All the layers of society were represented. All without exception related the

Vijaya Schartz

unnatural events of the rally in Washington, though in different shades of realism.

Interviews and picture-taking sessions occupied most of Michael's time now. The publicity worked. Demonstrating some paranormal powers on the air widened the audience while he imparted his message. Michael made the most of every opportunity to explain his views of a better world, of what could be accomplished and how. He planted in each listener's mind a seed of positive energy that would soon grow and bloom into the will to help his cause.

The Earth Crusade had become a powerful machine that gained momentum with each appearance, causing new ideas to germinate in millions of minds. Michael was hardly needed anymore, since other organization had taken over the program. In order to stop this positive force, Krastinios would have to intervene in person.

Walter and Debbie became inseparable. The threats stopped, and they went on warily with their lives.

* * *

"Earth Crusade, first take."

The black and yellow board clapped in front of Michael face, jerking his mind back to the recording studio. In the heat of the projectors, Michael remained cool by controlling body temperature. It didn't take much to control one's own environment. A few months ago he would have laughed at the concept.

"You see, this planet needs tender loving care, much like a human being..." The speech made sense, but what mattered was the thought pattern woven into the sounds. By now Michael had seen its effect many times and was still amazed at the power of his voice on regular human beings. He sometimes even had doubts about the ethical aspect of the Crusade, although it was for the ultimate good.

"If each person keeps in mind these most important values, they will affect everyday thoughts and actions. Ultimately, the course of events will change. When choices must be made, they will be made for the greater good of the planet and of the people who inhabit it."

Michael spoke for the cameras, constantly aware of the crew moving quietly about. As he had seen it happen before, a change occurred in the eyes of the man holding the long pole of the microphone, tears rolled down the face of the production assistant, and the makeup artist stood transfixed. Michael could sense emulating thoughts from the sound engineer at the console. Staring into the lens, Michael conveyed power to the words, and the light technician joined the quasi-religious experience.

In these moments of pure worship, Michael could choose to become a god. Aware of the possibility, however, he had no inclination to do so.

* * *

The morning of the seventh day since his first public appearance, Michael woke up before dawn in a sweat. In his dream, a long line of police cars

Vijaya Schartz

drove up the road toward Debbie's house, coming to arrest him. No doubt, he had been recognized and found out. His past had caught up with him.

Although no walls could hold him, Michael did not care much to be riddled with bullets. People feared what they could not understand. His mission had barely started. He also had to find and destroy Krastinios. Besides, he did not want to endanger Debbie. So he dressed quickly and mounted the Harley.

The police would find an empty house. Debbie had spent the night at Walter's condo. Michael left the doors unlocked, hoping the zealous cops wouldn't destroy anything.

It felt good to be on the road again despite the cold, rainy dawn. Before the transformation, Michael would have hated such weather. His stiff joints would have rebelled against the dampness. Since the training, the alien part of his mind had rejuvenated his body, allowing him to enjoy the rain without reservation. He'd remained sober during the Crusade, and his mind felt light and clear.

Making himself inconspicuous as a grain of sand on the beach, Michael rode on in the misty morning toward his brother's home in Arkansas. While his thoughts wandered freely for the first time in many days, Michael reflected on Jennifer. She had not contacted him in several days. He had been so busy that he hardly noticed the break in the pattern. He must reach her sometime today.

Later, as Michael traveled along the blue-crested Appalachian mountains on Route 81, thoughts of Veronica came to his mind, bittersweet and far away. How he missed her... Seeing Walter and Debbie so close made him think of his own solitude. Damn Krastinios! When would he finally show his face? Michael couldn't wait to destroy the bastard for taking away Veronica, the only woman he'd ever loved.

Vijaya Schartz

CHAPTER TWELVE

At dusk, among French geometrical gardens, lit from the inside like a monumental pumpkin, the seventeenth century structure loomed ominously. Krastinios' chateau dominated a marble esplanade, surrounded by a low, stone balustrade. A monumental stairway led through several broad landings to a maze of carefully groomed shrubbery, designed by the famous André Le Nôtre, gardener architect of Louis XIV.

Light as a dancer, the black knight ascended the steps to the first landing. Snapping his fingers, he then flooded the esplanade with flickering amber lights, enhancing the columns, windows, and the balconies of the three-story façade. Conveniently, he left dark alcoves and gray areas around benches and bushes for the privacy of the playful guests.

Muffled conversations and broken laughter rode on the cool breeze with traces of perfume, mingling with the more subtle scent of roses blooming ahead of the season. A nude nymph emerged, running and giggling from behind a fountain. The long red hair, pale skin and full breasts evoked the image of Venus from a Boticelli painting. Count Dracula's smooth chest shone, inviting against the red lining of his black cape as he followed the nymph with nonchalance.

Inside the great hall, the air felt pleasantly warm. In an intricate play of warm colors, dim lights and friendly shadows, the costumed party unfolded according to the master's fantasy. Louis XV, heavily rouged and perfumed with bergamot, lowered one knee to the thick, silk rug covering the oak parquet floor. Lifting Madame de Pompadour's crinoline, Louis admired the pubic hair, intricately braided with multicolored ribbons in the eighteenth century fashion.

In front of a replica of the Sphinx, Cleopatra, spread in a lascivious pose on a blue velvet sofa, toyed with a turquoise from the heavy necklace resting on her naked breasts. From a silver cup, she drank a red aphrodisiac, the nectar of the gods.

When Krastinios came near, Cleopatra winked at the knight in black leather. He smiled then lightly kissed her hard nipples. Cleopatra's blue eyelashes fluttered. She shivered under the caress, but Krastinios withdrew quickly and walked away as her heated scent flourished, leaving her wanting for stronger pleasures.

Ravel's Bolero, amplified by sophisticated sound technique and closed in by the hanging tapestries and heavy drapes, permeated the very air, lend-

Vijaya Schartz

ing its pulse to the game. The sweet smell of opium wafted high from the Chinese chamber. There, elaborate water pipes sat on low tables of red lacquer, attended by two young oriental maidens. Their thin veils parted as they moved, revealing creamy skin. A red glow softly lit the smoking room, soothing to the eye, inviting to the heart.

Walking through the crowd of guests, Krastinios made sure everyone enjoyed to the fullest the forbidden pleasures he had devised. He provided their favorite entertainment so they, in return, would see to his personal needs.

In an avant-garde corner, psychedelic lights exploded with life and merry sounds. An exuberant Greek huntress, a generous creature with gleaming eyes, hooked herself to Krastinios' shoulders. Her pale, hairless body, clad only in slave bracelets of green oak leaves with a headband of the same greenery, undulated at his contact. She nibbled at his ear, softly blew in it, then laughed. Krastinios gently peeled her off his chest to relinquish the woman to the care of the Marquis de Sade for further enhancement of their mutual pleasure.

"My dear friends," Krastinios announced to a small group including Rasputin and Elvira, "I want to issue a special invitation for an exceptional party. It will take place tomorrow night, at midnight, in the crypt of the greatest cathedral of all."

"Notre Dame de Paris?" a clear feminine voice exclaimed with a trace of wonder.

"Yes, my dear, under the heart of the city. I also have a very unique treat for you all, but it is a surprise. May I count on you? Please wear black, and nothing underneath. This is a very formal event. Spread the word. You may invite some friends, but make sure of their commitment and secrecy. You won't regret it. I promise you an unforgettable night."

In front of a delicately painted paper screen, a white-faced Geisha, artfully coiffed with long, carved ivory pins, exposed her small white breasts while plucking the strings of her *shamisen*. In a hypnotic trance, she recited to a captivated audience a very daring haiku, written long ago by a bored shogun concubine.

Nearby, a Michael Jackson look-alike in diamond studded blue leather cut neat lines of white powder with a gold razor blade on a slab of black marble. Feverish eyes around him, some with dark circles, stared avidly.

In an adjacent chamber, a passionate Chopin played a bewitching Nocturne. Around him, heavy breasts heaved above white lace corsets and satin petticoats, amidst muffled cries, in the sweet giddiness of champagne.

Farther away, on a decorated stage, a rare scene unfolded. Projected live on a video-screen occupying most of the wall, two hermaphrodites engaged in heated sex acts. They exposed their bisexual organs in giant close-up shots, penetrating each other simultaneously for the curiosity and arousal of the onlookers.

Silent as a cat on black suede paws, Krastinios enjoyed surprising his guests with sudden appearances, almost as if he had emerged from thin air, and often he did. He reflected now on Jennifer and Tori, Jennifer so innocent, and Tori so beautiful. How

Vijaya Schartz

would they respond to his depravity? Their fear, their shock, their disgust, their arousal, their terror... What a delightful sight to look forward to.

The Persian youth, in yellow silk and matching turban, sat cross-legged on a marble pedestal. He sent a delighted smile when Krastinios materialized. The innocent chestnut eyes greeted the man in black with a look of pure adoration.

Krastinios found blind idolization quite arousing tonight. He flashed a most charming grin in response, his mind already pondering the potential for pleasure. He then walked toward the young boy in a slow, deliberate stride and kissed the soft lips that opened willingly under his insistent pressure. In a lustful exchange, Krastinios' hands explored the hard muscles under the dark supple skin. "Come with me," Krastinios whispered urgently then started in the direction of a dark corridor.

The boy followed him along the purple maze of doors and passageways. They passed Barbarella and Barbie-doll, standing against the wall, mouths locked, short and long hair tousled, red and black leather gear open in front. Bare breasts rubbing against each other in a lustful fever, they tangled in a tight embrace.

Krastinios recognized a heavy fragrance: the scented oil used by the African enchantress who now tumbled with a sturdy stallion of a man, on a sofa hidden in a dark recess. Walking through the hall of many doors, Krastinios could hear the sounds of expectation and sweet madness possessing the junkies free-basing crack in the antechambers or shooting needles in the powder room.

The boy following him stared but kept smiling and took the man's hand for reassurance. Krastinios tenderly obliged. A narrow stone stairwell spiraled down to the basement where a dark hallway ended in front of a forbidding black door. It opened as they approached and closed by itself behind them, without a sound.

In the luxurious torture chamber, Krastinios whispered suavely, "Now, my beautiful Chosen, you are mine, and nothing can come between us. I will enjoy all the pleasures this gorgeous body of yours can provide, and no one will hear you scream... For you will scream as your life escapes to feed mine."

Uncertainty floated in the chestnut eyes. A timid smile started to curl the corners of the boy's mouth, but it all changed to terror when the dangerous truth finally registered.

And he did scream, but no one heard his desperate plea behind the mysterious door.

Vijaya Schartz

CHAPTER THIRTEEN

Rays from the rising sun filtered through the clouds while Michael rode east. The sky looked like the religious pictures of his youth, with silver beams of light piercing the dark gray clouds. After a few strategic turns, to make sure he was not followed, Michael headed west toward Arkansas. It felt good to ride through open country again after all these years. He had missed the smells, the fragrance of the dirt, even the grass.

The land represented the soul and the spirit of his young years. He remembered a day when, at twelve, some old cowboy convinced him he could ride a bull. Although Michael was underage, the man arranged for him to ride in the rodeo.

"Nothing to it," the rugged man said. "You're good on a horse. You can handle it. You'll become famous... It's good money. If I could do it at your age, you can. The girls will look at you for sure."

Archangel Crusader

Ranch hands hoisted him atop the meanest beast of the bunch and opened the gate. As soon as the Brahma bull bolted in the enclosure, young Michael realized his mistake. Under him, a ton of twisting, pounding, skyrocketing muscle kicked and spun. He held on to the rope as hard as he could, pale and screaming, while the cheering crowd whirled around and up and down. A deadly carnival roller coaster ride, the boy thought with terror, the frail body taking a severe beating. Michael did not get trampled but almost died of fright. It took him a week to recover, less than for one of his stepfather's regular beatings.

This was the law of the country, as Michael knew it as a child. He still respected that old cowboy for teaching him a lesson in humility. That young boy had quickly learned the values that later shaped his life. Freedom at all cost, respect for life, love and protection for the children. Women remained a mystery, however. Would he ever understand them?

All his romantic involvements ended the same way. Michael never found what he looked for or knew what to expect from a relationship...until he met Veronica, his first true love. How he hated that popinjay in black leather for taking her away. Michael could do nothing when he met him before, but this time it would be different. At least he had the tools to fight, and soon, he would.

Hungry and dirty from the road, he stopped in Nashville for the night. The streets smelled of burgers and fries. Michael kept an inconspicuous profile, using mind suggestion to alter his appearance. To passers-by, he looked like an old, solitary biker better left alone.

Vijaya Schartz

After dinner, sitting on the bed in a dark motel room with green and gold draperies that smelled of stale cigarette smoke, Michael called Debbie and Walter on his mobile phone. The FBI had contacted them. They'd honestly answered all questions, including the fact that they had no idea where he hid. Michael did not enlighten them either, only saying that they could contact him soon at his destination. He hung up the phone before the call could be traced. Satellites had a way of giving out locations.

When Michael called Dave, the FBI had been there too, but only briefly. Since Michael had officially cut all ties with his family at the age of fourteen, they seemed to believe the story Dave fed them and probably would not come back. Dave's farm still looked like the best place for Michael to wait. Besides, Jennifer might try to reach him there.

Jennifer... Was she safe? He dialed Tori's number but obtained no response. An inexplicable malaise seized Michael as he thought about his daughter. Time to establish mental contact. Relaxing on the hotel bed, he launched his consciousness to the French city of Paris and from there spread his awareness over the continents. Michael searched relentlessly for any sign of Jennifer's psyche. She couldn't possibly be lost, but he couldn't find any sign of her on the planet. She had to be alive. Michel would know if she were dead. Why couldn't he reach her? He could only hope Jennifer would call him soon.

Finally, Michael fell into a troubled slumber, the strong body giving up to physical exhaustion as well as mental strain. His sleep that night crawled with nightmares. They brought up the recurring face and atrocious cold eyes of the snake-alien Lufriec, surfacing from another dream weeks ago, out from under the silvery hood of a monk's robe.

* * *

Jennifer thoroughly enjoyed the Eiffel tower. She cringed with apprehension during the noisy elevator ride, amidst enormous beams of rough brown iron and closed her eyes a few times. Despite her fear of heights, the view from the top of the great lady of steel, proved rewarding. As long as she kept her eyes on the horizon, Jennifer was fine, but vertigo seized her every time she tried to look down. Below, magnificent palaces, museums, and white churches sprinkled the hills. Parks and streets formed a picturesque grid, like a gigantic map, with the lazy River Seine snaking nonchalantly through it.

For lunch, Jennifer and Tori took the cruise on the river in a Plexiglas boat. The food wasn't that great, but Jennifer's eyes devoured the scenery passing by. Old stone bridges decorated with statues, antique bookshops in the open air, cathedrals and churches. People in a hurry walked everywhere. Jennifer even saw Lady Liberty on the riverfront, saluting the passing barges. Who would have ever guessed she was French?

In the afternoon, Jennifer fed the pigeons in the square in front of Notre Dame. She marveled at the height of the elegant towers of the great cathedral, at the lace-like pattern of the stone carvings along the portals, at the stained glass windows and

Vijaya Schartz

rosacea. She looked up at the flying buttresses until her head reeled, frowning at the ugly gargoyles staring back at her. She wondered if the hunchback of medieval times still slumbered under the eves of the highest tower among the gigantic bells.

Following the left bank, Jennifer and Tori walked among the crowd of the Quartier Latin, mainly students of the neighboring universities. When they came upon the Place Saint Michel, Jennifer stopped and stared. A huge fountain dominated the intersection. There towered a colossal archangel, framed by magnificent wings. The bronze statue of Saint Michael brandished a snake sword and trampled the Devil in a demonstration of raw strength and righteous wrath. The handsome fiend writhed under the onslaught.

Somehow the statue of the archangel reminded Jennifer of her father, right down to the long wavy hair... She had not been able to reach him lately. She'd tried to concentrate as he taught her, but to no avail. She'd also called his mobile phone, but for some reason the lines did not connect.

"Maybe we should go home," Tori suggested. "We have to get ready for our big night."

Jennifer agreed. The very special night at the Opera was her first great event. Setting her worries aside, the young girl focused on the evening. She would wear the red dress Tori had bought for her.

Back at the penthouse, mother and daughter tried different hairstyles and makeup combinations. They giggled, striking poses in front of the mirror of the master bathroom. Jennifer marveled at the professional lights and drawers full of assorted lotions, creams, powders, blushes, eye pencils, nail polish, lipstick, and a variety of cosmetic tools she had never seen before.

In order to look alike tonight, mother and daughter had purchased two long, bright red silk dresses of slightly different styles: one flattering Jennifer's budding breasts with a frilly ruffle, and one that downplayed the voluptuous bosom of her mother. The back on each dress exposed much bare skin. Even the hairstyles would look similar, at least from the front. By cutting short bangs in the front of Jennifer's long hair, combing them in a boyish fashion, and pulling up the rest in a high chignon, Tori made their faces look strikingly alike.

Jennifer practiced walking in high heels. These, with her tall stature, added five years on her. False eyelashes, lipstick and careful makeup made her look like the little sister of her gorgeous mother. Jennifer basked in the feeling. She knew now without a doubt that she had found her real mother and felt very secure. Both enjoyed the same things, they even looked alike. If only her father could see them now!

* * *

The white limo pulled up in front of the brightly lit Opera House, which resembled a white wedding cake with gold and green bronze decorations. Krastinios, casually holding up the dark-green, velvet drapes, watched from the private office window above the lobby. His expert eyes appraised the two beautiful women who stepped out of the car, wearing

Vijaya Schartz

red silk and gold lamé stoles, diamond necklaces and bracelets covering their flawless skin.

"Thank you for the exclusive tickets," Krastinios said, turning back to the middle-aged man in the expensive suit sitting behind the antique cherry desk.

"This is nothing after all we owe you, dear friend." The gray-haired man looked fearful in the glow of the desk lamp. "Besides, it is such a privilege to serve you. We greatly appreciate your generous support of the arts, among other favors." The lecherous smile of the man told of depraved tendencies. "See you later, at your little party."

Bowing slightly, Krastinios smiled, more to himself than to the man, then left. Down the stairway of Venetian marble, his feet barely touched the red runners held in place by polished brass retainers. Krastinios reflected on the incompetence of simple humans. They could not be depended upon and usually found ways to fail in the most important tasks, like the Secret Services, that bunch of amateurs...

Krastinios should have gone to Washington himself. The agents in charge of organizing Debbie's accidental death had fumbled. "A slight error in timing," the Colonel had explained. "We could easily terminate her anytime, if you like." How could it look like a random terrorist act now? Krastinios could not kill Debbie without attracting attention to the Crusade. Too late... The opportunity had come and gone. Time to implement plan B.

As he crossed the landing, his eye caught a television screen displaying his archenemy. This Crusader, as the journalists named him, was becoming bothersome. This last week, his face had been

Archangel Crusader

showing up everywhere in messages packed with subliminal suggestions to restore the planet. Other speakers had picked up his cause, and his ideas spread with unexpected alacrity. A renewed interest in ecology, world peace and solidarity now surfaced in all the media. The little tramp had learned much in a short time, enough to become a major thorn in Krastinios' side. Like all Reptilians, he liked the heat and counted on the global warming. Without it, Earth would be a cold home for his people. Why had the Blue Angels bothered to teach a lowly Earthling? Didn't they know a mortal didn't stand a chance?

From the second floor, leaning nonchalantly on the marble banister, Krastinios kept the foyer in his field of view. There, Jennifer and Tori admired the grandiose architecture, the sculptures and the paintings while waiting for the curtain call. Krastinios had obtained for them the best seats in the house, first balcony, front row, also known as the presidential lodge which, however, presidents rarely used anymore. He would surprise them by showing up at the last minute, his seat conveniently reserved in the same box.

Krastinios had not come tonight for the premiere of Romeo and Juliette, although the ballet, remarkable in every way, featured the most reputable dancers in the world. No... He had come to stalk his chosen prey: two beautiful white doves, already wearing the crimson of their very blood.

Jennifer and Tori seemed to enjoy the social game. As they approached in all their glamour, they acknowledged a smile from a good-looking man, a glare from a less beautiful woman.

Vijaya Schartz

Krastinios followed them into the crowd of multicolored organza, shiny satin, starched pleated shirts and black neckties, with an occasional tuxedo or black hat. He was the only man there wearing fine leather, open on a smooth tanned chest. His rare elegance, perfect posture, ideal proportions and natural poise made Krastinios the most fashionable man in the crowd. Many women, and quite a few men, noticed and coveted him.

Taking a detour behind a pink marble pillar to better observe his doves, Krastinios chuckled at their surprise when the usher showed them to their seats. He waited a few minutes then ambled toward them. "What a delightful surprise!" he exclaimed, all charisma and smile. "I could not have wished for better company. Jennifer..." He formally kissed her hand. "Madame Fontaine." He reiterated the courtesy.

Mother and daughter caught their breath at the apparition. A question furrowed Tori's eyebrows, but she soon joined in the conversation already started between Krastinios and Jennifer. They talked about the magnificent ceiling, painted by Chagall a few decades ago. The modern style contrasted with the classic gold columns and centuries-old architecture. The angels sported black-contoured Picasso-like faces, and the bright colors and bold shapes won Jennifer's vote. Tori, who had seen pictures of the original ceiling felt it more suited to the style of the edifice.

"The new generation likes it," Krastinios concluded as an apology.

When the lights dimmed, the crowd hushed. In the low incandescence of a huge chandelier, the spectators held their breath while the majestic curtain of crimson and gold lifted slowly, revealing a diaphanous veil. The flimsy fabric caught the light but still concealed the rich decor behind. After a few customary tuning scales, the orchestra struck the first notes of the introduction.

Rather than stare at the stage and enjoy the music, Krastinios savored the closeness of the two very beings he would use to bring down his archenemy. Easy work indeed with such trusting, naive, and oh so enjoyable females. He checked once again on the psychic shield he had placed on Jennifer to prevent her from reaching her father. The invisible barrier held. Not a chip in it. A little more patience, and all would be won.

In the meantime, the ballet unfolded on stage in the glorious colors of old Italy. The dancers breathed in the passion of Shakespeare, swaying to the music of Tchaikowsky brought alive by the choreography of Nureyev. Krastinios allowed his mind to wander for a while to his next commitment of the night.

At the intermission, he said his goodbyes, promising to take Jennifer and Tori to dinner at La Tour D'Argent in two days. Jennifer, forgetting her manners, squealed with glee while Tori stared wordlessly, uneasy about something but agreeing nevertheless.

"Wonderful! I will pick you up the day after tomorrow, at six-thirty sharp," Krastinios said as he departed.

* * *

Vijaya Schartz

When he reached the bottom of the wide stairs fronting the esplanade of the Opera House, a black Mercedes with dark windows pulled silently to the curb. The back door opened and Krastinios slipped inside in a fluid motion. The door made no sound as it closed. The luxury sedan then took the Avenue de l'Opéra in the direction of the River Seine, the traffic lights turning green as the car approached them along the Quai du Louvre.

Within a few minutes, the Mercedes reached the Pont Notre Dame. Past the Prefecture de Police, in front of which two uniformed officers stood guard, the majestic cathedral appeared on the left, its front portals and south walls flooded with electric light. The north side, however, along the rue du Cloître Notre Dame, remained bathed in cold shadows. The quiet vehicle entered the dark street, slowed then stopped for a brief moment along the wrought iron fence. Krastinios exited quickly, then the car vanished into the night traffic.

The black metal gate turned on its hinges. A few stone steps led to a red portal. It opened under Krastinios' smooth hand, releasing a fragrant cloud of myrrh and incense from inside. The impossible height of the venerable ribbed vault was lit by the pale glow of the outside projectors, through the Chartres-blue stained-glass windows. A few votive candles added an amber light.

Krastinios entered the cathedral, light steps caressing the green and gold mosaic of the marble floor. When he reached the heart of the sanctuary, he knelt, looked up and invoked humbly the one Being he feared and depended upon, his Nefarious Father. Only Lufriec could understand what His son was going through.

"Father, you made me powerful but not as powerful as Thee. Why is it, Father, that I need to maim and kill for my very survival? I know they are simple, uninteresting humans, but isn't there any other way?"

Just then, a shimmer enlivened the very air. In the diffuse brilliance above the altar, a shape slowly came to focus. A green spark sizzled and smoked on the altar stone, leaving an electric scent. Hissing sounds reverberated, bouncing off the high stone pillars while tears of longing welled in Krastinios' eyes. The great shape came to life, a huge monk in a silver robe who pushed back the hood, revealing the green scales of a Reptilian face. The enormous dark eyes of the powerful alien changed color, swirling with emotions, from black to brown and dark green. A forked tongue lashed the still air.

"My son," Lufriec roared, the sound filling the gothic edifice to its highest arches, "For you there is no other way. You must gather the energy from many human lives lost in agony before you can reach the level required to fulfill our prophecy. Remember that, as we speak, your nemesis also accumulates strength. Do not underestimate the Crusader... We cannot afford to lose. You must prevail in the end. The survival of our race is at stake..."

"I know, Father." Krastinios bowed humbly.

"Make the most of tonight's offering, my son." Lufriec gaze around the cathedral. "By the way, I like your choice of place." There was a hint of cold glee in the voice now. "It is absolutely perfect."

Vijaya Schartz

"Thank you, Father, I thought you would like it." Krastinios smiled. Serious again, he implored, "Bless me, Father, for I need the support of your might."

"Rise, my son, my pride and joy. You have my unconditional support. I bless you, my child, with the powers of your birthright. May you succeed in your dangerous quest."

The apparition rippled and vanished in a vibration of hissing chords that lingered after he had gone. A small serpent of green light slithered and disappeared beyond the edge of the altar. Then silence and semi-darkness took possession of the medieval edifice once more, with only the smell of incense and the glow of the projectors filtering through the stained-glass windows.

Krastinios felt rejuvenated. He circled the altar to reach the hidden door behind it. A slight pressure of long fingers on the head of a golden cherub prompted the opening of a low door in the stone wall. The floor slid to reveal a secret staircase that led down to the buried crypt.

Krastinios descended into darkness. Materializing a lit candle, he set it in a niche in the wall to light the stairs then continued down to the low-ceilinged room. He inhaled the cool musty air and walked to the altar set on a central platform surrounded by stone steps. From the center of the circular room, his long shadow danced, caressing the thick pillars all the way to the stone benches. Stone effigies lay very still on the sepulchers lining the periphery of the wall.

Concentrating for a few seconds, Krastinios purified the place for the special occasion. Red torches suddenly appeared in sconces, illuminating the domed ceiling. The altar, floor and circular stone rims shone as if made of polished black marble. The temperature in the room rose to a more comfortable level while a red pentagram drew itself on the smooth black floor, the altar standing in its center.

Soon, several black-hooded silhouettes, each carrying a candle, shuffled silently along the outside perimeter of the circle. They took their places on the semicircular benches, setting the candles in the niches of the wall. A slumped veiled figure, supported by two sturdy males, was then led to the altar. The Chosen. Once there, she thankfully collapsed, her nudity under the black transparency of the muslin veil becoming evident in the glow of the torches.

Krastinios waved a hand toward the door. The opening in the wall sealed itself shut with a rasping of stone, then an eerie harmony echoed throughout the crypt. When a loud clap resounded, the hooded participants rose, then Krastinios intoned a ritual in Latin. "Oh Nefarious Father, deign to look upon us with compassion. We implore Thy presence and Thy blessing as we celebrate Thy power in the name of the Father, the Son, and the Holy Serpent. *Et cum spiritu tuo.*"

"Amen," came the chorus reply.

From nowhere, Krastinios produced gold decanters full of wine, with matching goblets that he passed around. He also distributed baskets of delicacies. The aphrodisiac in the wine and the cocaine in the food would soon enliven the mood.

Casting an appraising look on the sacrificial lamb, chosen for her beauty as well as for her sexual stamina, Krastinios ascended the three steps to the altar. At present, drugged as she was, the young woman had no knowledge of her surrounding. Soon enough, however, the narcotic would wear off.

Krastinios delicately removed the veil shading her face then stared into the unfocused pupils. Her eyes look darker than their natural pale green. How he liked the sweet helplessness, the vulnerable expression on the Chosen's face. Removing the pins from the lustrous coppery hair, he smiled encouragingly. The Chosen smiled back, as if charmed and comforted by his attention.

The participants stared, a few of them holding their breath. When he had everyone's attention, Krastinios pulled out the bejeweled dagger he used for human sacrifices. The sinuous blade gleamed dully in the warm light. Applying the exquisite razorsharp edge to the front of the woman's black veil, he slit the flimsy fabric then pulled her nudity toward him in a soft embrace, gently kissing her lips. The Chosen smiled nebulously and melted in his arms, slowly waking to her sensual cravings, still unaware of her plight.

Krastinios laid her down on the warm stone and covered her body with kisses first. As she writhed under him in arousal, he kept her down under his weight. Reaching for her hands, Krastinios produced soft black leather ties from under the edge of the altar and bound her wrists to a metal ring at the head of the altar stone.

The Chosen groaned in anticipation, inviting Krastinios to move down her body. How he enjoyed her eagerness to please! He spread her legs apart and bound them to the far corners of the sacrificial stone. Wanton hips contorted in sexual beckoning while hard breasts swelled and fell to the rhythm of the woman's heavy sighs.

Krastinios rose and straightened his clothes with nonchalant ease. "Since we are among friends, let's enjoy our special party... I think our lovely surprise is ready to be consummated. Make yourselves comfortable and suit your fancy. I will give a reward for the most creative sexual act."

The eerie music grew louder and the tempo accelerated. The participants removed hoods and face veils, unleashing thick tresses of perfumed hair. It suddenly felt very warm, the low ceiling and dim torchlight adding to the oppressive sensation. The eyes of men and women alike burned with shameless lust. Articles of clothing came off, revealing haphazardly muscular thighs, a hard male member, small firm breasts. Heavy bosoms rose to the rhythm of undulating bellies and rounded buttocks. Soft hairy triangles, alive with heat and exploring fingers, released a sexual aroma..

A powerful male, unclad except for a black hood, approached first the low altar. He stepped up and knelt astride the vulnerable chest of the Chosen. As the drug started to wear off, the bound woman blinked in wonder, shock registering in her green eyes. When she opened her mouth, the man seized her head roughly and shoved his throbbing member deep into her throat. She coughed and choked and cried. Meanwhile, the other participants came closer, to observe and prepare for their own desecration of the offering.

Vijaya Schartz

A full-figured woman neared the sacrificial table and lowered herself onto the highest step of the altar. Wetting her fingers, she worked the small sensitive knob of the victim's most private parts. The Chosen's back arched under the gentle but insistent pressure. The plump woman then teased her mercilessly with tongue and teeth, sending her quarry into a flurry of wild quivering. The man on top erupted in tremulous release then vacated the altar, making room for more to participate.

When the Chosen finally came back to reality, she was beyond caring. The scent of mating, the heat and the repeated stimulation contributed to her surrender. The participants quenched her parched throat with wine, soothed her with kisses. All took turns at the desecration.

The panting creature gasped but still showed wantonness. Her skin glistened. Drops and rivulets of perspiration dripped from her brow and upper lip. Her voice weakened, raw from groaning. Yet, again and again she gave in to the irresistible craving, never satisfied, never complete, never fully satiated. Even when overcome by several partners intent on satisfying her needs, the desperate soul begged for more.

When the giant with the whip came into her field of view, however, the Chosen paled. Garbed in a black leather mask and wide leather straps, the tormentor's stance made his intent clear. He laughed harshly at the dismay on his victim's face. She pulled on her restraints and started to plead, but he only raised the thick leather braid. Clenching her jaw, the woman tensed for the blow. It came hard, leaving a red snaky mark on the pale skin. The Chosen winced, then she howled like a wounded animal.

The activity around the altar stopped as everyone concentrated on this new entertainment. Aroused by the scene, several participants found a willing partner to appease their fancy. The bullwhip slowly rose then lashed, harder every time, each stroke extracting a broken scream and leaving a new angry welt on the soft skin. When he could not hold his arousal anymore, the tormentor threw aside the whip, straddled the altar, lifted the Chosen's hips, then crudely relieved himself in her bleeding rectum while the spectators cheered.

Only Krastinios had not participated... Yet. Fully clothed, relishing the heat, he presided over the ritual from his elevated throne. The black knight had waited patiently, bathing in the energy released for his benefit. Now, he rose, casually stepping down from the black marble seat. As he approached the sacrificial platform, his underlings respectfully made room for their powerful master.

Gently, Krastinios untied the whimpering woman then gathered her in his arms, offering understanding and comfort. With a sigh of relief, the Chosen collapsed and sobbed against his chest.

At a snap of his fingers, four stout men approached the altar. Each taking hold of a wrist or ankle, gently at first, they held the Chosen firmly down. She protested feebly, hurt and distrust fleeting on her face. Then Krastinios pulled the bejeweled dagger from the fold of his black leather tunic and held it aloft, in ritual offering, for his Father's blessing.

"You are doing fine," Krastinios assured the

Vijaya Schartz

trembling victim. "In this safe place, no one can hear you. You may scream all you like... The more the better."

Smiling all the time as if to reassure the woman, Krastinios waited until full understanding and terror registered on the Chosen's face. Too scared to scream, she stared as he lowered the knife, ever so slowly, to her spread genitals and penetrated her with the blade.

She screamed. Krastinios plunged the knife deeper into the abdomen, and she screamed again as the steel crushed the pelvic bone with an audible crack. Applying steady force, Krastinios bisected the heaving abdomen, all the way up through the sternum.

The screams stopped when the disemboweled victim lost consciousness. Blood and steaming insides spilled onto the warm stone and down to the floor.

Krastinios seized the exposed beating heart and cut it loose from the arteries. Blood sprayed the ceiling. The overpowering, coppery smell of it, as much as the sight, sent pulses racing and lungs breathing hard. With a hissing sound in his mother tongue, the knight placed the bloody organ on a gold plate and made a ritual offering to his Father. Then, bringing the heart still beating to his mouth, Krastinios took a bite, chewed the firm bloody morsel with relish then swallowed.

None of the followers observed the small green snake leaving the entrails of the Chosen to slither away into inconspicuous shadows, but Krastinios nodded in acknowledgment and smiled. Shaking the blood loose from the blade in a swift motion, he returned it to its hidden sheath.

On his order, the blood was poured into gold decanters and mixed with wine. In a ritualistic communion, the disciples partook of the mixture, the tormentor, winner of the contest, getting first blood and a share of the heart.

When no blood remained in the gold vessels, Krastinios turned to his disheveled and now bloody guests. They stared at him and he knew why. Not a drop had spilled on him. His face, hands and clothes remained perfectly clean. "Let the party go on!" he announced cheerfully. "I am expected elsewhere... Have fun without me. There are still a few hours before dawn."

The black knight headed toward the hidden door, a happy spring in his step, turned and waved to his friends, feeling magnificent and rejuvenated. Then he dematerialized, grinning at the surprise of his loyal subjects.

Vijaya Schartz

CHAPTER FOURTEEN

After Michael's struggle in the busy capital, Arkansas came as a welcome respite. A dog from a distant farm barked to the roar of his motorcycle. In front of a neighboring farmhouse, a small fire burned dead branches and leaves. Michael smelled the smoke on the cool breeze. Now close to his brother's small estate, Michael wondered how some people could enjoy the simple life of the country and ignore the problems that plagued the planet. In blissful ignorance, they partook of Earth's gifts without a care about the morrow, as Michael had done, before meeting Amrah.

On the horizon appeared the familiar blue haze of the Ouachita Mountains. In a pale green meadow, a mare and her colt grazed in the shade of a tall oak tree. Already, the sun lowered on the horizon, setting ablaze the open fields in various shades of green and brown.

Archangel Crusader

The vibration of the engine had numbed Michael's arms. Throat parched from the dust of the road, he longed for the cool serenity of a house in a shaded meadow. The headband, stiff with caked dust, made him look like the half Native American he did not like to be. *Boy, am I going to enjoy a shower!* Soon he came to the farm's landmarks: a dirt road leading to an old barn and a trailer home, a baby-blue pick-up truck discolored by the sun and, behind it all, the skeleton of a pretentious two-story house still in the framing stages.

Dave must have heard the motorcycle first. He'd waited all day, no doubt, so relieved did he look walking toward Michael along the dirt lane. "Mike?" he yelled over the noise of the engine.

Michael turned off the ignition, stabilized the big machine, dismounted and greeted his brother with a bear hug. Even though Michael had raised him, Dave, five years younger, looked older with his bushy beard and receding hairline.

Behind Dave's washed blue eyes, Michael could read his brother's thoughts. For the past five years, Dave had tried to instill some wisdom in his wild, older sibling, unsuccessfully. For Dave, Michael remained a hopeless alcoholic, a manic-depressive off medications, and a suicidal renegade suffering from a persecution complex. Dave loved him nevertheless, imperfections and all. Still, Michael would have to work hard at changing the image he'd carved in his brother's mind.

A young, giggling girl in a pink dress ran out of the mobile home, followed by a woman Michael recognized as Becky, Dave's wife.

Vijaya Schartz

"Hi, Becky!" Michael waved cheerfully, trying to forget old grudges to see her with new innocence. Becky waved back from the house, saying something Michael did not understand.

As the running child came to a stop, Dave introduced her, puffed with pride. "This is Clara, our newly adopted ray of sunshine!"

"I'll be damned!" Unbelieving, Michael stared at the adopted child, who stared back with round brown eyes in a clever chocolate-brown face. "Why didn't you tell me?"

"Tell you what? That she's black?" Dave guffawed.

Michael was delighted. "I was just surprised... Glad to see you've forgotten the old man's lectures about 'the evil nature of those goddamn niggers'."

"Damn right! What difference does it make? We love the kid, and the color of her skin doesn't make a bit of difference."

"Believe me, I know..." Michael looked at his brother with moist eyes, realizing the vastness of the transformation occurring in the world. Despite their upbringing, Dave had set aside his old beliefs to adopt an African American child.

Michael flashed the girl a big smile and scooped her in his arms. A sudden yearning for Jennifer seized him as he held Clara. Almost the same age... Clara was younger, shorter, but Michael felt in her the same need for love.

When he let her down, Clara took his hand, "Come see the new house, Uncle Michael."

Wiping wet hands on her apron, Becky joined them and kissed Michael on the cheek. She looked different, plain, with glasses and no makeup, a far cry from the exotic dancer she was when Dave had met her. She looked older, too. Michael could not help but think of them as older folks, although it had nothing to do with age. They seemed to have given up on youth. Michael would never give up. He would always be eighteen.

"You guys go see the house, I'll bring some cold drinks. Michael, you want a beer?" Becky asked, matter-of-factly.

"No thanks, Becky, got any soda?" There was a short hush.

"Sure... Pepsi okay?" She seemed at a loss.

"Fine... Pepsi's fine." Michael avoided looking at Becky, who stared at him in disbelief.

Dave broke the embarrassing silence. "Come see my work." He rested a hand on Michael's shoulder. "Let me show you how far I got. Your timing's perfect. I sure can use your talents now. I need some advice on how to frame the dormer windows on the roof... See, the bedrooms on the second floor have a slanted roof, and the living room will have double-height ceiling with full-length windowpanes... And I don't know as much as you about plumbing either..."

Clara followed the two men closely, curious as any child when meeting a famous family member for the first time. They sat on sacks of concrete piled up in a corner of the future living room. The elongated shadows of the naked frame crisscrossed in an elaborate pattern in the glow of the setting sun. Becky joined them shortly and sat with them, as if finally relaxing after a long day of domestic chores.

Vijaya Schartz

Clara stared, obviously fascinated by Michael. During a pause in the adult conversation, Michael addressed Clara. "I have a little girl like you, her name's Jennifer. You'll meet her soon. I'm sure you two will get along just fine. We can go fishing together sometime... Do you like fishing?"

Clara nodded vigorously. "But I don't know how!" She shrugged, staring at him candidly.

"Really? I'll have to teach you then... If you want to learn, of course..."

"I want to learn..." The tone in Clara's voice and the determination in the set of her mouth made Michael smile.

"I'm pretty sure you'll like it... I know a river where the fish come when you call them... I'll teach you how if you want..."

The little brown face beamed with pleasure, "Really?"

"Sure... And I can teach you much more."

Dave and Becky watched, exchanging quiet smiles and holding hands over the heavy sacks covered with gray concrete dust on which they sat.

* * *

A long shower left Michael refreshed. A shave and clean clothes made him feel civilized again. The trailer proved bigger inside than it looked from the outside. Although temporary, these adequate living quarters would allow him to enjoy privacy without imposing on his brother's family space. As the aroma drifting from the small kitchen whetted his appetite, Michael realized that he hadn't eaten all day.

Dinner consisted of chicken, potatoes, gravy and apple pie, all ingredients produced on the small farm. Becky was proud of her home-raised chickens. She fed them good grain, and they ran free on the grounds. She also kept rabbits in cages in the barn. Dave took care of growing the vegetables. He had a small tractor, sufficient for the acreage. What they didn't consume, they sold at the market. Dave also hired out his services here and there as a carpenter to supplement their income.

The whole family spent the evening studying the blueprints. Dave explained his ideas, and Michael offered technical solutions to the problems encountered. Raised in Seattle by Michael since the age of ten, Dave, essentially a city-boy, had only recently returned to the land of his birth. His tastes, too sophisticated for a farmhouse, created interesting challenges. Dave wanted it all and Michael, although he did not quite understand why they needed all these luxuries, enjoyed the opportunity to show the extent of his knowledge in the craft.

Dave was a dreamer. He'd learned the construction trade from his brother but never considered it a vocation as Michael did. The younger brother enjoyed intellectual pursuits whenever time allowed, considering physical work healthy for mind and body. He relied heavily on Michael's technical expertise for the building of the future home.

Clara helped Becky clear the dishes then joined the adults who discussed the new house over coffee. Michael's enthusiasm and novel suggestions fired the conversation, his creative approach stirring excitement into the life of the isolated family.

Vijaya Schartz

Late that night, since it would be morning in France, Michael called Tori in Paris. When the call finally went through, he was patched into an answering machine. A foreign male voice delivered a recorded message in French. It might have been Tori's husband, but since Michael did not know the man, he couldn't tell. Nevertheless, Michael left a message for Jennifer, not sure at all he had reached the right number. Lately, He had been unable to achieve a mind-link with his daughter and he wondered why. Maybe the girl was having so much fun that her mind was otherwise occupied.

His dreams that night took Michael back to the infernal planet of his earlier nightmares. Below the fiery glow, at the core of the underground city, he saw the frightening alien with a snake face and a forked tongue. This time, the Reptilian laughed under the hood of the silvery robe, a dry, icy cackle that brought goose bumps to Michael's skin. But in the dream, Lufriec was not alone. Krastinios joined in the laughter with a warm, rich baritone. The two talked in riddles about two chosen doves for a sacrifice. Michael knew it concerned him and ought to know what it meant, but comprehension floated beyond his grasp.

The next morning, over a real breakfast of eggs, bacon, biscuits, and gravy, Michael discussed humanitarian and ecological ideas with Dave and Becky. He related the two-week campaign in Washington, gave Becky news of her sister Debbie and, to impress Clara, made the spoons dance by themselves on the table.

"Whoa!" the child exclaimed, big round eyes full of wonder.

"Nice trick," Dave commented. You'll have to show me how it's done.

Michael only smiled. Typical for adults to disbelieve…

But Clara now asked, "Do something else!"

Michael thoroughly enjoyed her delight. "Now, what do you bet I can throw this glass through the wall without breaking it?"

"Can you do that, Uncle Michael?"

"All right, just watch." Michael sent his glass flying in slow motion toward the flimsy wall of the trailer. It stopped as it hit, melted into the wood, then disappeared into it. "Now go get it in the dandelion patch outside!"

Without a word Clara ran out and came back with a big grin, triumphantly holding the glass high for everyone to see.

Dave and Becky laughed, but Michael knew they didn't understand what had happened and wrote it off as a trick. Funny how they only saw what their mind could comprehend and lock away any unexplained phenomenon. Even when confronted with the facts, the conscious mind would invoke coincidence, freaky happenstance, and still refuse the unacceptable proof. Michael didn't condemn them. He had done it, too, on many occasions.

After Becky left for her daily chores, the mobile phone rang as the two brothers walked out the door.

"Yo!" Michael frowned at the French accent and semi-familiar male voice.

"Michael Tanner? This is Jean-Marc Fontaine, Tori's husband. I am in New York and a little concerned about Tori and Jennifer. I could not reach

Vijaya Schartz

them on the phone, I wondered if you had heard from them..." More than the words, the inflections conveyed real concern. Michael felt an immediate affinity with this stranger worried about Jennifer.

"No, I haven't. All I get is a machine."

"Could you call my office at Chemitek in New York, if you hear anything?"

"Chemitek, you said?" The name sounded familiar. "Isn't that the company that's dumping chemical waste in upstate New York?"

"You heard? My European colleagues and I do not agree with it. I am trying to stop it, but I cannot get the support I need. My American higher-ups have powerful connections. The newspapers are hungry for sensational articles, but not one is willing to help me fight."

Michael linked his mind to the voice of the stranger, all the way back to its source. There he found honesty, love, good will, and strength. "Well, I know someone in Washington who would love to hear your story and can do something about it besides, if you have inside information that is."

"Oh, I have all the information you need, including a nasty plan to eliminate a certain Crusader who stands in the way... You may have heard about him."

"I know him well."

"You do? What a small world. But recent rumors say this guy is a dangerous outlaw."

"Oh, he's been on the wrong side of the law a few times."

"Outlaw or not, he does not deserve to die. Who is this person in Washington?"

While discussing strategy with Tori's husband, his unexpected new ally, Michael watched, through the window. Dave and Clara laughed and horsed around on the grass in front of the trailer house. Michael felt a pang of sadness, thinking of Jennifer... God, he hoped she was all right...

Finally, Michael joined Dave outside. Clara, totally devoted to this cool uncle who knew so many magic tricks, followed the two men, showering Michael with questions and expecting answers for each and every one of them. Clara had an opinion about everything and expressed it whether Michael was interested or not.

"Go play and let us work," Dave told the child once they reached the construction site.

After a short discussion, the brothers decided to work together on the front of the big structure, so they could talk and enjoy each other's company as they worked. As usual when the two brothers met, Dave stirred up memories of their childhood. Having survived and now well adjusted, Dave firmly believed in therapy. Therefore, he used every opportunity to help Michael get over the deep-rooted hatred for his abusive stepfather and the mother who tolerated such mistreatment.

"She was afraid of him, Mike," Dave said soothingly.

"No she wasn't. How many times did I help her through the hole in the fence? She was seeing other men. She was beautiful... She could have had any man she wanted..."

"But he was the only one who offered to marry her. She did it for you, so you'd have a father, a provider... Of course, he never did like you! That's for sure. Us other kids didn't have it as rough... But you were always opposing him, that's why he hated you. I saw her try to protect you so many times, but no, you had to gall him, you couldn't help it." Dave returned his attention to the work.

"I hated his guts for taking Mother away from me. I would have rather lived without a father. At least I would have had Mom's love." Michael pounded on his nail with vengeful strength.

"You always had it, Mike. You always were her favorite, despite the fact that you rejected her. She often told me so." It was Dave's turn to vent his frustration with the hammer.

"Well, she sure knows how to lie. But at least now I understand her a little better since I know who my father is."

"You what?" Disbelief spread on Dave's usually calm features. He dropped his hammer.

"I found my real father." Michael grinned. "Or rather, he found me."

"You say that so calmly, I can't believe it." Dave had to sit down on a drum of plaster. "You'll never cease to surprise me, Mike. So... Who is he? Even Mom pretends she was a virgin when she married, two years after your birth. I never understood why she stuck to such an obvious fabrication."

"In that, she may have told the truth, Dave. I have to give her credit for sticking to her incredible story. And the truth is even more unbelievable, but I think you should rephrase the question. It's not who is he, but *what* is he?"

"What do you mean by *what*?"

Now Michael had Dave's full attention. "He's not exactly a person. Not in the usual sense. Let's say he's from very far away... He was just passing by."

"I expected that much. He couldn't have been from around here. He would have been known. It's hard to hide such secrets in a small town... So where's he from? And how did he find you? Even the police can't find you." Dave stared, waiting.

"He's not from this planet."

"Stop it, Mike." Dave laughed heartily. "I almost believed you for a minute here. Have a little respect for your brother. From another planet..." He shook his head and picked up the hammer. "Really, Mike... You'll never cease to amaze me."

"I'm not joking, Dave... Do I look like I'm joking? Where do you think I learned to throw glasses through the wall and make spoons dance on the table?"

"I don't fall for tricks to impress Clara! Didn't you put the glass in the dandelion patch last night and just pretend to throw it through the wall this morning? I still don't understand how you rigged the spoons though..." A frown creased Dave's forehead.

"Nothing was fake, Dave. It's for real."

"Good God, Mike, what are you saying? As much as I want to believe you, I can't even begin to imagine the repercussions. I knew my brother was many things..." He winked. "But such a joker?"

Dave had not quite finished the sentence when a piercing scream ripped their eardrums. Both men jumped up and turned toward the back of the house, just in time to see a small dark body in a hot pink

Vijaya Schartz

dress fall, flailing, from the highest scaffolding. The cry stopped short on impact with the concrete slab below. Becky came running out of the barn, but Michael was the first one to Clara's side. The child twitched for an instant, then lay very still, like a broken puppet, arms and legs at odd angles, eyes fixed, mouth open, no breath moving the inert chest.

Michael looked up to see how high the child had fallen from... Mentally, he scanned her body for signs of life and found none. She was an empty shell.

"Becky, call the ambulance," Dave yelled as he waved Michael aside and immediately started CPR. "There's no pulse, no breath, nothing... O God... Please... Please let her live..."

Bright red blood pooled under the crushed skull. Michael laid one hand on his brother's shoulder. Dave was frantically working the little body, as if he could restore some life into it, some breath, some heartbeat, something. He counted aloud the thrusts upon the child's chest: thirteen, fourteen, fifteen. He gave two mouth-to-mouth breaths, then thrust again: One, two, three...

"She's gone, Dave, there's nothing you can do." Michael's words slowly made their way to Dave's brain.

After a few more desperate attempts, Dave finally stopped, picked up what was left of his new daughter and held the frail, limp body close to him. Blood trailed from the head and soaked his jeans. When he raised his face to the clear morning sky, big tears rolled on his cheeks, wetting his bushy beard. "NO!" he screamed in anguish, as if refusing to give

Archangel   Crusader

up the child who had just recently blessed him. Sobs racked the big chest, the mouth contorting in a grimace of utter pain.

Michael couldn't stand Dave's plight, couldn't bear to see him suffer such a loss. With a surge of adrenalin came a familiar tingling in Michael's body. He centered himself, focused on the young girl for a minute then gently took the little body from Dave's arms, saying softly, "Let me try something..."

Becky ran back from the house toward the child, anxiety tensing the muscles of her face, but Dave stopped her and held her in his arms as Becky collapsed, wailing in agony, understanding the tragic truth.

Michael laid the lifeless form on a patch of grass in the shade and concentrated on the injuries. Strong fingers ran along the spine, broken in several places. In his mind's eye, Michael saw internal bleeding, a badly fractured skull, and brain hemorrhage. The child had lost a lot of blood. Michael sat crossed-legged by the slight frame of the child and set his mind to work.

Laying his hands on Clara's head, he visualized the mending of bones and arteries, willed the hemorrhage to shrink, fused the broken spinal cord, mended nerves and ligaments, muscles, and smaller internal injuries. After all that was broken or torn had been repaired, Michael conjured new blood and started the heart pumping. Then, he coaxed the spirit floating nearby to come back and inhabit its physical form again. When it did, the chest took a shallow breath and, under the stare of Becky and Dave, Clara blinked, swallowed, and smiled peacefully, as if waking from an afternoon nap. She looked at Michael first and said, "Thank you, Uncle Michael, I love you too."

Dave and Becky, astounded and beside themselves with joy, laughed through their tears and hugged the child. Then Becky led Clara toward the trailer, the child jumping and running around.

The siren of the approaching ambulance brought the adults out of their euphoria. Dave asked one of the paramedics to examine Clara, stirring them toward the trailer, away from the bloody concrete.

The male nursed inspected Clara. "She's fine," he finally declared. "All vital signs are okay. We can take her to the hospital to make sure if you like... She mustn't have fallen from very high." The medic turned to Dave and motioned to his blood soaked jeans. "What happened to you?"

"Nothing... Just butchering." Dave led the medics back to their vehicle. "Sorry to disturb you for so little."

Once in the ambulance, the medic turned to the driver. They thought they couldn't be heard, but Michael smiled as he witnessed their comments in his mind. "I don't understand parents, sometimes. She didn't even skin a knee..."

Michael watched the vehicle drive away then looked at the imposing height of the towering framework. No child could survive such a fall. Looking down at the pool of blood on the concrete slab, he made it disappear with a snap of his fingers.

From the trailer, Clara waved at Michael who waved back. Becky took her by the hand and led her toward the barn.

Dave approached his brother with new humility. "I don't understand what happened just now... What you did... I just know that one minute she was dead, and the next she was alive and well... It's a miracle. Thank you, Mike." Dave choked on a sob. "Thank you."

"Don't thank me, Dave, that's the least I could do under the circumstances." Such a display of gratitude embarrassed Michael. Relaxing, he felt the sudden need to lean or sit. His insides turned to oil. He grabbed hold of a stud then dropped onto a plastic pail, his mind drowning in thick liquid.

In his excitement, Dave did not notice at first. "This is really incredible. How did it happen? I thought only God could do something like that. I'm sorry I was so skeptical earlier. You weren't joking, were you? I'd like to hear the whole story, if you don't mind..." Dave stopped talking, staring at his brother. "Mike? Eh! Mike, are you all right? You look like a ghost."

"Nothing a good night sleep won't cure." Michael forced himself to smile. "I depleted my energy. There is always a price to pay."

"By all means, I'll get you inside. You must rest. Sorry about asking so many questions."

"Don't be. I was going to tell you the whole story but I wasn't sure how to begin. I guess Clara solved that for me."

They did not work anymore that day, but Michael explained to his brother the secret of his birth and his destiny as an avatar.

CHAPTER FIFTEEN

In the following days, the two brothers made good progress on the building despite the many breaks needed for the sake of conversation. Worried about Jennifer, Michael teleported to Paris, only to find Tori's penthouse empty. It was early morning there. He scanned the streets of the French capital all day in vain. He even explored the countryside with his mind, but Jennifer and her mother had disappeared without a trace. More worried than ever, Michael re-materialized in Arkansas. What could have happened to them?

Upon his return, the mobile rang. Out of area said the digital screen.

"Hi, Dad, it's me!"

Michael should have felt relieved at the sound of Jennifer's voice, but the call filled him with foreboding. "Jennifer? Did you get my message? Are you all right pumpkin?"

"Not really, Dad... We're not hurt or anything, but..."

"What is it Jen? Tell me what's happening."

The next voice that came over the line chilled him to the tip of his toes.   "So you call yourself Crusader now," Krastinios railed in a melodious voice. "That has a nice ring. A little rough for my taste, though… I warned you not to get in my way, Tanner, but you wouldn't listen. That is really too bad."

Cold sweat collected in Michael's eyebrows, and his upper lip trembled with barely controlled rage. "You better not touch a single hair on her head, understand?"

"My, my, my! What arrogance! As it happens, I am the one giving orders here. I want you to grasp the situation."

A fuzzy picture plastered itself on Michael's mind.   The vision was flat, two-dimensional, and lacked color and detail. It showed a dark room in a castle, low vaulted ceilings, the glint of metal over two black leather tables. Tied upon one, lay a beautiful woman that Michael recognized as Tori, naked. On a chair, struggling against the bonds holding her hands and feet, sat Jennifer. Michael's heart sank. The second table obviously waited for his daughter. Close at hand, an arsenal of sophisticated tools on surrounding tables showed what kind of refined torture Krastinios could submit them to.

"Now that you have a clearer view of who is in charge," Krastinios went on in a sympathetic voice, "I want you to publicly announce that you are a fraud, that you did it for money and that you do not believe in your own Crusade. I also want you to give yourself up to the FBI who will handle you as I ordered. Is that clear?"

Vijaya Schartz

"You...mother-fucker!" Michael exploded, unable to contain the rage any longer.

"Or else..." continued the suave voice, "both of these young females will be Chosen for a sacrificial ritual and put to death after much exciting foreplay..."

Michael felt the blood drain from his face. "I will have your head for this, I swear..."

"I see that you need some reflection time, my dear Tanner... Very well, I will call you back in exactly twenty-four hours. By then, maybe you will have come to your senses. Or else..." Krastinios left the sentence unfinished. The powerful jolt Michael sent through the lines hit him in the face, leaving him speechless.

"Take that, you, son-of-a-bitch! Don't you threaten me! I may not know where you are, but I'll find you, I swear to God." Michael was yelling.

"It will not do any good to swat at me like an angry bumble bee, Earthling." The voice had lost its usual cool. "Tomorrow night, you agree to give yourself up to the FBI or they both die. It is that simple."

The line went dead. In the silence that followed, Michael dropped into a chair, head in hands, shaking like a leaf. In a voice hardly a whisper, he whimpered, "Good God, what have I done?"

"What is it, Mike?" Dave looked awed by this outburst of emotions.

"Krastinios." Michael spat rather than spoke the name. "The bastard who killed Veronica... He's got Jennifer and Tori, and he'll kill them both if I don't retract the Crusade and surrender to the FBI."

Dave just looked at his brother. Michael knew he understood his dilemma.

"My God, Michael... " Concern filtered through Becky's simple words. "What are you going to do?"

As Michael had explained that afternoon, there was no turning back. The Crusade had taken a life of its own and didn't need him anymore. Even if he wanted to, Michael couldn't stop it. Under Dave and Becky's sorrowful gaze, Michael stood up and dragged himself to the liquor cabinet. From it, he extracted the bottle of Jack Daniels. Not bothering to get a glass, Michael unscrewed the cap, threw it across the floor, then looked at the bottle.

"I screwed up big time," Michael said to no one in particular. He needed an anchor to avoid being drowned by the irresistible flood, so he held on to the reassuring presence of the bottle. He couldn't look Dave or Becky in the eyes.

Suddenly, Michael realized the enormity of his behavior. No. He wasn't going to make the same mistake. If Krastinios counted on that weakness to defeat him, Michael would not give him the satisfaction. Not this time. Not ever again.

Under the stupefied stare of Dave and Becky, Michael, in a struggle to control himself, started shaking violently, knuckles white from the pressure on the bottle of Jack Daniels. The rage at his own weakness, the wrath for Krastinios, the thwarted love for Veronica, the turmoil and the guilt about Jennifer and Tori, all these emotions rose and crashed inside him like a violent storm against the rock of his new resolve.

The trailer started to shake. Bottles on the rolling bar knocked down the glasses like during an earthquake. A window shattered. As Dave and

Vijaya Schartz

Becky looked around in fear, Michael struggled to get out, staggering, still holding the bottle. Out of control, his powers would destroy the trailer, and Dave's family didn't need to suffer in Michael's fight to exorcize his own demons.

Once in the open, the fury of Michael's inner fight against his weakness lifted him from the ground. He twisted in mid-air while storm clouds gathered above. When a rod of his own lightning hit him, Michael screamed, hurling the bottle to the heavens so high it never fell back down. As the dry storm gained in intensity, lightning struck Michael again and again, accompanied by loud thunder. Each time, he screamed in pain, fear, and rage, until a massive jolt ended the trial.

When Michael fell limp to the ground, Dave and Becky, who had watched from a distance in horror, ran to him.

"Shall I call the ambulance?" Becky asked in a daze. "Is he alive?"

Dave checked for a pulse. "Barely, but I don't think the medics can do anything for him. His problem is not physical." He looked at the sky where the storm clouds were dissipating as fast as they had formed. "Help me take him inside."

"What's wrong with Uncle Michael?" Awakened by the commotion, Clara was on the brink of tears.

"He's ill, Love. He needs a lot of rest. Go to your room. I'll come tuck you in."

* * *

When he regained semi-consciousness, Michael felt a familiar presence. A bluish glow illuminated the bedroom.

"Children always expend more energy than necessary in their futile games." The statement came as an observation, without reproach. The gentle alien came to face Michael who lifted his head slowly.

"You? Look at the mess I'm in. None of this would have happened if it wasn't for you." Michael's head hurt as if about to rupture.

Amrah smiled. "You mean if you had never been born and if Jennifer had not been born?"

Taken aback by the logic of the reasoning, Michael paused for a few seconds before answering. Jennifer was a ray of sunshine in his existence. And despite his attempted suicide three years ago, he loved life with a passion, at least most of the time. "I guess I never had much of a choice, did I?"

"I am sorry it has to be this way, Michael, I really am." The kind sincerity in the alien's voice warmed Michael's heart with hope.

"What am I supposed to do, Father? All is lost, no matter what I do. In any case, I die and she dies. I feel so powerless."

"But what about the others, Son... Dave, Clara, Debbie, Walter, Bill... Do they deserve to die, too?"

"I care deeply, don't get me wrong, but what can I do? I wish I could just fight the son-of-a-bitch, one on one. Do you think he would accept a single combat?"

"Consider the personality of your adversary," Amrah suggested. "He is so much like yourself,

Vijaya Schartz

proud, arrogant, powerful. He wants you dead just as you want him dead. Above all, he wants to know which one of you is the strongest. He itches to measure his power against yours."

"You think so?" Michael's mind started to clear. "But why would he risk everything if he's already won?"

"Krastinios does not know that for sure..." Amrah's dark blue eyes didn't seem so alien anymore. "What if you decided to sacrifice Jennifer and go ahead with the Crusade? He would lose it all! He is gambling on your weakness for Jennifer. You could gamble on his own weakness by offering a personal challenge."

"What makes you think he'll accept?"

"Oh, he certainly will... Of that you can be sure."

"But he may be stronger than me. What if he wins?"

"At least you will have a fighting chance... And, my son,"

"Yes?"

"Do not underestimate yourself. You brought Clara back to life and conquered your own demons. I think you are ready. You can also draw strength from me if you need it."

"Thanks, Father, I think I will."

"You can win, my son. My strength will be yours."

The bluish light shimmered. All went dark again. Michael sat on the bed, painfully contorting himself into a meditation posture to start repairing his body. After a while, feeling better, he went out to get some fresh air. Sitting under the oak tree in the front meadow, facing east, Michael waited for the sun to rise on a day that might bring new hope.

Vijaya Schartz

CHAPTER SIXTEEN

The sun finally appeared in a pink, pale sky. It was Sunday. Dave would probably want to go to church. Even though Michael would not mind going himself for old times sake, he could not risk being recognized. The FBI was still actively looking for him.

So, after breakfast, while Dave, Becky, and Clara attended mass at Saint Joseph, Michael explored the property searching for fishing implements. He needed to do something normal, something relaxing to clear the mind in preparation for Krastinios' next phone call. Michael had a whole day in front of him but had no doubt that the bastard would call back. His heart went out to Jennifer. God, he hoped she was all right.

Michael opened the small wooden side door of the barn and stopped, allowing his eyes to adjust to the dim light. The packed dirt on the ground felt soft underfoot. One side of the barn was stacked to the roof with bales of hay. The smell of straw and chicken droppings reminded Michael of his childhood on the chicken farm.

As a boy, it had been his job to feed the chickens every day. Ever since, he had hated the damned birds. Once, a belligerent rooster had attacked him, beak and talons lashing in a flurry of feathers and savage screams. The beast slashed his bare legs, jumping and flying to get at more vital parts. Young Michael had seized the bird by the neck, twisted, and pulled with all his might, feeling a surge of triumphant elation.

Later, he'd paid dearly for killing the rooster. His stepfather tied him up to the bedpost, naked, and flogged his skin raw with a thick leather belt, making ugly bruises with the silver buckle across legs, chest and back. Too proud to cry or plead, Young Michael had endured silently under the mad ravings of his persecutor.

Now, in the cool shade of the barn, in the familiar smell of hay, a small flock of white hens stared sideways, then came closer, hoping for some food or treat. Sensing their expectations, Michael picked up a handful of grain out of a canvas sac, then threw the grain in a wide arc. Immediately, the fluffy birds, forgetting all fear, swarmed to his feet. Michael crouched to observe them better. "What are you looking at me like that for?"

One daring hen eyed him with interest. The bird came close enough to be touched, and Michael extended one hand, when out of the shadows came a russet and green cock making straight for him. Michael stopped in mid-movement. The rooster rushed

Vijaya Schartz

at him, cackling, but Michael saw no aggressiveness there. In a friendly gesture, the bird offered his head to the extended hand, requesting to be petted. Chuckling at his own fears, Michael willingly obliged and picked up the rooster to scratch him gently behind the head.

Past the rabbit cages, Michael heard noises and discovered the source of a smell he had not noticed right away. Pigs. A sow and three piglets, pink and clean, were penned on a wide concrete slab covered with fresh straw. The mother lay down, feeding the litter.

Michael found most of what he needed in shoeboxes stored on the shelves in the back of the barn. He packed the fishing supplies in the saddlebags of the Harley and attached the fishing poles along the frame of the motorcycle. The small automatic in the saddlebags reminded Michael of the mission. He felt for the knife sheathed in his boot. Could a bullet or a knife kill alien evil? The thought of Jennifer in the hands of Krastinios made him close his hand on the handle. The time would come, soon...

Michael was getting use to the idea that he might win. According to the myths, supernatural demons could be killed with silver daggers and silver bullets, vampires dispatched with wooden stakes, witches and sorcerers burned alive, others decapitated. What would it take to eliminate Krastinios whose powers seemed limitless? If injured, he probably could heal himself instantly. Michael would need to strike a vital organ with enough force, accuracy and speed to cause instant death. Surprise might be the determining factor.

Archangel Crusader

Back to the kitchen, Michael made some sandwiches then wrapped them in an insulated lunch box, along with a few cans of soda. He jumped when the house phone rang. It was way too early to be Krastinios. Besides, it was the wrong phone.

"Michael? I'm so glad you're here. Are you all right?" Debbie sounded relieved to find him safe.

"Yes, Debbie. Just the person I wanted to talk to. How is everything in D.C.?" For a second, Michael thought about telling her to abort the campaign. No. Quickly regaining confidence, he resolved to go ahead as planned. "Where are you calling from?" he asked, concerned about her safety.

Debbie sounded excited. "Don't worry, this is a payphone. They can't track the call. Besides, I'm only calling my sister. I have great news. The Crusade is alive and well. The fact that you're hunted by the police hasn't been made public yet. I guess they don't have any hard evidence, only suspicions, and if they didn't find you, they would look bad. Walter has contacted a lawyer, a very dedicated friend. Even if there's a public scandal, the authorities have no legal right to prevent other organizations from taking over the Crusade and using your material."

"This is great news, Debbie."

"All your prerecorded tapes have been distributed to the right organizations and are used regularly in meetings and over the networks. Not bad for only two weeks of campaigning. Green Peace just agreed to finance several runs of your subliminal message film regarding the ecosystem in a major chain of movie theaters around the country. Your voice is heard, and your message mostly well-received."

Vijaya Schartz

"Mostly? What about the rest?"

"There are some industrial cartels who would love to see you dead. You made some powerful enemies in denouncing the illegal disposal of radioactive and pharmaceutical waste. They resent the expense of safe disposal and the cost of publicizing it to keep their good name. Some of them may be more dangerous to you than the police, or even Krastinios."

Chemitek came to Michael's mind. "Did the Frenchman call you yesterday?"

"He certainly did. A nice man this Jean-Marc Fontaine... He was baffled when I told him you were the Crusader. Why didn't you tell him? Anyway, he was a great help. The threat from Chemitek can be circumvented now. But there are others."

"Did you get any feedback from the press?"

"The newspapers are delighted. Your disappearance adds to the mystery. As far as the public at large is concerned, you vanished without a trace, and this makes you a legend. Your recorded appearances become even more meaningful. Everything is going so fast, it's like magic."

Michael knew that Debbie's hard work was at the heart of that magic. His intervention wouldn't have been possible without her. "Wonderful. What else?"

"I see a definite change in the attitude of the people who witnessed your public display. They were touched, Michael. They are on your side, and they'll help you, no matter what the cost. Even if you never came back, the Crusade would succeed. People are changing attitudes, affecting everyone and everything around them in a constructive way."

"This is perfect, Debbie. Good job. How's Walter, how are you guys coping with the situation? Is the FBI still harassing you? No more threats?"

"No, everything seems to have calmed down and Walter is here, taking care of me. I hope you're safe, too. Did you hear from Jennifer?"

Michael took his time before answering. "Yeah, she called me last night." The image of Jennifer tied on the chair haunted him. Something about it wasn't quite believable, but he couldn't tell what.

"Good, you were worried about her. How is she getting along with Tori?"

"Good, I think... But I made a terrible mistake... She's in danger, and it's all my fault."

"What do you mean?"

"I should have known she couldn't be safe anywhere. Krastinios found her. He has her and Tori."

"Oh no! This is terrible, Michael, I'm so sorry... Poor child... She must be terrified... What does that monster want?"

"He wants me, of course."

"What are you going to do?"

"I'm going to give him his wish."

"Michael, this sounds dangerous. Are you sure you can handle him?"

"No, I'm not sure of anything, but what would I be if I didn't try?"

"Be careful, Michael. You're strong and powerful, but from what you told me, this guy is wicked and doesn't play by the rules."

"I'll be careful, Debbie. I promise."

The sound of the blue pickup truck coming down the dirt road interrupted the conversation. The

Vijaya Schartz

vehicle stopped in front of the trailer and Becky stepped out. Michael waved the receiver through the window and Becky hurried inside to pick up the phone while Michael went out to meet Dave and Clara.

The child seemed all excited about something and finally blurted it out. "We saw Grandma. We saw Grandma at church, Uncle Michael!"

Michael struggled with the thought. He knew coming back to Arkansas would create an awkward situation since he had not spoken to Maria in years. She still lived with the hated stepfather responsible for all his suffering.

When Michael did not respond, the little girl continued unabashed. "She wants you and me to go see her this afternoon."

"But I have everything ready to go fishing to-day." Michael felt terrible about the lame excuse.

Dave had observed the scene while unloading groceries from the back of the truck. "You can do both, go fishing now, and go see Grandma later this afternoon."

"Thanks a lot, Dave! I appreciate the fact that you are trying to get my mind off Jennifer and to-night's phone call, but I'm not prepared for this, yet."

"You'll have to face Mom sooner or later, Mike. You might as well get it over with. You'll feel better afterwards."

"Damn you for arranging it behind my back!"

"I'm just trying to make everyone happy, brother. Believe me, you'll thank me for it some day."

"Can we go fishing now and go to Grandma's later, Uncle Michael?" The child's big eyes shone with hope.

"Let's go fishing first," Michael grunted. "After that, we'll see..."

Clara smiled, turned toward her adoptive father and attempted a clumsy wink.

Dave winked back and said, "Knock those fish dead, kid. But you want to change clothes first or your mother will have a fit."

It felt good to cruise on the purring Harley with a child's arms holding him tight. Clara felt so much like Jennifer. Even though there was nothing Michael could do for her at this point but wait, he thought about her constantly. Krastinios wouldn't hurt her, not yet. Despite the picture of the torture chamber, Michael knew she was still unharmed, but for how long? He hoped fishing would help him calm down and think.

They headed north toward a bend in the Arkansas river, where Michael had gone fishing many times as a child, a secret place safe from his stepfather, a refuge of precious freedom and even a few pleasures. The motorcycle managed the narrow trail, splitting the tall grass along the river's edge, where kids' bicycles had trampled the wild vegetation for many years. Except for a little more activity on the water (pleasure boats had been fewer in his childhood), Michael found the place much as he remembered it.

Parking the bike in the shade of a willow tree, Michael took the fishing paraphernalia out of the saddlebags. The river did not look quite as wide and imposing as it did when he was a boy. Michael remembered dreams of flowing with the river away from his mother and stepfather, all the way to the mighty Mis-

Vijaya Schartz

sissippi. Unfortunately, he discovered later that there was no escape from one's unhappy childhood. Michael had to face the ugly scars on his heart and deal with them in the end.

"This is a nice spot. I like it," Clara announced solemnly, hands on her hips, looking around as if she were about to buy the place. "Do you take Jennifer here too sometimes?"

"I never have, but I'm going to make sure we both bring her here soon." Michael silently prayed this would come true.

"She'll like it," Clara declared with confidence.

"I think so." Memories of fishing with Jennifer in Pennypack Creek, her disgust at touching the worms, a clear laugh in the dappled clearing with the sun playing on the water, Jennifer picking wild strawberries, Jennifer... Michael took a deep breath of cool, moist fishy air and released it slowly in an attempt to relax.

Man and child sat on a log, ate the sandwiches, and drank soda while making up fishing stories. Michael discovered with surprise that, unlike Jennifer, Clara was not afraid of worms. She loved to touch them and laughed when they slipped between her fingers.

"How do you make the fish come close? You said you would teach me." Clara looked skeptical.

"That's easy. Just concentrate." Michael probed her thoughts and directed her young mind into the correct brain wave pattern. "That's it. Now call them and watch."

The child did as told, and the young face lit with pleasure as she pointed to a school of long gray silvery eels heading their way just below the surface of the greenish water. As the fish swam closer, Clara knelt at the edge of the river. Soon, the eels milled around while she fed them straight from the worm can with obvious delight.

A couple of young boys in a small rowboat waved from a distance. Clara and Michael waved back. It reminded Michael of Dave and himself, many years ago... The boys were heading straight for the deep hole, just down river, Michael wondered if they knew of the treacherous undertow that could and had on occasions pulled down a small boat and everyone in it... Obviously, they didn't. Michael yelled and waved for them to come back, but to no avail. They just waved and yelled back, unaware of the danger.

Michael concentrated in an effort to warn them telepathically. He saw when understanding dawned on the two boys, but rather than changing course, they panicked, rocking the boat in their desperate maneuvers, while the churning current pushed them faster toward dangerous waters. The boat tilted perilously as both boys tried to stand up. It dipped, thrashing into the muddy torrent. The two youngsters disappeared underwater. One head surfaced, then the other. The boys swam, but the rapids pulled them mercilessly toward the undertow.

The great body of water between him and the two boys dampened Michael's paranormal abilities somewhat. He had to get closer if he wanted to help. Mind searching ahead, Michael started the Harley and rode down the river trail. Still too much water between them... Making up his mind, Michael drove the roaring machine straight toward the middle of the river. Levitating the heavy motorbike was the least of his worries.

Vijaya Schartz

In a heartbeat he reached the scene, emerging through the spray, as if materializing out of a white cloud. Stretching down as he had done many times when practicing to pick up beer cans, Michael fished one boy out of the water. The child relaxed a little at the sight of this savior out of nowhere but seemed stunned to find himself on the back of a motorcycle. Shivering with shock, cold and fear, the dripping boy hung on to Michael's waist.

The other boy remained out of sight. Mentally scanning for signs of human life, Michael rode the motorcycle above the muddy current. He sensed the younger child, deep under but alive still. Michael hovered at the same speed, gauging the depths, and by sheer mental strength pulled up the struggling kid from the deep cold hole toward the light of the shining sun. The boy was propelled out of the water like a big, jumping fish. Michael caught him in mid-air and held the coughing boy in front of him as he made for the shore with the precious cargo.

To avoid the onlookers, Michael headed up-river, landing in the secluded spot where Clara waited, in awe. For once, she had nothing to say.

The boys were fine and glad to be alive. Michael mentally altered their memory of the event. As far as they knew now, they had been rescued by a stranger on a Jet Ski.

After that, fishing seemed out of the question. Mentally exhausted, Michael sat against a tree to meditate, hoping to recuperate while Clara took a nap in the shade. When she woke up, the little girl insisted on going to Grandma's.

Michael felt uncomfortable about facing Maria after all these years. Although there was no danger now, the hatred for his stepfather was still very much alive. Nevertheless, it was impossible to refuse Clara and, as Dave had said, Michael would have to face his mother sooner or later. He had known this all along. Deep down inside, he desperately wanted to make peace with Maria, but could he?

Michael and Clara picked up their gear and left the riverside. Riding first in the direction of town, they turned south on a little county road Michael remembered well. He slowed down, unconsciously trying to delay the dreaded confrontation. At the sight of the old chicken farm through a clearing in the cluster of birch trees around the bend in the road, memories rushed back. The place had not changed much. It looked old and decrepit, the hen house abandoned. The fence was new though, and pink and purple hydrangea grew in the shade in front of the old house. The front door stood wide open, a dirty screen door obscuring the dark interior.

Michael stopped the Harley and helped Clara off the warm machine. The girl immediately ran to the screen door and opened it, yelling, "Grandma, Grandma, Uncle Michael is here!"

The figure that appeared then in the black frame of the open doorway hesitated then froze. Maria Tanner had aged a little, the jet-black hair now short and streaked with gray. She looked plumper and shorter than Michael remembered, but still beautiful with copper skin and liquid brown eyes. Fine lines only added to the depth of Maria's smile. She seemed overwhelmed, wiping away tears with a small handkerchief, but Michael had learned long ago not to trust Maria's theatrical displays.

Vijaya Schartz

"Mikie? I have been praying for this moment for the past eighteen years... I missed you so much... You always were my favorite, you know... My God, you've become such a handsome man." Maria hovered in the doorway, as if hoping for a kiss that didn't come.

"Hi, Mom... How've you been?" No, she hadn't changed a bit.

"Come in, come in, don't stand outside like that." She led the way inside.

As his eyes adjusted to the cool darkness inside, Michael noticed that even the furniture stood exactly where it had when he left. The same musky perfume permeated the air. Michael almost felt nauseated but checked himself. He had to go through with this.

"Sit, sit down there on the couch... Here you go... I'll get you some nice cold tea. Don't pay attention to him." Maria motioned toward a corner of the room. "He can't understand anything anymore."

When Maria disappeared in the kitchen, Michael suddenly saw what she was referring to. In the far and darkest corner of the living room, in the same old armchair, slouched the silent shadow of a man, so frail and weak that Michael did not recognize him at first.

Michael stood up to get a closer look. The drooling mouth gave the white face a blank expression, and the eyes did not see anything, lost in some internal nothingness. Michael trembled with rage. Not only the bastard was here, but he'd robbed Michael of his revenge. How many times had he imagined the day when he'd send his fist into the hated face.

"Clara, would you like anything?" he heard Maria call outside. She reappeared with a tray and two tall plastic goblets of amber iced tea. "She's playing with the goat. I don't know why she likes that goat... You kids didn't like the animals on the farm very much, except maybe for that black mutt. He was run over by a car shortly after you left... Anyway, how's Jennifer. I heard so much about her. I hoped to see her, but Dave told me she's in Europe."

"Yeah... I hope to get her here soon." As he said it, Michael fervently hoped he would succeed.

"I'd love so much to see her. To think I have a ten-year-old granddaughter I've never seen."

"What happened to him?" Michael tried to sound casual, indicating the corner where his stepfather sat.

"Oh, him? I tend to forget about him sometimes... He just belongs with the furniture. The last stroke three years ago left him like that. The nurse takes care of him everyday. He doesn't eat much and doesn't bother me anymore. I can't say I'm sorry. Now I can live my own life, do what I please, when I please."

"I see you didn't keep up the farm."

"Too much work for a woman alone. Besides, your stepfather had a good insurance policy. About the only thing he did right in his life. I harassed him for years before he finally bought it though. The insurance man was a good friend of mine," she explained with a mischievous smile.

"You still fool around at your age?"

"You know what the good thing is about all this, though? I don't have to sneak out anymore. I could do it right in front of his nose, and he wouldn't know the difference."

The righteousness in Maria's tone shocked Michael, who felt almost sorry for the bastard in the chair. After making life a living hell for those who could have loved him, the abuser ended up sick and forsaken at the end of a useless life. Michael looked at his mother. "Well, I meant to tell you I recently met someone who knew you a long time ago."

"An ex-boyfriend?" Maria sounded excited, eyes sparkling.

"My father."

"What? Don't play with me Mikie... Your conception was a mystery from the start. I could never figure it out myself." She paused before adding, "I never told you this before, but now you might understand better. The only thing I can think of is that day when I went to the sacred cave."

"A cave?"

"Yes, on the reservation. I knew the place inhabited by powerful spirits. White Eagle had told me so, and at the time I could feel it too. So I went there, one night, unnoticed. I hoped the spirits would understand and grant me the special son I wanted for myself. I was very young, a virgin, and I didn't care for any of the men on the reservation. Beside, I was taboo."

"Taboo?"

Maria hesitated. "I had just killed a man... In self-defense... He was drunk and tried to force himself on me. I took an empty bottle by the neck, broke it against the bar, and with all my strength I stabbed his chest with the jagged edges. Blood splattered everywhere. The man looked at the red stain on his shirt as if surprised, then he collapsed. A narrow shard had pierced his heart. He died on the spot." There was no remorse in Maria's voice.

"Didn't the reservation police arrest you?"

"No. I was under age, and it was self-defense. They didn't like the guy anyway. He was trouble. After that, I couldn't have loved any Indian man. I wanted a white man who would treat me right. I wanted to live in a nice house and have a nice car."

"We knew that, Mom."

"But first, I wanted a special son, one that would be like no other child, a great seer, like White Eagle. A son who would make me proud and make my miserable life worthwhile... I really believed it could work if I offered myself to the Great Spirit, but during the ritual, after I smoked the peyote, I must have passed out. Someone must have entered the cave. If I knew who it was, I would have the bastard killed for taking advantage of me like that."

"I know who it was, Mom, but it was not a man... Not really. He gave you your wish though. Remember, you wanted a son?" Michael smiled.

"I still believe in spirits, even though I go to church every Sunday, but I had enough time to think about this and I don't believe that it was a spirit. Besides, if it was a spirit, you would be a man of great wisdom, not a drifter and a runaway."

"Did you ever see the Crusader on TV, Mom?"

"No, but I heard about him from friends at church. They say he can perform miracles. No one knows who he is or where he comes from. And he disappeared just as mysteriously as he came. They

Vijaya Schartz

say he's very powerful. He could be a new Messiah.
Now, that's someone I would be proud to be the
mother of. You kids just brought me trouble all my
life, I swear."

Michael chuckled. He toyed an instant with
the idea of confounding Maria then had a better idea.
Through the window, he checked on Clara, busy with
the goat outside. He would get back before she
missed him.

"The traveling spirit who visited you then is
back in the neighborhood," he told his mother. "I met
him. He might like to see you again. Do you think
you can get back in the same kind of trance you used
to as a young girl?"

"I don't think so. It was wonderful though. It
was like a dream, but I could not remember it afterwards. I felt light and happy. My spirit floated high,
like on the wings of an eagle. All I remember is a
beautiful blue light. I was in love with that blue light.
It made me feel whole. After a while, my attempts to
call the blue light failed. I never saw it again. Then I
met my white man. I thought it was the end of my
bad times, but it was only the beginning."

"Mother, please just relax and try to remember
that blue light." As he spoke, Michael summoned the
powers to convince his mother to relax and visualize.
Then he opened both arms to a luminous blue shaft,
wide enough for both of them. As he glanced toward
the corner where his stepfather sat, Michael thought
he saw a glint of awareness touching the staring eyes
and twisting the drooling lips. Michael dismissed it
from his mind and proceeded to elevate Maria bodily
along the vertical beam. She looked at him with awe

and delight. "Let's go visit Dad." Michael brimmed with love.

When they reached the spaceship Michael immediately became aware of unusual tensions aboard the vessel. The fluctuating colors pulsated more violently and in brighter shades. The previously quiet craft now echoed muffled electronic sounds of activity and conversations. Amrah did not appear immediately upon their arrival although Michael had sent a telepathic message. Something troubled the usual serenity of the place.

Michael sat his bemused mother on an invisible chair and smiled to reassure her. Maria looked around with wonder. Her eyes shone with recognition when they gazed upon the blue being coming toward her.

"Greetings, my son." Amrah's voice, as kind as ever, betrayed a worry Michael had never noticed before. The Blue Angel turned to the beautiful Indian woman staring at him in ecstasy.

The alien face softened, and the tone conveyed more feelings than Michael had ever seen Amrah express. "Maria... You came back... I hoped you would... You are still very beautiful... In your heart and in your mind, as well."

"I know you... Are you a spirit?" asked Maria.

"No, a live being. We met many times. We used to get along well and had much happiness together. Thanks to our son, we are a family again." Amrah brought about a blue cloud that enveloped Maria.

When the cloud dissipated, comprehension lit the woman's face. "So, that's what made me so

Vijaya Schartz

happy then. And that's how you happened to give me Mikie, the son I asked for?"

"Not just any son, Maria, an avatar, I should say a Crusader, that is what he is called on this planet today." The Blue Angel studied Maria's face.

"Mikie? The Crusader? Well, I'll be..." She looked at Michael with new respect then turned to Amrah. "What did I do to deserve such an honor? Why did you choose me? I was unworthy... There were lots of other girls."

"Yes, but you came to me and asked..." Amrah explained melodiously. "And with convincing fervor I should say. How could I resist such innocence?"

Michael still had difficulty with the story. "You, the level-headed, rational, wise old alien fell in love with a young murderess?"

"A beautiful, lost child, Michael, as it was meant to be. And I will love her forever."

"Maybe that's what I couldn't explain," Michael reflected aloud. "I hated her and I loved her at the same time... But you... You can forget all the ugliness and just love the beauty and the innocence..."

"Look at her, my son, and tell me what you see."

"I see a radiant woman, happier and more beautiful than I have ever seen her."

"This is the miracle of love, Michael. This is what happens when you give unconditionally. This is what your world should be, what you can make it, if you succeed... But this may prove more difficult than I thought at first."

"More difficult? In what way?" Suddenly, Michael's first impression when boarding the ship came back to him. "Something's happening, I can feel it... What is it?"

"A great evil spawned from the red planet where you saw Lufriec in your dream. After millennia of inactivity, we presumed the troublesome Reptilians extinguished. Recent reports, however, describe a fleet of ominous war crafts heading this way at great speed. They originated from that planet and resemble in technology the vessels of an ancient power so great and destructive that we are not sure we can hold it off. Lufriec is the key to that power, and Krastinios is his son. Since we are not geared for destruction, you are witnessing the conversion of our energies into weapons."

"War? How can you wage war? You taught me love and peace and now you prepare for war?" This new development shook the foundation of Michael's understanding.

"Basic evil cannot be won over," Amrah explained. "We tried before, and it failed. All we can do at this point is destroy it or perish in the attempt. If you have to fight Krastinios, do it fast, before his father arrives. The son gets stronger as Lufriec gets closer. Besides, defeating Krastinios might weaken his father."

"So much destruction... I still wonder where and how to fight him."

"In the Nevada desert," Amrah said confidently. "A place called Yucca Lake."

"I heard the name before, but why there?"

"There lies the perfect weapon to fight your powerful foe. Get there before he can claim it."

"What is it?" Michael asked.

Vijaya Schartz

"You will see..." Amrah answered mysteriously.

Michael shivered, thinking of Jennifer and Tori. "I better get back down there now."

Maria had quietly come closer and stood next to the Blue Angel, a blissful look on her face. Michael bent to kiss her cheek.

Amrah turned to Michael. "Take care of yourself, my son. Leave Maria to me, I will protect her."

"I know you will. Wish me luck, Father."

"Luck has little to do with it, Son. I wish you courage."

The look of compassion in the blue alien eyes touched Michael and, forgetting all previous restraints, he stepped forth to embrace the Blue Angel, feeling the need for physical contact. The tide of warmth and love took him by surprise, but Michael held on tight, letting hot tears flow freely. When they disengaged, they waved goodbye, as any loving father, mother, and son would, knowing they might never see each other again.

* * *

Back at Maria's house, Michael considered the paralyzed body in the chair. He felt some pity for the helpless son-of-a-bitch who had caused him so much pain. But the man had hurt enough people. At least, now, he was harmless.

Leaving his crippled stepfather in the nurse's care, Michael collected Clara outside.

"Where did Grandma go?" Clara asked.

"She's visiting an old friend in heaven, but she'll be back."

Clara looked at Michael dubiously then laughed. "Can she do that?"

"You'd be surprised." Michael smiled mysteriously.

Dark clouds gathered strength and the wind picked up as he drove back to Dave's home in the gathering storm. Soon, Krastinios would call.

Vijaya Schartz

CHAPTER SEVENTEEN

Tori sat at a round table with a white table-cloth. The golden light of the morning sun danced through the delicate white lace of the curtains draping the French doors of Krastinios' chateau. Across from her, Jennifer spread marmalade on hot toast. Both dressed for horseback, mother and daughter chatted gaily about enjoying the country for the weekend, such a peaceful place, yet so close to Paris.

Outside the many small glass panes, the es-planade overlooked neat geometrical gardens with bright red, pink, white, and yellow roses. Perfectly groomed shrubbery in geometrical designs alternated with fountains and ponds, surrounded by wide alleys of packed dirt designed only for the hooves of horses. Farther, beyond the artificial lake where white and black swans glided, the French garden turned into an English park that gradually became a forest. There, reindeer, boar, jackrabbit and fox cohabited peace-fully, the serenity disturbed only once in a while by a small party of horseback hunters in red coats making much noise with horns and dogs.

Since she liked to be thought of as an animal lover, Tori had refused to have a hunt organized on her account. She did accept a morning ride around the domain, however. Jennifer, although weary of horses, agreed to come along when Tori intimated that any well-bred woman should know how to ride a horse in style.

"Listen to this," Tori exclaimed, scanning the newspaper she held over her cup of coffee. "'Under the mounting pressure of various international eco-logical groups, Japan finally renounces the hunting of whales in the Pacific.' Isn't that terrific? I love it."

"Hum..." Jennifer's response sounded less than enthusiastic.

"And here," Tori translated further, "'The U.S. is actively negotiating with the Baltic countries to stop the genocide, while international Red Cross hospitals in the main cities treat the wounded of all ethnic groups without discrimination.'"

"Anything about home?" Jennifer asked. "Something a little less boring?"

"Boring? This is so interesting. Here, you may like this better. 'MacDonald's is funding a project to help save the Amazon. Florists from New York buy exotic leaves from the Indians for expensive flower arrangements. This encourages the local tribes to depend on the forest for their survival rather than on its conversion into ranch land."

"That's good." Jennifer's answer could have pertained to the news or to the piece of toast she was chewing.

Vijaya Schartz

"Mr. K has a picture in the paper for the inauguration of a new exhibit of rare pre-Columbian art today. Apparently he financed it and most of the pieces come from his private collection. They call him a prince and even wrote his name in full... Truly unpronounceable."

Tori returned to her breakfast. "I really don't understand how that man survives. I have never seen him eat or drink or sleep or work... He's always impeccable, never a wrinkle on his spotless clothes or a hair out of place. He always looks happy. I'd really like to know how he does it."

Krastinios, who overheard, smiled as he entered the breakfast room. "No, believe me, charming beauty, you do not want to know." He walked straight to Tori, took the perfectly manicured hand with long red fingernails, then slightly pressed his lips to the pale fingers. "And how are my chosen doves this morning?" he asked with a winning smile. Turning to Jennifer, Krastinios took her hand in the same gallant gesture.

"We are fine, thank you," said Jennifer, mimicking Tori's intonations.

"As soon as you are ready, meet me in the stables. I shall be with the horses." Krastinios saluted, turned around and left through the French doors, letting the fresh morning breeze play with the white lace of the curtains.

Something in Mr. K's attitude bothered Jennifer this morning. "Tori, I kind of remember talking to Dad on the phone yesterday, but I'm not sure what he said or what I said to him," Jennifer whispered as soon as

Mr. K was outside. "It was like a dream... Did we call him or did I dream it?"

"This is strange," Tori said. "To tell the truth I can't quite remember myself... I think Mr. K talked to him, too. I wonder if there was something in the tea... I remember feeling good, but that's all." She paused, as if reflecting on these disturbing thoughts. "Since rehab, I've never lost touch with reality."

"Well, maybe we can call him again today after we ride the horses," Jennifer offered, proud of her suggestion.

"Maybe we can..." Tori answered with a frown.

"Well I'm ready." Jennifer left the napkin in a ball on the table and rose. She hoped to hide her nervousness by speaking with determination. The black riding breeches tucked in black stiff leather boots made her look very slim, while the lime green shirt tied in a knot on the flat belly added color to the outfit.

"Let's go then, young lady." Tori, also wearing black riding breeches and boots, had opted for a romantic poet shirt from the extensive wardrobe Mr. K made available to them.

So far, Jennifer enjoyed this unexpected weekend at the chateau. She could sense some tension in her mother's attitude, however, but except for a few blank areas in her memories, Jennifer felt great, having a wonderful time.

Although the day promised to warm-up later, the cool morning would be perfect for a ride. They walked out on the flat terrace along the length of the three-story building, built in the seventeenth century by the Count de Saint Germain as a hunting retreat.

Vijaya Schartz

The curved slate roof housed the servant's quarters while the architecture, quite advanced for the time, provided for vast rooms with fireplaces, oriental rooms, modern rooms, classic rooms, even an Egyptian room, complete with a sphinx. The huge bathrooms, equipped with all the creature comforts and walk-in closets, constituted a more recent addition.

From the outside, however, the castle kept its historical character with white marble columns, Renaissance esplanade, and exquisite French doors and windows that brought in much light, giving the place an airy feel. A short distance from the main building, toward the woods, the freshly painted white stables attested to the owner's inclination for expensive horses. Mother and daughter headed in that direction.

Jennifer pinched her nose at the odor of straw and horse dung as she entered. The place looked clean though, with perfectly ordered white stalls, all bearing names and each containing a magnificent horse. Jennifer stopped breathing altogether when she saw Krastinios petting a tall, shiny black stallion by the name of Lucifer. At her sight, the proud beast reared in the stall in a clatter of hooves, exhibiting a fantastic impetuosity. Jennifer stayed clear of the stallion, eyeing him with what she hoped would be interpreted as only great respect.

"Do not worry, Jennifer, I have a perfectly well-behaved mount for you." Mr. K indicated a small bay mare being fitted with an English saddle by a stable attendant. "Faustina is an Arabian purebred, a little older and extremely docile," he assured her. Mr. K held the reins and offered a hand to help her mount.

Archangel Crusader

Jennifer stood on a little step-stool brought there just for this purpose. Too late to recant now, she thought, climbing onto the animal's back. It was the first time. She sat very proud, like a queen overseeing her subjects. The mare did not make any unexpected move. Neither did Jennifer, very careful not to jeopardize her precarious balance.

Tori mounted a young white mare of slightly hotter blood, a little too skittish for Jennifer's taste. The name on the stall said Kalinka, and Tori had to pet her neck to calm her down. Tori, an accomplished rider, could handle a little temper. Finally, Mr. K mounted the black beast from Hell, who calmed instantly and became tractable under the master's control.

The threesome set out at a leisurely pace for a grand tour of the property. The early morning sun made the dew sparkle on the newly opened roses, and on the white lilies of the French garden. Jennifer inhaled the smells of freshly cut grass and turned up dirt. She especially enjoyed the playful songs of the larks and the trills of the robins as they rode on, exchanging mundane thoughts in the morning breeze.

They turned into the cool green shade of English gardens, then into the woods where the vegetation grew thicker as the trail narrowed. Jennifer's bay, comfortable with a slight rider, took the lead. Much like an old circus horse would do out of habit, the bay led the younger ones on a well-known circuit.

Krastinios, while exhibiting the attitude of the perfect host, seethed inside. His cheek still burned from the jolt the Crusader sent him over the phone line. What an arrogant title. The success of the Cru-

Vijaya Schartz

sade irritated him more than he cared to admit. As long as Tanner lived, Krastinios could not feel safe, for as ignorant and uncouth as the upstart seemed, he must have some hidden strength. That worried Krastinios. Although he deemed himself superior, he wished he knew the outcome. Impeding the progress of the Earth Crusade took too much energy from him.

As a result, he did not concentrate enough on keeping his prisoners' memories under control. Already, Tori questioned his motives and Jennifer started remembering. Even though the torture room picture was fake, there was much he didn't want the women to remember. Krastinios also had to maintain the shield to prevent them from contacting Tanner on their own. So many tasks scattered his energy, causing the uncomfortable feeling of losing control. Nevertheless, a smile lit Krastinios' dark eyes as he returned his attention to the pleasant conversation of the two enchanting guests.

Suddenly, Jennifer heard the stallion behind her whinny a warning. Out of the thick underbrush, a reckless black boar darted right in front of the bay who shied and reared. The mare rolled wild eyes, neighing in a frenzy of hooves at the scent of danger.

Jennifer tensed on the reins and felt herself lifted up and backwards. Losing balance, she fell back, sliding in slow motion along the horse's flank. When she finally hit the ground, right under the frightened mare, she saw a huge hoof coming down on her face. Paralyzed, Jennifer tried to scream but no sound escaped her mouth, then the hoof hit, and all went black and silent.

Krastinios swung off the stallion with the agility of an acrobat, mentally cursing his distracted mind. He calmed the mare and led her away from Jennifer who lay inert in the dirt.

Screaming, Tori dismounted to kneel on the ground beside her daughter. At the sight of bright blood gushing out of the deep depression in Jennifer's forehead, Tori's breathing became erratic. Tears filled her eyes as she looked at Krastinios. He found her stunning with raw anxiety on the pale face.

"Please, get the car, quickly. Where is the hospital?" Tori asked in panic.

"There is no hospital close enough. The brain is damaged and the cervical cord severed. She is dead. They cannot save her."

Tori covered her mouth in horror. "It's impossible. How can you tell?"

"Trust me. I know what to do." The power of persuasion in Krastinios' voice compelled Tori to surrender the child. Jennifer was too precious to Tanner to lose her, yet. She was the Crusader's weakness. Krastinios cursed his carelessness. How could he have let this happen?

So, faking an honest look of concern, under Tori's tortured gaze, Krastinios lowered himself to the forest floor and laid one hand on Jennifer's forehead, the other on her heart. Eyes closed in concentration, Krastinios assessed the girl's injuries, then murmured an incantation in an alien language, with hisses, clucks and rattles.

Next to him, Tori fidgeted and twisted her hands even under the spell. Shortly, Krastinios stopped and gave her a serene smile, erasing the seriousness of the accident from her memory. Tori ex-

Vijaya Schartz

haled relief when Jennifer opened her eyes and sat up apparently unscathed.

"Are you all right, Baby?" Tori pressed Jennifer against her chest.

"What happened?" A look of wonder on her face, Jennifer seemed fully recovered.

"Not much," Krastinios lied. "You fell from your horse. You better get back on it before it starts back home and leaves you behind."

Jennifer looked embarrassed for a few seconds. Brushing herself clean of the dust, she regained composure to climb back onto the horse with Krastinios' help. As the trio headed back for the castle, Tori glanced surreptitiously at the prince in black leather, a puzzled look on her face. Krastinios caught her confused thoughts and flashed an engaging smile.

* * *

Michael could hear Dave and Becky in the next room. They too felt the tension of the gathering storm and couldn't sleep. It smelled like rain. Almost twenty-four hours since Krastinios' ultimatum. The phone would ring any minute. Despite training and psychic powers Michael found it hard not to let feelings get in the way. He worried about Jennifer and about all those he loved.

All evening, Michael had been reviewing his plan, trying to clear his mind before issuing the challenge. He'd thought of many stages for the duel, away from populated areas, since the destruction might be extensive. Even a forest would be hard to protect. He had first thought of an atoll in the Pacific, the snow-covered Himalayas, the Arctic ice cap, or the Sahara desert. Following Amrah's suggestion, Michael opted for the Nevada desert. Near some rocky slopes lay the dry sandy bottom of Yucca lake, an abandoned nuclear test site.

Drained by the effort of transporting Maria to the ship, Michael must have dozed off for a while, for something jolted him awake. Gusty winds shook the trees. A squall rattled the TV antenna on the roof. Something else caught Michael's attention, the phone: it was about to ring. He flipped the cover before the ring. "Yeah, I'm here."

"So, my dear Tanner, are you ready to renounce your ridiculous Crusade?" The arrogance in the voice unnerved Michael to no end, but he had to remain calm.

"How's Jennifer? What did you do to her? I want to talk to her right now." Michael didn't feel like playing games.

"My, are we edgy today... I didn't touch her yet, she is too precious."

"So why that torture chamber business?"

"I cannot believe you fell for such an unrefined subterfuge. That was all I cared to improvise on the spur of the moment. I'll show you kindness and put her on."

"Dad? Is it you, Dad?"

"Jen? Thank God. Are you all right, sweetheart? Is Tori there, too?"

"I'm fine, Dad. Tori and I... We had a lot of fun. This morning, we went horseback riding."

Vijaya Schartz

"I thought you were afraid of horses."

"Mr. K is very nice. He gave me a very gentle horse. Her name is Faustina." The innocent voice of Jennifer conveyed no fear or anxiety.

"That's enough, Tanner."

"So it's Mr. K now? How cute."

"You hurt my feelings."

"You should be ashamed of preying on a weak child."

"Not so weak, really. I happened to get into your daughter's mind to mend her broken skull this morning, and I saw traces of raw psychic powers. She will be quite a handful when she reaches puberty."

"Broken skull? You asshole! I'll make you pay for that."

"Riding accidents do happen, my dear Tanner... Now, what about our deal? Are you giving up?"

"Never!" Michael's definite tone made the ensuing silence frightening.

"Then, I may dispose of these two pretty girls for my personal pleasure, right?"

"Not so fast... I have something better for you, something a little more challenging, something you want very much."

"Do you presume to know me that well?" A hint of curiosity crept into the casual tone.

"You and I are alike in more ways than I care to admit." Michael found it to be the truth.

"What a disgusting thought... So, what is it?" Krastinios sounded almost interested. Was he taking the bait?

"The chance to kill me yourself! A personal challenge, a duel... Just you and me." Michael held his breath.

"You do know me a little after all." That curious tone again. "Interesting... Weapons?"

"Anything goes." The dice were cast.

"How crude! Place? Time? Conditions?"

"In two days, at noon, Yucca dry lake in Nevada, bring Jennifer and Tori with you." As he spoke, Michael prayed it would work.

"Tempting... Very tempting." There was a short pause on the line then, "Yes... I like it. You have a deal! But why not right now?"

Just as impatient as Krastinios, Michael knew that he needed to rest. After using up so much energy in the past few days, he couldn't teleport to Nevada and still have the strength required for this ultimate fight. "I want to test your patience," he said instead, trying to sound confident. "In two days, then, with the girls?"

"In two days." The smug disembodied voice made Michael wonder if he had made the right choice. But as in chess, once the move was made, he couldn't turn back.

When Michael switched off the phone, a swift, cool breeze caressed his skin. He heard a steady downpour battering the flimsy roof. Heavy drops pelted the window and a fresh, humid scent pervaded the room. All the tension fled from his body. For a little while, at least, Michael could relax. Jennifer would be safe until he saw her in two days.

Vijaya Schartz

A soft knock on the door brought Michael back to the present. Dave poked his head through the crack. "Are you all right?"

"Yeah, I'm okay... Thanks for asking... Come in, I'm going to need your help."

CHAPTER EIGHTEEN

"Did you ever jump from an airplane?"

Dave's voice drowned among Michael's thoughts as he stared at the slick road through the metronome of the windshield wipers. The blue Ford pickup purred under the hammering of raindrops on the metal roof. The radio played a country song. On the floor of the truck lay the black leather bag in which Michael had packed some camping gear, a blanket, a knife, an Uzi and ammunition, although it seemed useless.

"Are you going to get Jennifer?" Clara had asked him before he left.

"I hope so," Michael had answered while Becky wished him good luck. Michael had jumped in the passenger seat, long hair curling from the chilly morning rain and tumbling over the sheepskin vest.

Now, Michael scanned the newspaper articles Debbie had mailed. They highlighted an international foundation for accelerated research and distribution of new treatments for AIDS. The organization received approval and financial support from several private and government agencies. Another article estimated that with all the new dispositions taken to limit air pollution, the ozone layer would repair itself within three years. A third article outlined a new trend in advertising strategies for chemical companies: the new campaigns focused on how well they disposed of dangerous waste products.

Dave's voice took Michael out of his preoccupation.

"You said something, Dave? Sorry, I wasn't listening."

"I said, did you ever jump from an airplane before?"

"No... Why? Shouldn't be that hard, is it?" Michael hoped his apprehension did not show. He wouldn't want Dave to think he was nervous about something so trivial.

"I don't understand. Why don't you just transport there, since you have the ability?"

"It'd take too much energy from me. I'll need my strength to fight the bastard."

They veered onto Interstate 440 loop, in the direction of Adams Field Municipal Airport.

"How well do you know this guy?" Michael's mind returned to the immediate situation. "What do you call him? The Weasel? Are you sure he's not going to chicken out at the last minute?"

"No way," Dave protested. "The Weasel can handle it all right. He's pulled that kind of stunt many times. He used to smuggle drugs over the Mexican border."

Michael whistled appreciatively. "I didn't know you had such colorful friends, brother."

"Well, he straightened up, but he owes me a big favor from way back when... He'll try to find out what you're up to. Don't tell him anything. He may be a snitch in his spare time. I'm sure he's more than happy to settle his debt."

Just as the rain stopped, the first hangars appeared, gaping wide open. Soon, a timid ray of sun sparkled on the bright logos of the few small planes lined up in front.

Dave parked the pickup along the fence. They jumped over it and walked across the field toward a row of small aircraft. The vibration of a bigger plane taking off drowned out all other sounds. Light fuel fumes polluted the air, mixing with the smells of wet dirt and tar. Puddles on the concrete slabs glistened with purple and green oil stains, and wild dandelions sprouted through cracks in the loose cement joints.

Michael looked toward the eastern sun. As he reached for the dark glasses in the pocket of his sheepskin vest, he smiled at the segment of rainbow spreading across the morning sky.

The Weasel did deserve his nickname, short and skinny with sparse, light-brown hair. The nose looked too long for the face while beady eyes constantly moved, as if searching for a clue or a minute detail that would give him an edge. The man's smile, however, only touched the lips. The gaze remained worried and scheming while the Weasel talked to Dave with exaggerated deference. Michael decided that the little man would do the job but could not be trusted.

Vijaya Schartz

Dave negotiated efficiently. Everything worked as he said it would. On such short notice, he had pulled the right strings and obtained results. Michael felt paternal pride for his younger brother, mainly when he excelled in areas where Michael himself did not feel very comfortable, like diplomacy.

While the four-seater Beechcraft Bonanza finished refueling, Michael thanked Dave in a bear hug.

"You sure you don't want me to go with you?"

Michael shook his head. "You did all you could, Brother. The rest is up to me. I'll see you soon." Michael's voice carried more confidence than he felt, his throat constricting at the thought that he may never see Dave again."

Half an hour later, Michael rode the blue skies on his way to Nevada in the company of the Weasel. With sixty-knot head-winds, they flew steadily over lush forests and great, wide rivers. The map unfolding underneath did not bear names, but Michael thought he could tell the Red River by its slightly rusty color. They crossed Oklahoma, a vast expanse of dry Texas lands, and the Indian reservations of New Mexico.

Glad for his aborted flight training, Michael knew how to read instruments and maps and, therefore, understood their position. The plane ride took longer than it would have on a jet. It would take nine hours to reach the destination. Plenty of time for Michael to think about Jennifer... He didn't want to think about what would become of her if he lost the fight.

The odd pair landed to refuel twice, once in Lubbock and once in Albuquerque. Michael welcomed the chance to exercise his long legs and eat a quick meal. Conversations with the Weasel, easier on the ground, away from the ever-present vibration, remained strained since Michael did not volunteer any information about the object of the trip. The distrust seemed reciprocated.

Gradually, the scenery turned from the green hills of northern Arizona to ocher valleys and deep canyons. In late afternoon, they reached the Nevada desert. As soon as they approached the test site area from the east, the Beechcraft dropped altitude. The Weasel flew as close to the ground as possible to avoid radar detection. It would not do to be chased by a squadron from Indian Springs Air Force Base. Since a parachute would not have enough altitude to deploy, the plan was to come as close to the ground as possible without landing, allowing Michael to free fall at his own risk.

The little man had received half the price before takeoff. The rest of the agreed-upon money made a slight bulge in the breast pocket of Michael's shirt. He took the money out and handed it to the Weasel who flashed a smile of pure delight.

Down below, the rocky desert unfolded its dun-colored ravines. According to the coordinates, they were now inside the restricted zone, although no sign in the landscape differentiated it from the surrounding wilderness.

"Here is Yucca Lake, straight ahead!" the Weasel yelled above the roar of the engine. He sounded relieved to see the end of their partnership.

"I see it." Michael looked at the misshapen shadows lengthening on the ground below. The

Vijaya Schartz

white sands of the dry lake basin contrasted with the rocky slopes of the nearby mountains.

"I can't land on this terrain," the Weasel said bluntly.

"Just get as low as you can, okay?" Now was the time to jump. Michael hoped his levitating skill would not fail him. He would need all his assets to get out of this situation unscathed.

The plane slowed down and dropped to twenty feet. Michael grabbed his equipment bag and opened the small side door. Stepping onto the wing, he held fast to the doorframe and concentrated on breathing. The ground below sped by at sixty miles an hour, but he had to do it.

Michael dropped the bag and watched it fall. Still hanging to the bottom of the doorframe, he crouched to the edge of the wing, then hung down from it, held his breath and let go, closing the distance to the ground.

In a short burst of power, he slowed his fall a little, landing hard on his toes, knees bent, rolling forward with all the grace of a martial artist. As he rose, Michael waved a hand in the direction of the retreating Beechcraft, which gained altitude and disappeared in a purring sound over the Sierra Nevada.

As he backtracked to retrieve his bag, Michael scanned the area through enhanced vision for any terrain particularity that could give him an advantage in tomorrow's duel. Some unusual pull attracted his attention to a rocky incline in a northwestern direction. Michael smiled, unfastened his black leather bag, checked the contents for damage, then headed northwest on foot.

Archangel Crusader

The sun dipped fast behind the high peaks to the west. What he, at first, thought might be a cave came into focus now and revealed itself as an abandoned mine. The last of the daylight showed the entrance, a small hole in the rock. The main beam, supported by wooden shafts on each side, looked at least a century old, preserved by the dry, hot winds.

Michael felt the temperature dropping and shivered at the sight of a white, desiccated bovine carcass staring at him from empty sockets. The call of a coyote in the distance reminded him that the desert supported life. He also noticed sagebrush and tumbleweeds.

The mine must have brought riches once, silver, or gold maybe. Michael wondered where the people of yesterday had found wood for the supports. It was a long way on horseback from the nearest big trees.

Michael ventured inside, lowering his head to get in. Immediately darkness enveloped him. Taking a flashlight out of the bag, he started exploring. If not for the fact that the old tunnels had remained intact for at least a hundred years, Michael would have hesitated. Dirt fell at unexpected times and places. Some corridors ran short and stopped. Others had collapsed, obstructed by rock and sand. In this maze, strange loud noises echoed through the empty shafts. Once, Michael thought he heard water running deep underground.

Around a bend, he came upon old sticks of dynamite, left against the rock wall in a small recess at an intersection. Quite volatile after so many years, he thought. Soon, Michael reached a well too deep

Vijaya Schartz

for the flashlight to show him the bottom. Throwing a rock inside, he counted the seconds to impact. Surprised as no sound came back, Michael then closed his eyes to scan the depth using his paranormal training.

What he saw through the mind's eye surprised him. A huge deep-seated cave permeated with moisture. An underground lake lay deep under the desert. Further down, however, something else lurked... A soft humming that almost reminded him of... Could it be what Amrah suggested? It would be so perfect. Michael had to make absolutely sure. Pushing the mental probing, he explored further. Yes, victory could favor him tomorrow.

Michael let his disembodied mind float down inside a cylindrical chamber of smooth stone. As he had done many times before, he willed his body into the mind picture and found himself standing at the bottom of an underground silo, in front of a black capsule...a fully operative nuclear bomb, the weapon Amrah hinted at.

It seemed perfect, but at what price... Mentally reviewing scientific data, Michael tried to weigh the goal against the means. The explosion would not release any radioactivity in the atmosphere. The silo was too deep, and under a body of water. It would create a tremor that would be felt a hundred miles away. It could melt the deeper crust and possibly create a weak spot in a tectonic plate. It could also pollute deep underground streams.

Not daring to make that choice alone, Michael decided to ask the prime party concerned. Sinking to the ground in lotus position, eyes closed, Michael felt a breeze ruffling his hair. He became the mountains, the oceans, the valleys, the rain clouds, and the volcanoes. He felt Her come into him.

"Earth, Gaia, Pele, Mother Nature by any other name, I am Thy Crusader. I come in love and in anguish. I beg Thee, for the sake of your many children, for the destruction of a great evil."

From deep and away came an answer, a whisper on the breeze, a breath of life and infinite love. "I am Gaia, Pele, Earth, Mother Nature by any other name... My beloved Crusader, I understand your distress. Know that I have made greater sacrifices before. Pain is a familiar friend. I will bear it for you and support your fight. I will seal the contaminated waters and contain the disease. May you save my children and lead them back to me in love, harmony and togetherness."

"I am grateful, Gaia, Pele, Earth, Mother Nature by any other name... I will do my best to win, for my race and for Thee."

"I know, Crusader. I know you will."

The breeze abated. Cold and stillness attested that the presence had gone. Michael opened his eyes. The black capsule still sat on its narrow pedestal. Tapping into the universal knowledge, Michael powered the control panel and surprised himself by deftly overriding the security codes. A few more minutes allowed him to set up the mechanism for telepathic detonation. Standing in front of his handiwork, he grinned. "Krastinios, I'm ready now." Then he willed himself back to the surface.

Now, under the full moon, looking at the benign entrance of the century-old mine, Michael understood what had caught his attention earlier. Not the

Vijaya Schartz

cave but the weapon. He concealed his discovery behind a mental shield. In order to win, Michael needed the element of surprise. He'd take any advantage he could get.

* * *

"Tori, look!" Jennifer pointed excitedly at a picture in the French newspaper lying on the black leather couch of Mr. K's library. "It's Dad, it's Dad. Dad is in the paper. What does it say?"

"Are you sure? God, he looks so mature, but yes, I recognize him." Tori sat, holding the newspaper upright.

"Hurry, what does it say?" Jennifer crowded next to Tori.

"Let's see... 'The mysterious Crusader who recently stirred waves of peace, love, and ecology awareness in Washington, D.C., and seemingly performed miracles, has disappeared without a trace. Contradicting rumors allude to a shady past as well as a holy mission. Some concerned citizens suspect a cult and asked for an investigation. Direct witnesses think he is a saint while official religious sources denounce him as a fraud. The FBI refused to comment on his identity or his legal or illegal status.' Michael? Michael is the Crusader? I know he always liked to shine and impress people, but this is unbelievable."

"Dad is not a fake. He really has powers. I've seen them."

"What do you mean powers?"

"It's true. He can read minds, he can make things move without touching them. He can make the fish come to the shore. I swear, I've seen it."

"You don't need to swear Jennifer. What did Michael tell you he was going to do after you left?"

"He was going to help Uncle Dave build his house, but he said I would be safer in Paris with you. He said he would get the bad guy who killed Veronica."

"This sounds more like the Michael I used to know."

"Look, Tori, there is a picture of Mr. K also. What does it say?"

"It says, 'Prince Krastinios attended the opening of the special Aztec art exhibit in the newly opened rooms of the Louvre yesterday. More than a hundred of the priceless pieces shown come from his personal collection.' I knew he was rich, but a prince?"

"You said Krastinios?" Jennifer could hardly speak.

"Yes, what a strange name! That's what they call him also right under the picture. He's very photogenic." Tori held the paper farther as if to get a better look.

"Mr. K is Krastinios?" Jennifer repeated in a daze, suddenly cold, feeling the blood drain from her extremities. "But he is so nice!"

"What do you mean?" Tori looked at her daughter. "Jennifer! Are you all right?" She dropped the newspaper to support Jennifer who was ready to faint.

"Krastinios is the bad guy who killed Veronica," Jennifer said weakly. "He tried to kill Dad too, and he said he would. When Dad sent me here, he said I would be safe. I'm scared." She buried her head in her mother's shoulder, crying softly.

"What are you saying?" Tori suddenly paled. "What do you know about this man?"

"Krastinios has powers like Dad, but he is mean," Jennifer said, unable to control her sobbing.

"My God, no wonder there was something strange about him. That would explain why we do whatever he suggests and can't remember what we did yesterday."

"What are we going to do?" Jennifer asked, not daring to hope.

"I'm not sure." Tori frowned. "I think he would have hurt us a long time ago if he had wanted to. Let's play the game until we find a way to get out of here."

"You know what? I felt him in my mind when I fell from the horse. Just like Dad used to do."

"He behaved in a very bizarre way that day. I didn't like it, even though he brought you back. It bothered me. I've read about supernatural things many times, but actually seeing it gives me the creeps."

Jennifer turned cold at the sound of a suave voice behind them.

"Such a pity that you had to find out just now!"

At the sight of Krastinios emerging from behind a drapery, the woman and the girl recoiled in horror, speechless. Tori stepped in front of Jennifer protectively.

"I would have much preferred to take you with me on this trip of your own free will." The gentleness in Krastinios' voice did not ring true anymore. "Then again, a little terror might add spice to this expedition." The charming smile raised goose bumps on the back of Jennifer's neck.

"Why did you kill Veronica?" she challenged. "She didn't do anything. I hate you!" Jennifer launched herself at Krastinios who stopped smiling and swiftly stepped aside.

"I'm afraid you will have to be restrained," he declared seriously. "Let's hurry, my craft is waiting."

Vijaya Schartz

CHAPTER NINETEEN

Michael walked toward the light as she came to meet him in the cave where he was meditating. He could not see the face in the shadows, just the shape of the lithe body through soft, streaming silk. He could smell her perfume and knew who she was even before he heard her voice.

"I welcome you, my love, but it isn't time yet. You still have much to do before we can rejoice."

"Veronica... Is it really you? I missed you something fierce... Why did you have to die?"

"It was necessary, Michael, or you wouldn't be here."

"I'll pulverize the bastard who killed you, I swear."

"Set aside your hatred, my love, or he will feed upon it. Forget your fear. Forget your doubts. Your victory can come only from selflessness." She looked so strong...

"Veronica... I want you to know that I love you. I never could express my feelings well enough to make you know it, but I did care very much, even in the short time we had together. I wish we could have another chance."

"There will be other times, my love. That, I can promise." Her image vacillated slightly.

"Other times? How?"

But she had turned around and floated deliberately toward the light, an invisible current moving the veils about the slim silhouette.

When all went black, Michael found himself staring at the complete darkness of the cave. Against his bare back, the rock felt cold. The soft breeze on his face told him of subterranean air currents carrying a strong odor of sulfur. Bubbling water sounds reverberated, covering the ominous presence underneath.

Easing out of the lotus position, Michael flicked the flashlight on, setting it on the ground to illuminate the ceiling. The light lost itself in shadows. The roof stood so high that only the near wall and rocky floor to the edge of the underground lake could be seen in the beam.

Michael went to the dark brink and knelt to splash his face with chilly water. He tasted it before drinking freely. A little sulfur couldn't hurt him. Splashing noises echoed, bouncing off the towering walls like a din of whispers resembling voices. Michael stopped to listen. Funny how the imagination could trick us sometimes…

A stubby beard made him feel uncouth. He wished he had thought of bringing a razor. Remembering the warmth and the dust of the desert on the

Vijaya Schartz

surface, Michael stripped and waded into the shallow pool.   Enjoying the refreshing feeling, he lowered himself into ink-black coolness.

In other circumstances, he would have felt scared and vulnerable, naked in the dark waters, but today this communion with the secret side of nature elated him. He willed his eyes and ears to scan the cave. Now, Michael could make out the outlines of the huge cavern. It seemed that several rivulets fed the wide central lake. Floating on his back, he guessed at the height of the vaulted ceiling, and at the small shaft communicating with the mine above.

Something on the cave's roof moved, making faint noises. Adjusting his mind vision, Michael discerned a multitude of small creatures hanging head down. Bats. Surprised to find them here, he recorded the information for further use.

Now totally refreshed, Michael stepped out of the water. He shook the dust from his clothes before putting them on, mentally readying himself for the task ahead, then willed his body back to the tunnels. Before leaving the mine, he inspected the dynamite he had carefully prepared the night before. Age had liquefied it into an extremely volatile explosive, nitroglycerine.

The mental shield he'd placed on the silo would hold. Michael also cloaked his own thoughts, remembering how Krastinios had read him on their last encounter. A shift in vibrations told him the enemy was near. Michael checked the knife in his boot, took the Uzi out of the bag, loaded it in two short motions, placed it on a rock outside the entrance of the mine then walked purposefully out into the noon sun.

Archangel Crusader

Despite the moral support of Amrah and the dream of Veronica, Michael felt utterly alone as he walked in blind sunlight to meet the challenge. Nevertheless, he braced himself, ignoring the heat and the parched rocks. As relaxed as he could get under the circumstances, he cleared his mind and headed toward the white sands of the dry lake bottom.

A subtle whistle made Michael look up as a triangular craft materialized in the sky, descending fast, then hovering in mid-air a foot above the ground. No engine noise. No wind. No displacement of sand pattern. Krastinios was right on time.

Michael closed the distance. The small hermetic vessel seemed to absorb the light through its dull, black surface. It had a V-shape. A familiar smell pervaded the area, not unpleasant, rather sweet, like burned licorice, not unlike the smell of Amrah's spaceship. Michael puzzled over the lack of noise and wondered whether the craft used the same mode of propulsion as Amrah's.

One side of the hull slid open, revealing the loathsome smile of his archenemy. Michael kept his anger in check and chose a rough, sarcastic approach. "What'd you do? Steal an Air Force prototype?"

"You disappoint me, Tanner. I am hurt. This is much more advanced technology." Krastinios leapt down from the craft. "Don't you like it?"

"Where's Jennifer, you, filthy snake?"

"Tsk, tsk, tsk. Such lack of manners! She is here. Would you care to go inside?"

"Thanks, but no thanks, let her come out. Did you bring Tori, too?"

Vijaya Schartz

Krastinios beckoned to someone inside, and both Jennifer and Tori appeared in the opening, hands bound behind their backs, squinting against the mid-day sun.

"Daddy!" Jennifer exclaimed, both surprise and relief evident on her face.

"Michael?" Tori looked confused and a little embarrassed.

"Get them out, away from that thing." Michael reinforced his natural authority with a mental command.

Krastinios flinched, as if resenting the coercion. "I believe they would be more comfortable waiting inside, really."

"I don't trust your sneaky ways. Let them out, and untie their hands."

"You have no sense of humor whatsoever, Tanner. And you are spoiling all my fun." Krastinios sighed. When he snapped his fingers, the ties fell off the prisoners' hands.

Jennifer jumped off the hovering craft and ran into her father's arms. Tori massaged her wrists and looked around. She hesitated for a second then stepped out of the craft, blinking under the glare of the bright sun. When her gaze met Michael's, ten years of guilt seemed to weigh on her shoulders. Still holding Jennifer, Michael looked at Tori with steady understanding, sending waves of forgiveness to soothe her suffering mind. She responded with a smile.

"Tori, I'm glad you're all right. Would you please take Jennifer to the shelter up there? There is shade and water. I have some business with Mr. K."

The pseudonym rang like an insult but Krastinios didn't seem to notice. "What a touching family portrait. Unfortunately, in a few minutes there won't be anymore family."

Ignoring the threat, Michael watched Tori and Jennifer retreat to the flimsy shade of the makeshift tent he had pitched the night before, then turned his attention back to his enemy.

"How lovely," Krastinios mocked. "Now, it's just you and me, alone at last, free to consummate."

"Cut the crap. Let's get on with it."

"A little impatient, aren't we?" Krastinios obviously enjoyed the idea of the duel. "For myself, I would like to savor the moment. I have been waiting for this."

"So have I, asshole. It's pay-back time."

"You have learned a few tricks since last time. Closing your mind to my scrutiny will not help you."

Michael composed himself and relaxed his stance, turning slightly to face Krastinios straight on. As he unfocused his eyes, he flashed lightning at the exact spot where his opponent's head was a moment before. It hit the black aircraft in a shimmer of disrupted electromagnetic fields. A strong licorice smell filled Michael's nostrils as loud, impudent laughter resounded behind him.

Michael faced about, just in time to sidestep a much stronger jolt coming straight at him. The fire bolt scorched the sand where Michael had been standing.

Another peal of laughter... "You provide the finest entertainment, my dear Tanner. I enjoy it immensely."

Vijaya Schartz

Michael aimed again, this time igniting a ball of tumbleweed while Krastinios evaporated to reappear on the right, laughing in the same infuriating way.

A cloud of sand and dust started to rise when Krastinios summoned a fierce whirlwind. Blinded, Michael struggled to stay erect. The tornado threatened to sweep him off his feet and throw him to the heavens. Michael held fast, concentrating his energy, rooting himself deep into Mother Earth. He choked on dust, arms covering his face protectively. Quickly, the vortex subsided.

Suddenly blotting the sun, a wingspan of nine feet dropped upon Michael's head, talons and claws slashing. A gigantic eagle... It took several deep cuts in the skin of his arms before Michael could collect his wits and mentally send the bird of prey packing with a cry of dismay.

From the relative safety of the tent, overlooking the dry lake, halfway to the entrance of what looked like a mine, Jennifer and Tori stared in horror. Every time Michael faltered under an attack, Jennifer cried out. She wanted to rush toward him, but what could she do? Throw rocks? It seemed childish. Shielding her eyes, she looked in the direction of the mine and saw something on a flat stone. Some kind of gun... She ran toward it.

"Jennifer!" Tori called after her.

Jennifer ignored the call. When she returned to Tori, out of breath, she proudly held in front of her Michael's Uzi. "I found something." She handed the weapon to Tori. "Can you use it? We've got to help him."

Archangel Crusader

"Dear God, I don't know..." Tori took the weapon and looked it over. "I've seen it used in movies." She tried the grip. "It looks armed, I just have to pull the trigger."

"Try it!"

Resolutely, Jennifer and Tori walked down toward the lake.

Now bleeding from many gashes on face and arms, mad as hell, Michael faced Krastinios again. He struck, strong and true. Krastinios did not vanish this time but somehow deflected the jolt back to its sender. The bolt hit Michael in the chest, paralyzing him with pain and fear. He staggered and fell, tasting blood and grit on his lips. Willing himself to get up despite the crippling wound, Michael dragged himself to his feet, only to fall again.

Krastinios loomed now, blocking the sun, filling the air with vexing laughter. At such close range, Michael could not avoid a fatal blow. He felt so weak, ready to faint. If only he had a few seconds to recover...

A round of firearm exploded nearby.

Krastinios stopped laughing. His eyes narrowed with surprise, mouth twisting as he clutched his stomach. With green blood seeping from several wounds, the black knight fell to his knees.

Closing his eyes for an instant, Michael thanked Jennifer for the respite while mentally healing his worse injuries. No time to rest, though. Half running, half limping, he rushed toward the mine entrance, gesturing to Tori and Jennifer. "Get away from there!"

Krastinios, already on his feet, didn't follow Mi-

Vijaya Schartz

chael but went straight for Jennifer and Tori. Jennifer scrambled up the slope like a rabbit, but Tori stood her ground, a figure of righteousness and wrath in her dirty, sweaty dress, firing at will. This time, however, the bullets hit an invisible shield and ricocheted in every direction. Tori gasped, stopped firing then dropped the weapon to run. When she tripped, a net stretched in front of her. She fell, tangled in the web. A few yards away, Jennifer met the same fate.

Krastinios laughed. "Maybe I shall kill you first." Taking a deep breath, he prepared to strike. In that instant, lightning hit him hard on the side of the head. Krastinios pivoted, eyes full of hatred, to face Michael who stood in the black entrance of the mine. "Do not interfere, Earthling. I will take care of you too."

"Pick on someone your own strength, coward!" Michael held his chest as he limped further inside the dark tunnel. This time Krastinios followed him.

Michael went straight for the dynamite, ignited it with a mind jolt then lightly dropped into the shaft, slowing his descent by levitating. He landed on the floor of the cave a little harder than expected, waiting for Krastinios to get caught in the explosion. No such luck. The dark knight was already next to him when the conflagration shook the cave, sending a shower of dust and rock through the communicating chimney, disturbing a thousand screaming and flapping bats.

While struggling to get out of the net, Tori and Jennifer heard the explosion that shook the mountainside. Tori freed herself first, then helped Jennifer out and held her in her arms. "God help us!" she cried in despair, pressing the girl against her chest. Several smaller explosions followed.

Dust and heavy smoke came out of the entrance, but neither Tori nor Jennifer dared enter the collapsed tunnels.

Jennifer attempted to contact her father's mind. "Dad is alive!" she declared triumphantly, wiping the sweat off her forehead. Then, she stayed linked to Michael's mind, offering her small supply of energy to supplement his.

Despite the explosion, the cave itself was still intact. The deeper rock had not been affected much by the shock, but the two combatants now threw lightning at each other, illuminating the cavern with their fireworks.

Regaining control of his body, Michael fired relentlessly to keep Krastinios busy while mentally exploring the silo underneath. The alien envoy did not relent. Obviously he had access to limitless energy. Michael would have to end the fight soon, or else die of pure exhaustion.

When he finally located the device, Michael discovered with dismay that the countdown sequence had already started without his intervention. The tremors had triggered the sensitive mechanism. The seconds rolled down on the red dial, seven, six, five...

Using telekinesis, Michael attempted to reverse the process. Distracted by the problem at hand, he failed to sense the boulder Krastinios had detached from the rock above him. Too late... The force of the blow on his left shoulder made him lose all control. Michael felt himself falling into darkness...

Vijaya Schartz

"*DADDY! DADDY!*" Jennifer's frantic screams in his mind called him back to awareness. Behind closed eyelids, Michael gathered all his remaining strength to call all the screaming bats to fall on Krastinios. A brief distraction was all he needed. In the silo, the seconds ticked, five, four... In a supreme effort, Michael willed himself out of the cave, in the same fraction of a second when fifty megatons of blazing energy imploded, burning the oxygen, melting the rock of the deep cave, volatilizing the lake, and mutilating Mother Earth who rumbled in protest.

Michael re-materialized outside, under the bright sun, next to Jennifer and Tori. "Down!" he yelled, dragging Jennifer to the ground and covering her with his body. Tori sprawled down at his side, protecting her head.

The seconds that followed happened in slow motion. First, a piercing screech froze bodies and minds. Then, a low rumble amplified as it shook the very ground they lay on. The tremor contracted, then expanded. Soon, a violent wave, like a ripple in water, coursed from the epicenter, throwing and displacing everything in its wake. Hills collapsed, hillocks rose. The ground shook under a shower of rocks and a cloud of dust.

The three of them were ejected then thrown to the ground, coughing and choking on the dust. Michael raised a mental shield against falling rocks and other projectiles. The angry infrasound of the wounded planet covered Jennifer's screams. When it was over, they didn't dare move, waiting for the aftershock. It came within a few minutes, but with minor effects.

Michael finally raised his head, surprised to be alive, eyes screwed against the stinging sand particles. The cloud above was only dust. Mother Earth had swallowed the pain and the poison. Michael closed his eyes in infinite gratitude. Covered with white powder that resembled salt, the three sat up, checking themselves for injuries.

Jennifer looked at her father, then at Tori's piteous state and said, "We look like the three stooges after a flour fight in the kitchen."

"I'll be damned if that was a flour fight." Still shaken, Michael didn't feel like laughing.

But Jennifer started chuckling then Tori joined in. Soon Michael laughed, glad to relieve the tension.

Suddenly, Michael saw something slithering on the ground and blanched. Jennifer and Tori stopped laughing, frozen in place. Slowly, Michael brought one hand to his boot, reaching for the knife. "Don't make a move," he whispered under his breath.

The blade flew in a quick silver-blur, impacting in a fleshy thud, followed by a faint rattle. Michael relaxed. Jennifer looked behind her at the downed target and screamed. Tori looked horrified at the sight of the fangs. Mouth open, the rattlesnake writhed around the blade that had nailed it to the ground.

"I hate them snakes," Michael spat before collapsing from exhaustion. As the adrenalin wore off, the pain of his multiple injuries made itself felt. Tori and Jennifer tried to make him more comfortable and brought him the water bottle retrieved from the collapsed shelter.

After they all drank, Michael took the time to see to his wounds. Jennifer offered to join her mind to her father's to help. Pleased by her willingness to learn the skill, Michael showed her how he reset bones, repaired tissue, neatly cleansed and closed wounds and cuts. Soon, with the sun setting behind the western mountain range, the exhausted Crusader fell asleep.

A few hours later, Michael awoke to gaze upon a field of stars. He felt whole again. Immediately, he noticed the eerie glow of an unnatural object hovering about a foot above the dry lake sands. Tori and Jennifer awoke as Michael started to move.

"Are you okay, Daddy?"

"I'm fine, sweetheart."

"What do we do now?" Tori's asked.

"Let's get out of here. How about Dave's home... I don't know about you, but I wouldn't mind spending the rest of the night in a bed."

Tori looked skeptical. "But how do we get there? The phone battery is dead."

"Seems to me like we have a craft waiting right here. The vessel doesn't look damaged by the quake. It must have ridden the wave."

The three of them walked toward the black flying object. The open door looked inviting. Michael stepped first into the softly lit interior. The cabin was spacious and totally empty, except for structural beams, reminding him of Amrah's ship. Tentatively, Michael sat down and found supporting pressure to accommodate his bottom. Jennifer and Tori did the same with much dignity despite their ragged clothes, dirty faces and disheveled appearance.

Michael addressed his daughter. "So Jen, how did that creep work this thing?"

"With his mind, I think."

"You think... Hum... Let's see... First, maybe we should close the hatch. Jen, could you do that for me, please?"

"I don't know if I can." Jennifer screwed up her face in concentration. The sliding panel closed a bit, then stopped, then slid a little further.

Michael wondered how his daughter picked up telekinesis so easily. She must be very powerful. "You got it... Easy does it, nice and smooth..."

When the panel closed shut, Jennifer beamed with pride.

"The rest shouldn't be too hard." Michael recognized the technology. Amrah had taught him to fly such vessels. It was just a matter of linking his mental vibrations to the magnetic field. The magnetism made the object float easily, and the mind gave it direction and speed.

Michael concentrated on the coordinates, willing the light ship to fly to its destination. "Let's go home, wherever that is. We won the first battle, but galactic war is coming our way. We better get ready to help."

Jennifer and Tori looked dismayed by this news.

In a spray of diamond dust, the small craft shot off, illuminating the desert night. None of the passengers, however, saw the wondrous display in the starry sky.

Vijaya Schartz

CHAPTER TWENTY

"Mr. Fontaine, I have your wife on line two." At the sound of his assistant's excited voice on the intercom, Jean-Marc Fontaine stopped the relentless pacing. He threw his gum in the wastebasket and snatched the receiver.

"Tori, at last. Are you all right? I was worried-sick. I called all our friends trying to find you. Where have you been?"

"I'm fine, Love. And Jennifer is fine, too. We are in Little Rock, Arkansas."

"What are you doing in Arkansas?"

"I'll explain when I see you. I need you. I'd like to come to New York right now."

"Listen, I have a better idea. I'm driving to Washington D.C. today. I could join you in Little Rock afterwards for a few days."

"I'd love it. In that case, I'll need a favor... Not for me, for Jennifer..."

Archangel Crusader

* * *

Later that day, driving his company Mercedes, Jean-Marc Fontaine found himself sharing his impressions in French with a huge black and white feline answering to the name of Shadow. From the back seat, the cat oversaw his every moves with disdain. On the passenger side lay the attaché-case containing the compromising file on Chemitek Enterprises.

Thinking back, Jean-Marc Fontaine had never seen Miss Goldbloom so animated or so worried. She'd surprised him, losing her reserve like that.

"I hope you weren't joking about offering me a job if I lost this one!" She'd dropped the heavy folder on his desk, her questioning eyes looking straight at him for a change. "There is enough in there to sink this company with fines and send the CEO behind bars for a few years. I broke all the security codes but I was careful. They won't find out anytime soon." She'd blushed a little. "Are you sure you know what you're doing?" The crimson had claimed her whole face.

"We are doing the right thing," Jean-Marc had assured her. "Do not worry so much. Except for the culprits, everyone will be fine."

While driving, Jean-Marc usually reverted to French whenever thinking aloud. Shadow the cat listened between naps, one ear shivering once in a while. Fontaine could have sworn the animal knew he was going to meet Jennifer from the minute he'd picked it up. A good man this Bill Jensen... If nothing else, it said something about Michael Tanner's choice

Vijaya Schartz

of friends and business associates. "Right, Shadow?"

The cat yawned in approval. Obviously he knew that already.

When Jean-Marc stopped for gas, he bought a paper and scanned the headlines. What was the world coming to? Even the serious *New York Times* reported UFO sightings in France, Arkansas, and Nevada, linking the latter to an unexplained earthquake!

* * *

Within a few hours, Jean-Marc sat in Debbie's office in Washington, delivering the dossier on Chemitek. Hopefully, it would guarantee an indictment. With the support of several environmental organizations involved in the Crusade, he could now rest assured that the harmful dumping would stop.

"I do not understand how or why Michael does all this," Fontaine told Debbie over another cup from the coffee machine.

"It's extraordinary, isn't it? I still don't quite understand it myself. The story he tells is unbelievable and I suspect he did not tell me all. Such selfless dedication amazes even me, a friend since childhood."

"Tori says he used to be different." Jean-Marc sipped the tepid brew.

Debbie nodded. "He's changed so much, I can hardly recognize him. Last time I saw him he seemed empowered by the Crusade and the results are beyond any reasonable expectation. It's almost as if he wasn't human anymore, Mr. Fontaine." Debbie's hand shook a little when she drank from her coffee mug.

"Please call me Jean-Marc."

"All right, Jean-Marc. I'm worried about Michael. His own life does not seem to matter to him anymore. If it weren't for Jennifer, I doubt that he would still be among us. He always had charisma and passion, but now he shows great control. Yet, something in him scares me, as if he has become some kind of mystic."

"What do you mean?"

"Since Jennifer's return, he acts like a secluded monk. He hardly sees or talks to anyone. He spends most of his time in deep meditation. He has withdrawn from the world he's trying to save, as if he was no longer part of it."

"But, I thought he was active in the Crusade!" To Jean-Marc, this didn't make any sense. Fishing for gum in his pocket, he offered a piece to Debbie.

She accepted with a smile. "The campaign he started gets stronger and more successful as time passes, but without his physical presence. He manages all of it in total isolation. Apparently, the Crusade only needs the power of his mind."

"Really?" Jean-Marc felt renewed respect.

"Frightening, isn't it, to know that one person can have so much power."

"How do you know all this if he does not keep in touch?"

"Jennifer keeps me informed. She's worried about her father too. He speaks in riddles, scarcely eats or drinks. I fear for his health... And his sanity... Since you're going there, could I ask you to keep an

Vijaya Schartz

eye on him, and let me know if we can help him in any way?"

Jean-Marc rose from his chair. "I will be glad to oblige, Debbie. Thanks again for everything."

Debbie walked him to the door.

Winking, Jean-Marc added, "I'd like to talk some more, but I hate to think what that cat will do to my car if I leave him alone too long."

* * *

Immediately after his victory over Krastinios, Michael understood that he had only won a battle. Although he had destroyed his archenemy, the war itself had yet to be fought. Meditating in isolation, he hoped to achieve the level of consciousness that would allow him to participate in the great conflict to come: his father's war.

Daddy? Jennifer sent the mental request as she entered the small alien craft where Michael had established his new quarters.

"Yes, Jen. Come in, honey." He eased out of his meditating position.

"I brought you something to eat." She hesitated only an instant before setting the tray aside, then settled in a comfortable position, sitting in mid air close to her father.

"Thank you, Sweetheart, but I'm not hungry. Don't worry about me. I'm fine. This is a purification ritual. I want to become a better person."

"I was wondering... About Krastinios... How come he was so nice and so mean at the same time?"

"No one is all good or all bad, Jennifer. The best people can be mean at times, and the meanest people can be sweet as honey. Although in this case, I believe the sweetness was fake."

"Isn't there anybody who is only good and never mean?"

"I don't think so, but there is someone close to it. As a matter of fact, I was just on my way to see him. Now that you met your mother, how would you like to meet your grandfather and your grandmother?"

"The one who hurt you when you were a kid?"

"No. My real father... He may seem a little strange at first, but he's a really good guy. He lives in a spacecraft like this one, but much bigger. He's not from this planet."

"An alien? My grandfather? Cool..."

"He only looks weird."

"How weird?"

Michael sent Jennifer a mental picture of his father. He knew how sensitive his daughter was and wanted to prepare her.

"Wow!" she exclaimed. "I've seen him before... In a dream, I think..."

"I thought you never dreamt."

"I just remembered now. Let's go see him."

They straightened into their invisible chairs, and Michael guided Jennifer's mind to focus on the controls of the alien craft. She followed his mind patterns, observing how he set it in motion, ever so gently. Michael could sense her curiosity and her excitement. He enjoyed surprising the young girl with exhilarating experiences. She picked up the challenge every time. He liked that in his daughter.

Vijaya Schartz

The ride, despite the incredible acceleration, proved smooth and light. No jolts, no temperature changes, no eardrum sensations, not even a swishing sound. Just a smell of sweet licorice... It took only a few seconds to leave the atmosphere. Once in space, the whole section of the hull facing Earth became transparent and Jennifer stared in awe at her native planet. Michael guided the craft toward the shaded side of the moon where his father's vessel waited.

The Blue Angels' ship was in uproar when they docked inside. Even Amrah's private quarters bustled with activity. Maria, in a turquoise leather gown decorated with beads, gave orders to naked aliens who hurried to bring the things she mentally ordered. The new addition of southwestern furniture attested to her personal touch. The material, although replicated, looked and felt real enough. Maria stopped in her tracks at the sight of the young girl holding Michael's hand. She stared, and tears betrayed her joy when she touched Jennifer's long silky hair.

"Such a beautiful child, Mikie... Jennifer, you're even prettier than I imagined. No wonder your dad is so proud of you. Would you like some chocolate? I had some replicated."

"Chocolate?" Jennifer's eyes lit up as Maria seized a crystal cup full of chocolate candy in gold and silver wrappings.

"Mother, you said the magic word," Michael teased. Then he looked around and finally asked, "Where is Amrah?"

"Your father is very busy with the coming invasion and all, but he should be here any minute, since he knows you are aboard." Maria nervously fingered the arrowhead of her necklace.

Jennifer, munching on chocolate, stared openly at the nakedness of the bluish beings apparently working to furnish the place to Maria's wishes. The older woman made her guests sit on a couch, like the perfect hostess of her strange new home.

Jennifer glanced with surprise at the dream catchers decorating the bulkheads, the Kachina dolls on synthetic shelves beside long pipes that smelled like sweet burnt leaves. Brightly colored rugs covered the smooth floors.

"Dad, lots of people don't believe in aliens. Why?"

"I guess it takes seeing to believe. Human nature tends to fear the unknown. For many, it's more comfortable to deny than to fear. Right, Mom?"

Maria chortled, playing with a lacy handkerchief, obviously delighted by the discovery of her granddaughter.

"But there is nothing to fear if they are nice, right?" Jennifer asked.

"Nothing at all," Maria answered. "They are so powerful, they can protect you from any evil spirit. Your grandfather would never let anything bad happen to any of us. Right, Mikie?"

"I'm afraid they are not all like that, Mom," Michael objected. "Krastinios was the son of a particularly bad one, a snake-alien."

"I don't like snakes," Jennifer declared with conviction.

"Neither do I..." Michael echoed. "Here comes your grandfather."

Vijaya Schartz

Maria bent toward Jennifer and whispered, "Amrah is very old and wiser than a medicine man. You should treat him with great respect."

Amrah appeared then, and his mental presence entered the three minds at the same time. They all stared at each other for a few seconds, sharing in a warm, silent greeting. Jennifer stayed in contact with Amrah longer than her father or Maria, while Michael marveled at the obvious link transfiguring his daughter. She smiled, expressing more wonder than any word could.

"Well, my son, your daughter will be easier to train than you. She already masters complex principles."

"Really?" Michael felt a little uncomfortable at the thought of Jennifer being trained by Amrah.

"She has wide open pathways and no mental objection of any kind. She will be very powerful some day." Amrah sounded confident.

"I'm glad to hear that," Michael answered automatically, but inside he was not so sure he liked it. Power usually meant dangers to confront, and he preferred for his daughter the comfortable life he himself never had. To change the subject, Michael announced the purpose of his visit. "How long do we have until Lufriec gets here?"

Upon a subtle sign from Amrah, Maria took Jennifer by the hand. "Come with me for a tour of a real flying saucer," she said to her granddaughter. "These two have business to discuss." As she led Jennifer away, the child looked back to her father for reassurance. When he responded with a smile, Jennifer followed Maria with no more hesitation.

Archangel Crusader

Sitting on the couch, Amrah looked as comfortable in the new earthly arrangement of his quarters as he had always been in his barren alien decor. "In three or four days, we expect them to reach our vicinity." He sounded preoccupied.

"Will you be ready then? How can I help?" Michael shifted position. He thought about the irony of it all. In three days it would be May Day. How many would remember that is also was Earth Day?

"We are as ready now as we will ever be, but time does not matter as much as timing. Nevertheless, the Reptilian fleet is several thousand strong, and we have no precise idea of how sophisticated their weapons and defenses are."

"How much do you know about them?"

Amrah shrugged, a strange movement for his slim frame. "We know very little since they evolved along a different path. Long ago, they used magic and rituals. Their strength always lay in numbers. They thrived on adversity and conflict, burning with a passion we could not understand. Blindly they followed their warlord and seemed to enjoy cruelty... A disconcerting trait."

"Sounds familiar. We've had a few of those throughout history."

"Unfortunately, as a peaceful people, we have lost the will and, I fear, also the ability to fight. I thought maybe we could use your wild instincts. You could teach us by sharing the passionate side of your personality with us."

"I'd be glad to help in any way I can, but I may not be the expert you need for the job." Michael wondered what kind of savage his alien father thought he

Vijaya Schartz

was. "Did you ask for reinforcement from your home planet? You cannot face a whole fleet with only one ship."

"You see, my people do not have fighting ships." Amrah smiled at Michael's surprise. "Besides, they never get involved in other worlds' conflicts. My interest in Earth is very... Personal, as you may have guessed. My ship is bigger and hopefully more powerful than any of the Reptilians', but it cannot withstand a whole fleet."

The odds didn't look good. "So, we'll have to fight on our own?"

"Earth technology is no threat to the Reptilians. It would help, however, if your people participated mentally."

"How So?"

Amrah hesitated. "If you lent us the energy of your collective minds, it could give us an edge, but we would need at least a third of the population to participate."

Michael whistled. "One third? That's no small feat. I wonder if I can rally that many. The population at large is not quite ready for the full impact of this news. It could mean panic. I can see the headlines, 'Aliens waging war in our sky with Earth as the coveted prize.' No. We would achieve panic, not a pool of mental energy. How about a mass visualization? Can you draw on that kind of energy pool? Would that help?" Michael was running out of ideas.

"It might work," Amrah said with some enthusiasm. "We could use the power generated by a dynamic picture, something hypnotic that would focus the mind."

"How about all the media on Sunday showing a picture of Earth seen from space, revolving slowly, bathed in a blue aura of health, peace, and harmony?" Michael pictured it in his mind.

"Good. We can broadcast an image of your planet, live from space via your telecommunication satellites. Maybe we could add an appropriate soothing sound, something they never heard before, something compelling that would induce concentration... We could maintain the broadcast for twenty-four hours on all frequencies. Do you see any problem on your end?"

"I like it. I can see it from here, a big, blue planet on the front page of the newspapers. I have only three days to warn the TV networks, though. We could make up a story about an international space program experiment in conjunction with a worldwide meditation for Earth Day."

Michael wondered briefly about the ethical implications. He would be lying, but he saw no alternative. "With Debbie's help, we might be able to wing it. By the time the space committees officially deny any scientific experiment, it will be too late. Some governments may even take the credit."

"I hope they get a chance." Amrah's dark eyes rested fondly on Michael.

During the short trip back to Earth, both Michael and Jennifer remained silent. Michael grimly pondered the slim chances to repel the oncoming invasion while Jennifer, unaware of the threat, obviously tried to digest all the wonders she had just witnessed.

Vijaya Schartz

* * *

Jean-Marc Fontaine felt relieved when he finally saw the landmark he was looking for around the bend. This Arkansas farmhouse had proven harder to find than he had imagined. He longed to hold Tori in his arms and could hardly contain his curiosity as to this newfound child of hers.

Jean-Marc wanted to find out how his wife had ended up in this place. Relinquishing the ever-appraising cat would also come as a relief. Not that the animal caused any worries or complications. It was well behaved. Despite multiple attempts at French dialogue, however, neither man nor feline trusted the other.

"Well, Shadow, my reluctant friend, you should see your rightful owner soon." The cat perked one ear, showing some interest.

The stately car bounced ahead of a trail of dust toward the isolated cluster of wooden structures constituting an ordinary farm. Two children emerged from the barn and stared at the silver car coming down the road. Tori came out of the trailer, flushed, arranging her hair in haste and checking her slim-fitting jeans. When Jean-Marc opened the door and stepped out, she rushed into his arms.

He gathered her in a tender embrace and kissed her mouth with hunger. "*Mon amour*, it's been so long. I missed you so much..."

"I know... I missed you too," Tori answered, as soon as he let her breathe again.

By then, the children had joined them, and the curious head of Shadow peeked through the open door. One child spotted the cat in a flash and called its name. That was all the feline needed to overcome his mistrust of strangers. He ran into the girl's legs. Jean-Marc assumed it was Jennifer. She picked up and hugged the poor thing too tight, but the cat did not seem to mind and purred all the same.

"How did you find me? I thought I'd never see you again," Jennifer purred back to the pet. Then, re-membering the company she was in, she made for-mal presentations. "Clara, this is Shadow... Shadow, this is my cousin Clara."

Tori laughed and, still clinging to Jean-Marc, introduced him to everyone.

"Thanks for bringing Shadow..." Jennifer felt a little intimidated by this elegant man who was so nice to her and her mom. She didn't know quite what else to say, but her smile must have been explanation enough.

The Frenchman smiled back. "You are wel-come, Jennifer. Nice to finally meet you... It is a pleasure to see the happiness in your eyes." Then he turned back to Tori and lavished her with his atten-tions.

* * *

How could Michael possibly meet the required participation? He had teleported back to Debbie's of-fice in Washington D.C. to take part in the craziest campaign of all. How could he promote such an event in three days? One third of the population? It was far more than rallying ten percent of the votes at election time. Michael doubted his ability to succeed. It took most of his energy just to contact enough key people on such short notice. Thank God for the Internet.

On day two, Michael found himself sending and receiving faxes, phone calls and e-mail at an accelerated rate. Press releases traveled back and forth across the planet in every known language. The twenty phone lines rang like on a TV marathon drive. Electronic equipment, loaned or donated, crowded the small Washington office. The official website went on overload several times. Fortunately, computer experts had rushed to the rescue.

Michael's concentration was put to the test by the constant racket. The buzzing and beeping tones, the rings, the excited conversations of the volunteers helping him… Even the radiating disturbance of computer monitors and keyboards affected his ability to visualize a positive outcome. The smell of strong coffee permeated Debbie's office, transformed for a few days into World Visualization headquarters.

Michael felt tense despite his training. "Debbie, how's it going on your side?"

"Most TV networks refuse to believe that the worldwide transmission of a single image from space is even possible. Advertising it may prove tougher than I thought. Good thing some of the executives in charge, touched by our previous campaigns, do trust our sources."

"Well, that's a start. Don't get discouraged Debbie, you're only human. Do your best and be proud of yourself for your successes. I personally think you do a hell of a job, damn it!"

"Thanks for cheering me up, big guy, I needed that." Debbie smiled and went back to her phone. Her voice sounded hoarse from too much talking, too much coffee, and not enough sleep.

She looked emaciated. Her careful makeup did not hide the blue smudges under her eyes anymore. Michael noticed the vial of Zantac by the coffee mug. He felt guilty, putting her through such stress in her condition. The thought of curing her had crossed his mind many times, but Debbie had refused, still troubled by his unusual powers. In any case, he couldn't spare the energy right now, and in two days the whole human race might die anyway. Michael had to concentrate on the task at hand.

Fortunately, devoted Walter backed Debbie up without question. His network at least would support the project. Thanks to the communication system initiated at the beginning of the Crusade, a constant flow of information could be processed and expedited. The data, propagated by a domino effect, spread to the most isolated corners of the world, bouncing off computers and fax machines in remote places.

Volunteers from all walks of life had answered Debbie's call for help. The place resembled an anthill feverishly preparing for an incoming assault. Little did they know how much was at stake, Michael thought, thankful for their dedication.

Of course, the *New York Times* requested references from the scientific community before publishing a single word. Of course, no reputable expert would comment. The lack of data made the facts impossible to verify.

Vijaya Schartz

The various tabloids couldn't care less about World Visualization or space technology. That piece of news was not sensational enough for them. So, Michael gave them the true but incredible story of aliens waging war nearby, needing help to protect the planet from certain destruction. He provided computer-generated pictures of Amrah, surrounded by other blue aliens with big elongated heads and huge dark eyes, and a scary portrait of the snake-like Lufriec. He even pinpointed on a space map the location of the starship hiding in the shadow of the moon.

When Debbie read the article, she looked shocked. "Do you really want to send that garbage? How can anyone believe such a distasteful story?"

"The truth has many faces, Debbie, and this, as unsavory as it seems to you, is one of them."

"Well, whatever it takes. Bad publicity is better than none at all I guess, right?"

Michael could feel that she didn't care much for it. "Right." This was obviously not the time to tell her the whole truth. To her and the crew, Earth Visualization on Earth Day was just a neat challenge to promote solidarity and save the planet from Man.

Each and every group involved in the previous Crusade was presently engaged in the race against the clock, actively printing pamphlets to distribute on the street, inviting the masses to participate in the World Visualization.

High-quality color photographs of Earth viewed from space made their way to each and every newspaper, with sufficient ideological data to issue a decent article. Michael had imprinted each picture with a psychic compulsion to publish it on the front page.

The formidable *Asahi Shinbun*, the most widely read daily newspaper in Japan, surprised everyone by responding enthusiastically.

Michael read aloud from the computer screen, "The Japanese people welcome the opportunity to improve their image in the eyes of the world. By participating in a noncommercial event, they hope to demonstrate high morals and team spirit."

This bit of good news was received with cheers from the tired team as congratulations rained on the lucky volunteer who had dealt with the paper.

Radio disc jockeys all over the world proved easy to sway. Some saw the event as an opportunity to promote world peace. Others saw a chance to get ahead in their ratings. Sometimes, the little guys could make a big difference. Michael couldn't afford to neglect any involvement, no matter how small.

Russia, or what was left of it, had everything to gain from participating, but in central Europe, where violence still smoldered, participation would probably be slim. Western Europe responded with quiet reserve, as usual. Poring over the reports told Michael where he should concentrate his efforts.

Not every country reacted with Australia's eagerness. Some Moslem countries even claimed a conspiracy of infidels against traditional Islam, while others welcomed the prospect of American military support. Central Africa picked up the challenge of peace as one more game. South Africa embraced the project. Central America had mixed factions, and South America's participation would stay partial. India at large, however, agreed to take part with *'colossal enthusiasm,'* according to the bulletin.

Vijaya Schartz

The great unknown remained China. Its huge population could mean the difference between victory and failure. Michael needed their participation to save the human race. The greatest efforts had been deployed to provide information and pictures, but little information filtered back on how the event might be received or if it would be publicized at all. Hong Kong sources sounded optimistic, but nothing transpired from Beijing.

Through it all, Michael watched Debbie who fought courageously, losing herself in a battle that wasn't hers. This remarkable woman gave away all her strength selflessly for his cause, but he knew all along that each effort brought her closer to her grave. She deserved the title of Crusader.

* * *

Meanwhile, at the FBI headquarters, a special witness gave a deposition. "Yes, that's him all right." The Weasel stared with a crooked smile at the photograph on the desk, a picture of Michael Tanner.

"Are you absolutely sure?" The federal agent in the three-piece suit looked interested. The other agents listened quietly.

"I'm positive, sir, I swear on my mother's grave. That's him. I never forget a face. I would recognize him anywhere. He's a big guy, six foot tall at least. Mean..."

"Please, tell us where and when you saw him?"

"Always a pleasure to be of service to my country, gentlemen. Where do I start... I picked him up at Adams Air Field in Little Rock, Arkansas. You see, I was supposed to take him to Las Vegas, but he pointed a gun to my head and demanded that I drop him off over Yucca Lake in a military zone." The Weasel shifted his gaze from agent to agent, evaluating the risks he was taking against the amount of the reward. It wouldn't do to reveal that he willingly accepted the run to settle an illegal debt.

"How did he contact you?"

"He didn't. His brother did. His brother lives in Little Rock. I know exactly where. I can show you on a map. I'm very good with maps..." He produced a folded map from his inside pocket as he went on. "Last time I flew over, there was a weird aircraft parked behind the barn. Looked like some kind of prototype straight out of Area-51. Never seen anything like it..."

"Really? Please go on..."

And the Weasel went on and on...

Vijaya Schartz

CHAPTER TWENTY-ONE

In the middle of the night, Michael teleported back to Little Rock. This was possibly the last day before the destruction of Earth's civilization, and he'd be damned if he wouldn't spend it with Jennifer. He had thought of sending his family to Amrah's spaceship for safety but realized they would stand a better chance to survive on the planet.

When Michael materialized in his brother's trailer home, late at night, everyone was asleep. He petted Shadow, wondering at the cat's presence when the phone rang. It was Walter. Debbie had collapsed and been rushed to the hospital in a coma. Her prognosis was poor. In the late stages, cancer did not respond well to exhaustion, but no one foolish enough to try could stop Debbie after she'd made up her mind. Nevertheless, Michael felt guilty about saving his energy for the great battle, but he must. The future of humanity depended on it.

Archangel Crusader

Three straight days of exhausting preparation in Washington D.C. had drained Michael's reserves. In the small UFO that now served as his residence, he slept for three hours. He awoke rejuvenated and ready for D-day, but first of all he was hungry. In the dim light of dawn, he explored Becky's kitchen and decided to cook breakfast for everyone.

He wedged potatoes, sliced onions, fried bacon, beat eggs, brewed coffee, even baked frozen biscuits and made gravy. On special occasions, he forgot all about his vegetarian diet.

The first little head to peek into the kitchen was Jennifer's. "Dad, you're back!" She rushed to hug him, nearly knocking the mug of hot coffee from his hand.

"How many times have I told you to be careful with my drink, kid," he said jokingly.

Jennifer stopped in her tracks then smiled. "Sorry, Dad!" She stretched her arms around his neck to kiss his cheek. She was growing fast, but in many ways she still reminded him of the baby she once was.

Michael set down the coffee cup. "Now, you can hug me all you want. I hope you want a lot." They hugged and laughed. A pang tugged at Michael's chest. Jennifer didn't know this could be their very last day, but it wouldn't serve any purpose to frighten her. "How do you want your eggs, young lady?" He tried to sound cheery.

The noise in the kitchen, as well as the rising sun and the delicious smell of breakfast, brought bleary-eyed Becky, Dave, and Clara out of their beds into the kitchen.

Vijaya Schartz

"My brother's cooking. What a treat!" Dave poured himself some coffee.

"I know, I know. I can't help it if I'm perfect." Michael smiled, remembering old times. As the cat jumped on the kitchen counter to be included in the rejoicing, Michael fed him a bit of bacon. "How did he get here?" Around his family, he did not like to read minds and preferred asking questions, like an ordinary human being.

"The Frenchman brought him," Dave confirmed. "He's staying at the Inn with Tori."

"Yes, and he's real nice. I like him," Jennifer added with enthusiasm.

"Oh, is that so? You like him better than me?" Michael rolled his eyes in mock anger.

"Dad... I never said that... I never would." Jennifer paused then laughed. "You're pulling my leg, aren't you?"

The same good humor persisted all through breakfast. Clara and Jennifer went outside to play with Shadow. Michael watched them through the window for a few minutes, then turned on the television. Of course, he already knew what would play all day.

Dave and Becky had planned to go to church, but instead they sat down, gazing at the screen in pure fascination. Encouraged by the effect on his brother and sister-in-law, Michael decided to do some meditation of his own. So, he retired to the small alien craft behind the barn.

All over the world, anyone turning on a television set or a computer couldn't help but stare in wonder at the living, breathing planet, occupying the screen. Some talked about it, but most just gazed in pure awe. They pondered the pettiness of their quarrels over differences that did not seem to mean much when viewed from so far away.

The papers published the same picture plastered on every front page. Most headlines used the conditional tense, however, as to whether the space-generated satellite broadcast would actually take place, using phrases such as, "If all the technical requirements are met today," or "According to unofficial sources," or even, "Hoax or technical feat? Find out by turning on your TV set." Some publications only mentioned Earth Day, safely omitting the worldwide television broadcast.

This was the quietest day on Earth in a very long time, even by alien standards. No big rally, no demonstration, not much traffic on the roads. The flight attendants were dumbfounded to find an image of the blue planet, complete with ethereal sound, coming out of their on-flight projection systems. Since no one complained, however, they didn't try to fix the video. All the passengers seemed engrossed in listening, staring, and meditating in utter ecstasy.

As for Michael, tuning in his long-range psychic search, he shivered in the invisible seat when he saw a crimson fleet of a thousand craft converging toward Earth from the outskirts of the galaxy. The mother ship looked much smaller than Amrah's vessel but ominous, with sharp angles and crab-like claws.

Even at this distance Michael felt the dread like a cold spot in his chest, the same fear that seized him every time he caught a glimpse of Lufriec, the

Vijaya Schartz

Reptilian lord. Michael shuddered, realizing that this was Krastinios' father, ten times more powerful and wicked than the son.

"O, dear Lord," Michael prayed, with all the powers of his enhanced psyche, "wherever, whoever, or whatever you are, please help us and be on our side today."

* * *

Jennifer and Clara had fun chasing Shadow around. The cat didn't seem to mind the game too much, as long as he didn't get caught, pouncing on them from above every time he had a chance. This time, however, the feline found refuge on a high branch of the oak tree. Clara, who knew the tree quite well, proceeded to climb after him.

"Careful, Clara, I'm not sure this is a good idea." Afraid of heights, Jennifer didn't dare climb herself.

When the little black girl reached the fork in the tree, she sat as was her custom and looked in the distance toward the road. "I see lots of cars coming this way," she said, proud of herself.

"What kind of cars?" Jennifer knew there was no traffic on that road on Sundays.

"I dunno... Cars, lots of them."

Jennifer couldn't resist the temptation to see and, spontaneously, without even thinking, she linked her mind with Clara's. "My God, they're police cars. I've got to tell Daddy." She ran off toward the small spacecraft concealed behind the barn. In her haste, she let her thoughts race ahead.

* * *

A rustling and a hiss made Michael turn around.

"You called me?" The suave voice came out of a tall, creature, a greenish humanoid with no hair, scaly skin, spurs and sharp ridges, in full red armor. He stared straight at Michael through black mesmerizing eyes. Only the lashing forked tongue indicated some excitement on the monster's part. "I am your Nefarious Lord, Lufriec," the Reptilian announced regally. "I came ahead to meet you personally. Interesting craft you have here, Earthling."

Michael's heart jumped in his chest. Had he provoked the apparition with irresponsible thinking? No. The powerful alien had chosen to grace him with his physical presence, scales, stink and all, but Michael did not feel ready. He had not anticipated a personal confrontation with the Reptilian warlord. Hiding his panic, Michael recollected every piece of information he could muster about Lufriec and his race.

"I could use someone as resourceful as you at my side," the Reptilian lord went on, gracefully pacing about the vessel, scales gleaming, spurs rising and falling gently as he walked.

"You, Lufriec, interested in me?" The unexpected offer surprised Michael. "What do you want?" He watched the Reptilian's slightest moves.

"I want you to help me colonize this planet peacefully. With your skills, you could convince your people to accept me as their ruler." Lufriec moved with ease, strong armored arms punctuating his words. "There would be less bloodshed if the leaders

Vijaya Schartz

surrendered without resistance. Your race should serve us best as slaves. I can reward you better than the Blue Angels..." The fanged monstrosity smiled.

At that instant, the on-board screen came alive under Lufriec's prompting, showing Michael adorned with gold, dressed in luxurious clothes, stepping out of a limousine, smiling at the crowd rushing to worship him while armed Reptilian soldiers kept his adoring fans at bay. Michael could hear them call his name. He could feel their love, their awe, their submission. He could smell their sweet devotion. "Power is my favorite," Lufriec commented insidiously.

Without transition, the screen now showed Michael relaxing in his own palace, as dozens of slaves attended to his every wish. Some poured him intoxicating drinks while gorgeous concubines vied for his attention by slowly removing their skimpy outfits.

"There are worlds to be owned, riches, powers, potent drinks, drugs, women, you name it. Consider... I could even spare your daughter's life."

The screen switched to Jennifer running toward the small spacecraft, chickens scattering in her path.

STAY AWAY! Michael's mental broadcast to Jennifer came too late.

When the little girl saw Lufriec through her father's eyes, she let out a horrified scream, brought a hand to her throat, eyes bulging under an invisible choke. Michael sent his strongest jolt to get Lufriec's attention away from her, but the Reptilian only laughed and increased the pressure on Jennifer's throat.

"Stop it!" Michael rushed the Reptilian warlord.

Lufriec avoided Michael but released the mental grip on Jennifer. "All right, as long as we understand each other."

When Jennifer collapsed unconscious in the dust, Michael spread his awareness. She was still alive. "You, coward. Leave her out of this," he spat at Lufriec. "Your business is with me."

"And very fruitful it can be for both of us. Think about your future, the power of my gratitude..." The Reptilian smiled horribly.

"My future? With your kind?" Michael thought of Jennifer raised with the likes of Krastinios and Lufriec when suddenly, in front of him stood Veronica in the flesh. Her loveliness made his body ache.

"Yes, you could have her back." The alien voice rang in his ears, corrupting every fiber of Michael's integrity.

Damn, this is hard... Tears blurred Michael's vision.

Veronica implored him. "I miss you, my love." Her sweet voice sounded like music. "Please, for my sake, give him what he wants. We can be happy together again." The daunting eyes he could never resist pleaded now as Veronica, touched his arm.

Moved beyond words, Michael stepped forward to caress the soft skin of her shoulder. Veronica smiled and kissed his tears, then took his hand, guiding it though the folds of her dress...

Something snapped in Michael's mind. He punched Veronica's face with unrestrained anger. Veronica snarled, her expression changing as her

Vijaya Schartz

distorted voice sent the warning. "Be careful Earthling, I could kill you in an instant." Her skin grew scales while her body reshaped itself into the form of Lufriec.

"How dare you tempt me?" Michael couldn't contain his anger anymore. "Your son killed the only woman I ever loved, and there is nothing for me on any of your worlds."

"You dare refuse?" A dangerous aura was building around the Reptilian lord, dark red, like his armor.

"Yes, Lufriec, I refuse... I would rather fight you and die in the process than listen to your lies."

"And die you will, Earthling." On cue, Lufriec sent a finger of electricity that nailed Michael writhing in pain to the metal floor of the small craft. "Did you really think you could get away with slaying MY son? Did you believe I would spare you? I don't need you to annihilate all resistance and enslave your race for labor or consumption."

Michael, still pinned to the floor, looked at Lufriec in shock at the revelation.

The Reptilian smiled. "Ah, Yes... My kind is quite carnivorous. I don't want to butcher all of you at once, though. First you will see your only child obliterated. But you will suffer more than anyone else, Earthling. I will kill you slowly before roasting your carcass on a spit for our victory feast."

Michael's mind raced despite the agonizing pain coursing through his body. Could he tap directly into the mental pool? Could he hope to destroy this monster even now? It would take enormous energy to blast the evil thing that rendered him defenseless.

An idea surged in his mind. Maybe Amrah could help...

"No one can prevent me from taking this planet!" Lufriec's arrogance knew no limits. "My people need a home with plenty of food, and I happen to like this Earth best. It was taken away from me once, long ago. But not this time! This time I win." Lufriec studied Michael's face. "I see your pain, Earthling. Show me some fear... I like fear."

A flash connection occurred between Earth and moon as Michael and Amrah linked minds in a quick debate.

Are you sure, my son? It is a most unusual sacrifice, Amrah argued in Michael's mind.

No, Father... But it's the best way... Please... He's only three feet from me. You can destroy the bastard now. Use my body as an explosive device and blast this craft with all you've got.

Very well, my son, if you insist... I'll redirect the energy from the meditation pool for one concentrated strike. Farewell, dear child.

Farewell, Father... Be quick.

In a flash, Michael saw billions of faces of all races. All over the world, people of all nationalities stared at a television screen, a monitor, a newspaper. Tension built up, pulling at the fabric of their subconscious. A great current of energy coursed around the globe, affecting all in its path.

In California, a man about to enter a convenience store gun in hand suddenly stopped in his tracks and looked at the sky. Shaking his head, he threw the gun in a garbage can and walked away.

In Nebraska, an inebriated father about to hit

Vijaya Schartz

his boy with a leather belt lowered his arm, touched by understanding. Scooping the frightened child into his arms, he cried, asking for forgiveness.

In Florida, a bigot about to scream obscenities at her gay neighbors suddenly saw them with compassion and understanding and smiled instead. In France, a politician in the process of embezzling government funds allocated the money to education where it was due. In Germany, a rapist stalking a young victim, appalled by his own thoughts, turned away to buy flowers for his wife.

In Rome, a highjacker about to board a plane looked at the passengers then left the airport. In Israel, a group of terrorists preparing to storm an embassy abandoned the project. In Russia, a hunter aiming at a deer lowered his gun and allowed the game to flee. In the Middle East, a dictator gave the order to release a hundred hostages. In Japan, an abductor returned the child unharmed to the frantic parents. Off the South American coast, a drug lord threw his whole cargo overboard and ordered coffee plants for his farm.

In Little Rock, Arkansas, the FBI swat team in bulletproof jackets storming Dave's farm dropped their rifles to stare at the strange glow coming from the small craft behind the barn. Dave and Becky came out of the trailer home, Clara ran back from the meadow with Shadow on her heels, and Jennifer opened her eyes, regaining consciousness.

In that instant, the creatures of Earth felt great pain, then relief followed by a vast peace. The electromagnetic wave that blanketed the planet shrunk to a single beam directed to Amrah's spaceship.

By then, the blood-red fleet approaching the Blue-Angel vessel had started firing, shaking Amrah's ship with powerful jolts. At their battle stations, the Blue Angels ignored the relentless fire hitting them. Responding in kind would compromise the delicate operation. Instead, they concentrated on monitoring the energy beam through their leader's brain. Flinching under the tremendous effort, Amrah enhanced and channeled the deadly ray into Michael's mind, making him the target and the weapon of Lufriec's destruction.

Michael felt the raw power burning through his neural pathways. Unable to speak, he reached for Lufriec.

The Reptilian stiffened at the daring touch but didn't break it. "You want to grapple with me, Earthling?"

Michael gripped Lufriec's shoulder, staring into the red depth of the creature's eyes.

The snake face exulted. "You have lost! Your planet is mine!"

Not yet, Michael thought but said nothing, holding on to his mark.

Fear finally registered on the Earthling's face. Lufriec rejoiced for a split second, savoring his victory. The Earthling stared, face contorted. Apparently the simple contact caused him great pain, so why did he hold on? Doubt wavered at the edge of the warlord's awareness. Had he underestimated his opponent? Suddenly, the Earthling smiled through his agony, and Lufriec realized his mistake.

Vijaya Schartz

Too late... A white blaze enveloped them both and engulfed the craft.

Jennifer screamed. A blinding flash, then a conflagration sucked the air. Every atom of every particle of matter in the immediate periphery ignited. A hot wind pulverized the barn. Rifles, gunmen, cars, all flew up with the dust, falling hard on the ground and on each other. A shock wave coursed, shaking in its wake the trailer and the farm buildings, the cars, trees and fences.

An eerie screech raised Jennifer's hair at the roots, followed by empty silence. A long silence... When the dust settled, nothing moved inside the circle of overturned cars. All that remained was a scorched patch of bare dirt. Jennifer looked around for her father, mentally scanning for any sign of his mind... Nothing.

"DAAADDYYY!" was all she could scream in her anguish. Her father was no more. Powerless, she shed hot tears, staring through the moisture of her eyes at the spot where, seconds before, her father had been alive.

* * *

In space, Amrah's ship, partly disabled by the first attack wave, now returned fire, further depleting its energy reserves. Repeated enemy assaults had claimed several lives among Amrah's crew while life support systems failed in succession. Among the smoke and barely breathable air, the Blue Angels kept fighting, improving their aim and causing as much damage as possible in the enemy ranks. Not enough damage...

Amrah himself started to lose heart when, suddenly, the Reptilian mother ship exploded in a shower of crimson fire, crippling many of its own vessels in the vicinity. Amrah felt the blast displacing his ship but mentally compensated for the impact without slowing the firing of his weapons.

Half the enemy fleet was destroyed, but Amrah's crippled ship was losing power, no longer able to defend itself. While the Blue Angel crew in their moribund vessel prepared for a last assault, the enemy regrouped, only to turn around and flee.

Amrah then realized that Michael had been right. His sacrifice had won the battle. For the first time in two million years, the Blue Angel let go of his emotional reserve. Tasting the wild elation of victory, he laughed shamelessly, soon joined by his surviving crew.

* * *

Among the rubble of the farm, The swat team came to, coughing and brushing the dust off their black uniforms. Some looked hurt, but not too badly. Jennifer felt a nudge at her feet. Sinking to the burnt grass, she picked up Shadow and held on to him, all the time staring at the charred empty spot. She must have lost track of time and jumped at a gentle voice behind her.

"Come on, Jennifer. You cannot stay here. Come with me darling, Jean-Marc and I will take care of you and Shadow." Tori lifted Jennifer gently by the shoulders. When the cat jumped off, Jennifer hugged

Vijaya Schartz

her mother. Through burning eyes, unable to speak, taking a last look at the scene, the girl took her mother's hand and started walking toward the waiting silver-gray car.

* * *

The two days that followed, although filled with sadness, saw Tori and Jean-Marc actively helping Dave and Becky with judicial matters, keeping them out of jail, assuring that Clara was not taken away from them, and providing a roof over their heads.

The trailer had been destroyed by the after-shock, but the naked structure of the unfinished house, further away from the blast, still stood. Dave would have to complete the construction as fast as possible. His family needed a roof.

All this time, Jennifer neither drank nor ate. Her shallow sleep crawled with nightmares. In her misery, however, a new window had opened on the world. She found herself wandering in and out of other people's minds. The shock of her loss had cleared mind channels that would otherwise have stayed blocked until puberty. Jennifer's young intellect reeled with the shock of knowledge and feelings too mature for her years. She now understood the deep, loving relationship between Tori and Jean-Marc. She also experienced the full scope of pathos of any stranger coming within range of her newfound abilities.

Overwhelming emotions kept her hidden from the cruel world, hugging her cat, cowering from this unmerciful society. She could feel Tori's deep concern and that of her stepfather. She marveled at the love her mother felt for her and at Jean-Marc's compassion. These were good people, and she felt safe and loved among them. A chunk of her heart was missing, however, and Jennifer could not help but cry every time she thought about her father.

* * *

On the third day, Jennifer ran into her mother's hotel room in Little Rock. "Mom, Mom! I felt him. He's alive... Daddy's alive!" Her smile illuminated tears of joy.

"He will always be alive in your heart, Sweetie." Grateful for the change in her daughter, Tori smiled. Jennifer had called her *Mom*.

"No, you don't understand, he really is alive. I felt his mind, far away... But I'm telling you, he's alive."

Tori remained neutral, unwilling to break the magic. But she could not allow her daughter to wander too far from the truth. She took Jennifer's hand. "Maybe you felt his spirit. He loved you very much... Maybe his soul floats around before going to heaven. You should not nurture false hopes... I understand how hard it must be for you to accept it, but your dad is not coming back, darling." She pulled her daughter closer for a hug, but Jennifer playfully escaped and laughed.

"He's alive, he's alive, he's alive!" Jennifer giggled and ran out of the room, jumping like a monkey.

Tori watched her leave, hoping Jennifer would not lose her mind over the loss.

Vijaya Schartz

CHAPTER TWENTY-TWO

"How is he?" Maria inquired of her alien mate. She looked twenty-five years younger and more beautiful than ever, her hair now long and shiny black.

"The regeneration cycle is complete. He will awaken soon." Amrah smiled, something he did more of, since Maria joined the ship. "His heightened intellect is fully functional, but he will have to get used to the new body."

Around them, the Blue Angel crew went about restoring the spaceship back to its former condition, a peaceful activity that soothed the mind and the spirit while erasing the physical scars of battle.

"He'll like the change." Maria knew he would. "I loved it the first time I saw myself in the mirror. Who would resent eternal youth, beauty, and health?" She adjusted the oval mirror and caressed the black tresses of her shiny hair. The happiness on her face betrayed deeper changes though, from being loved, and also from the subtle improvement of her neural pathways.

"Are you ready for such a long commitment, Maria?" Amrah stepped closer. "Forever takes on a whole new meaning. Are you sure you will not miss earthly pleasures? It may be a long time before we return. And when we do, you will be the same, but the people you love will have aged." Amrah came up behind Maria, resting his hands on her shoulders.

"I know... I'll miss Dave and his family, and seeing Jennifer grow up. Strange, isn't it, since I just met her? But I know my happiness is with you and our son. Will I get a chance to say goodbye?"

"Certainly. We have a few weeks of preparation before the ship is fully operative." Amrah rubbed her shoulders.

Maria gave herself to the soothing massage, relaxing for a few seconds then turned to face Amrah. "You know, I'll have time on my hands. Maybe I could help. If someone could teach me a few simple tasks..."

"You will do better than that, Maria, have no fear. Some day you will run this ship as efficiently as the best captain in the universe."

Maria smiled. "And who might that be?"

Amrah raised a smooth brow. "Me, of course... Didn't you know?"

"Now I know where Mikie got his attitude problem." She laughed and hugged her handsome blue lover.

* * *

Vijaya Schartz

Michael awoke in an empty room full of soothing colors, pastel blue, lavender, rose, and turquoise, vibrating in slow changing patterns. A soft purring matched his contented mood. He felt good but couldn't remember a thing.

A little disoriented, Michael stood up, naked, and stretched. He flexed one hand and stared at it, intrigued. Since when did he have such flawless skin? Not one hair on his legs or chest! Michael contracted an arm muscle, rolled a shoulder, flexed a knee. He felt incredibly limber. He took in the strange surroundings, something about the place felt familiar. A metal panel slid open and Veronica appeared, smiling. Michael smiled back. Something wasn't right.

"Hi, honey, I see you're awake." She seemed to study him behind the smile. "A little confused? Don't worry, you'll be just fine."

Michael suddenly remembered. "Stay away from me, you filthy snake." Bits and pieces of memory came rushing back. He was at the farm, in the small spacecraft, facing Lufriec, not Veronica. The battle raged on.

Suddenly, he felt Veronica in his mind and reeled with the realization that they were linked. She witnessed all his thoughts as he witnessed hers. Open channels allowed them to communicate at all times. Nothing could interfere with their full understanding of each other. "Veronica? Is it really you? I'm dead, right?"

Veronica smiled again, white veils from her dress floating around her. "Guess again. Welcome back, my love." The touch of her hands on his naked chest, the feel of her lips on his, and the fierce response he felt in his loins convinced him on the spot that he was very much alive. She laughed. "Well, would you like to get dressed this morning, or will you adopt the fashion of the place? It looks good on your father, but of course he has better control of his physical reactions." She pointed at his erection.

"I'm dreaming," Michael muttered to himself, expecting to wake up any moment. "But I saw you dead!" Who was he trying to convince?

"Not anymore... Do I feel dead to you?"

She wrapped her arms around him, and the warm smell of her skin threatened his self-control. Michael found his body responding with prodigious vitality as he held her. They read each other's mind in the same instant. Veronica's green eyes filled with infinite love. Her head tilted back, soft lips opening slightly. Michael had never been able to resist her call, but this time, despite the violence of his own attraction, exerting a restraint he had never shown before, he carried her to the airbed and laid her gently down.

The colors in the room changed to brighter shades of oranges, reds, bright blues, and purple. The humming became a soft harmony of musical tones. Although he felt about to explode with desire, Michael took his time peeling off her veils one at a time, caressing her apricot skin, running his fingers through her auburn hair. How wonderful to be able to read her most secret yearnings! Michael covered her with soft and hard kisses, hands working up and down the beloved body, overwhelming her.

"Please," she begged in ragged breaths, "Make love to me. I've been waiting for so long..."

Vijaya Schartz

"So have I." He covered her lips in a long, passionate kiss.

Cupping her small breasts, Michael teased her hard nipples with his teeth, tantalizing her while Veronica squirmed under his weight, emitting little cries that became more frantic. Soon, at the edge of insanity, neither of them could take anymore temptation.

Even then, Michael refused to succumb to his need. Enjoying her pleasure more than his own, he kept on teasing her, this time kissing her most private place, softly, insistently, holding her down with strong hands while she moaned and shuddered in ecstasy. Michael shared Veronica's delight in her mind, shaken by the intensity of his own feelings and physical sensations. Never had he felt so attuned to anyone, so sensitive, so vulnerable and yet so strong.

"Did I ever tell you how much I love you?" he whispered in her ear, nibbling it, preparing to enter her as he knew she wanted him to.

She seized his manhood and pulled him inside her. The contact almost caused Michael to faint with exhilaration. His heart beat hard, colors flashed in front of his eyes. Veronica's perfume, the sound of her cries, the softness of her skin, the love in her mind overwhelmed him.

Finally, unleashing the wildest instincts he never knew he had, he rode her with surprising fierceness. To his amazement, Veronica shared in his furious assault, enjoying it, urging him on. When the intensity reached the paroxysm, they both released their energy at the same time, in great tremors of shuddering sounds, colors and vibrations, followed by a great peace.

"Wow!" Michael commented.

Veronica smiled. "I know... I hope we never get used to it." She kissed him gently. "It took me a while to understand my new body. You remember when I met you in the cave, before the fight with Krastinios?"

Fragments of memories flowed back slowly. "But it was a dream, wasn't it?"

"No, it wasn't. My body felt so vibrant, even my enhanced brain could barely control it."

"New body? Enhanced brain? What are you talking about?"

"I'm talking about the two replicas in the embryonic tanks. Don't you remember, the future Adam and Eve?" Veronica seemed amused at his surprise.

"What? The improved specimens of you and me, built to last for millions of years?" Michael's mind reeled with the possibilities.

"Exactly. Made for each other, unable to think a negative thought... Well, they've been put to a better use."

"I'll be damned! This dad of mine is full of surprises."

"Wait till you see your mom... She's magnificent. They make such a handsome couple."

"Oh Lord, where does it stop?" Michael still didn't dare to believe. "What's the catch?"

"What do you mean?"

"When something sounds too good to be true, it usually is. So what's the catch?"

"I guess you could consider being stuck together for all eternity some kind of a catch."

Vijaya Schartz

Michael laughed, for this was the part he liked best.

But Veronica went on. "Another thing is, Amrah has plans for you. I think he needs you to travel with him. This means you'll have to leave Jennifer behind, at least for a while."

"I see..." A shadow passed over Michael's mind. This would be the hardest part. "Better be important, but coming from Amrah, I'm sure it is..." Michael reflected in silence then shook his head to dispel the uncomfortable thoughts. "Still sounds better than death." Suddenly remembering, he asked, "Is the battle over?"

At that moment, the door slid open. Amrah entered, answering the question meant for Veronica. "Over for now. Upon the death of their Warlord, the lead vessel exploded mysteriously. Our shields deflected their blows long enough. We destroyed many of their fighters. Losing their leader shattered their fighting spirit. They did not put up much of a fight after that. When the mother ship exploded, they turned back." The Blue Angel smiled.

Michael wondered how the gentle soul had coped with warfare but didn't ask.

Suddenly grave, Amrah added, "Lucky for us. We sustained many losses and severe damage during the battle and could not have held on much longer. It will take weeks to get the ship space-worthy."

"The Reptilians ran when they could have won?"

Amrah remained serious. "They didn't know that. But they will come back, believe me, Son. And next time they will be prepared. I need you to help hunt them down, find where they hide before they plan a new attack. With your wild instincts you could figure them out. I need an Archangel on my side. What do you say?"

"An Archangel?"

"Yes, Michael. Do you think this name was given to you by chance?"

"God damn you, old blue goat! Not anymore I don't. Do I have a choice?"

"You are absolutely free, Michael. You can go back down there if you choose."

"And do what? Help Dave build his house, dodge the police, struggle in the hell I created for myself? I wouldn't enjoy it anymore. Jennifer's my only reason to stay, but she doesn't seem to need me as much, now that she found her mother. Soon she'll grow-up and make her own life... It'll be hard to watch over her from afar, but you win, old man. I'm game."

"In about forty days, we will be ready to leave orbit. Is it enough time to settle your affairs on the planet?"

"It'll have to do, I guess."

* * *

Michael's first visit took him to a green hospital room in Washington D.C. In the middle of the night the hallways remained relatively quiet. The air smelled of rubbing alcohol and disinfectant. Looking with compassion over Debbie's emaciated body lying between the white sheets, Michael remembered how

Vijaya Schartz

she had labored for his cause with selfless abandon. He smiled, letting his heart go out to her.

The monitors attested to a faint heartbeat. Under the oxygen mask, Michael could see the bruises around the eyes. Probing Debbie's mind he realized that she was unconscious and heavily sedated. She did acknowledge him, though, in a dream. Her spirit embraced him with enthusiasm when he told her what he had come to do.

A nurse poked her head through the doorway. Michael waved, smiling, then closed the door as soon as she had passed. Approaching Debbie's bed, he disconnected the network of tubes and intravenous lines, took off the oxygen mask and admired his handiwork. Debbie slept peacefully.

Satisfied, he dimmed the lights before vanishing into thin air.

When Debbie opened her eyes, she felt weak, but the pain was gone. She could see the white sheets of the bed. She knew she was in the hospital, but she did not remember getting there. How long had it been?

She only remembered a dream. She saw Michael who told her that she was cured. Soon Debbie would go home and lead a normal life. And he had wished her happiness with Walter. Now, the pain was gone... She was hungry.

As her eyes adjusted to the faint morning light, she saw Walter enter the room in a blue suit, staring in disbelief.

"Good morning, darling," Walter exclaimed. "You look much better today... Your color has returned. The bruises are gone. How do you feel? The nurse told me you had a visitor late last night, after I left. A handsome guy too. Should I be jealous?" Ever solicitous, Walter sounded especially cheerful.

After days of numbness, pain, and silence, Debbie felt like talking again. "I'm hungry," she enunciated through a dry mouth.

"Nurse!" Walter called out in his excitement, beaming with hope. "She's awake... She talked... And she's hungry!"

The heavyset nurse came in and gawked, incredulous.

"What's the matter?" Debbie's speech improved by the second, "I'm hungry, that's all. Could I have some breakfast? I'm starved."

"Sure, I'll get you something." The nurse disappeared through the door.

"You'd think I came back from the dead or something," Debbie joked, but Walter's expression made her wonder.

"Well, to tell the truth, your physician didn't think you'd wake up this time."

"Really? I don't understand, I feel great. Ever since I saw Michael..."

"Michael? My God, you don't know about that either."

"About Michael? What about him? You know what, I thought I had a dream, but when I think of it, he was the visitor I had last night."

"Debbie, I don't know how to tell you this, but Michael..."

The nurse came in with a tray, helped Debbie to sit up with great care, and lifted the lid off the plate.

Vijaya Schartz

Debbie smelled the eggs then stopped and looked at the nurse. "Were you here all night?"

The nurse nodded. "Yes, I was. My shift ends in half an hour."

"Did you see my visitor?" Debbie turned to Walter. "In your wallet there's a picture of us with Michael at the studio. Show it to her..."

"But, darling, I'm trying to tell you that..."

"Please, Walter..."

Walter shrugged, searched his wallet and found the picture. He gazed at it for a second then handed it to the nurse.

She took it and after one glance said, "Yes, that's him, that's the young man I saw last night. I wish all visitors were as nice as him. You've got good friends, Miss. God knows you deserve them. Do you need anything else?"

"No, thanks." Debbie attacked her breakfast.

"But that's impossible..." Walter mumbled, scratching his head. "Becky told me he was..."

"He was what?"

"Nothing... If he was here last night, then he's alive." Walter stared at Debbie, who ate with a healthy appetite. "It's a pleasure to see you so energetic. I was scared. I thought I'd lost you these past three days."

"It's a comfort to know you're watching over me. I love you, Walter. Get me out of here and I'll prove it. I feel fine today." She stretched and smiled, pushing away the tray with the empty plate.

"I don't know if this is the right time, Debbie, but I can't think of leaving you without asking."

"What?" she asked, alarmed by his seriousness.

"Since it looks like you made it this time..." He looked at her with tears in his eyes. "Debbie..." He hesitated. "Will you marry me? Please say yes."

She gaped at him then felt her face blush with excitement. "Walter," she stumbled on the words. "Yes, of course I want to marry you, especially now..."

Walter held her hand, but she pulled him into a healthy hug. He laughed in her ear. "I see your strength is back too," he humored. "I wish I could stay longer, but I have to be on the set."

"All right, but come back as soon as you can. I miss you already."

Walter kissed her lips softly, and Debbie kissed him back with wild fire.

After Walter left, Debbie sank into the pillows. She could not stop smiling. Somehow, she believed that Michael had done it. She was cured. She felt re-generated, as if the cancer had died in her and only healthy cells remained.

Grateful, she watched the sun rise above the city. She wondered if the purity of the air was due to her state of mind or to the enforcement of the new, clean-gasoline regulations. Could there be a better time to be alive and well?

* * *

In a convalescent home in Little Rock, Arkansas, an old man, paralyzed by a stroke, had a vision. The name on his bed said Robert Tanner. In his dream, he had a visitor, a young man who looked like Maria's boy. Robert had never liked that boy, a smart ass, too proud for his own good. The kid was scared

Vijaya Schartz

of him but would never admit it, no matter what. In the dream, however, the boy offered apologies, peace, and forgiveness. He offered something else, health, that's what he said. The boy could give him his health back, if he promised never to hurt a living soul again.

Robert Tanner was too proud to accept any favors or make any such promises. So, he refused. He still didn't like the boy and did not want anything from him anyway. Curiously, the young man had looked sad as he wiped the drool off the corner of Robert's mouth and said he'd be back. Robert hoped he wouldn't. Maria's boy made him uncomfortable.

* * *

Michael materialized under the big oak tree on the front lawn of Dave's farm and called, "Jen!"

"Daddy! I knew you'd come, like you told me in my head." Jennifer climbed down from the lowest fork where she sat and rushed into her father's arms. "They think you're dead. I thought you were too, for a few days. But when I felt you in my mind, I told the others. They didn't believed me..." She stopped talking for a moment. As if noticing something unusual, she asked, "Are you okay, Dad? You look different. You're not saying anything."

Michael let Jennifer down gently and gazed into her eyes. "Nothing escapes you, does it?" He took his time before going on. "See, sweetheart, I really was dead... But I'm alive now. Amrah gave me this new body that can live forever, but it's still me, your dad, inside." He sat down in the grass, letting her digest the information.

"But you're okay?" She sat across from him.

"Better than ever. I'll stay with you for a little while, but in a few weeks I'll have to go with Amrah, far away. I'll be gone a long time... But I'll be back, I promise."

Jennifer was silent for a while, staring at the grass. Michael observed the process in her mind, feeling the pain and the disappointment she did not want to show. She raised her big green eyes full of resignation. "You really have to go? How long?" Her voice choked with repressed emotions.

"A few months, a few years, as long as it takes to eliminate the threat of the likes of Lufriec and Krastinios. It needs to be done, Jen, or this planet will never be safe."

"I know." She lowered her head in resignation.

Unable to withstand his daughter's pain, Michael entered her mind. *I'm not abandoning you, Jen. I'll be with you all the time. You can contact my mind whenever you like. I'll be there for you whenever you need me. Think, you'll have me around as long as you live and you won't have to take care of me in my old age. I'll still be here to take care of you.*

She raised her head and smiled. In that instant, Michael took away the pain, the disappointment and the grief. He would carry it for both of them.

She sounded happy as she said, "Cool! I'll be grown up when you see me again. Mom likes having me around. She'll be glad to keep me."

"I'll miss you, Jen." He took her hand.

"I'll miss you too, Daddy. But I know you are alive, and I know you'll come back."

"That I will. Can I get a hug?" He rose,

Vijaya Schartz

scooped her in his arms, and held her tight. Soon she wiggled and he let her down. "It seems to me that you have developed some new mental abilities in this very short time. You'll need some training, kid. These forty days are going to be very busy."

"Please, Dad, don't call me kid, I'm not a kid anymore."

Michael laughed at her seriousness. "All right, Miss, come with me. Let's teach the grown-ups to believe in ghosts."

Father and daughter walked side by side through the grass, toward the only building left standing on Dave's farm, the naked frame of the new house. Several cars were parked in front, Dave's blue pickup truck among less familiar vehicles. At the very end of the row, Michael's motorcycle stood alone. The debris of the old barn and the remains of the trailer had already been cleared up. The surviving pigs had been penned outside, and the chickens ran wild everywhere.

Michael and Jennifer approached the group of men bent over a set of blue prints. "Hi there, Dave, need a hand to build that big house of yours?"

The men stopped talking and looked at the newcomer. Dave dropped his tape measure and stared, white as a sheet. "My God... I must be tired, I'm seeing things."

"No, you're not dreaming, little brother, I figured you'd need some help, and I'm free for the next few weeks. What do you say?"

"But I thought you were..."

"I was. I just came back. I'll tell you about it later. For now, there's a job to do. Let's hurry, I haven't much time." Michael casually picked up his brother's tape measure from the ground and handed it to him. "You'll need that, little brother." He patted Dave on the shoulder.

* * *

"Why didn't you just make a miracle, rather than work hard when you didn't have to?" Dave asked one day, towards the end of Michael's stay. The house had much advanced by then.

"Building a house makes for good memories," Michael answered. "We're forging bonds that only hard work can seal. We don't value things given as much as things earned. Besides, It may be a long time before I build another house, and I do enjoy the work."

During that happy time, Jennifer often disappeared for several hours at a time. Only Michael knew that she was with Amrah, getting trained to control the powers recently awakened in her.

"I wish we could always be like this," Jennifer told Michael on their last night together, sitting under the big oak tree, watching the stars.

"It will happen again, Jen, but not for a while. Eternal life comes with obligations. Always remember that we'll never be apart. You can reach me anytime. Don't be afraid to contact me. I'll check on you as often as I can."

"I know. Still, it's not the same. Why don't you take me with you?"

"I can't this time, sweetheart. Next time, maybe."

Vijaya Schartz

The next morning, near the big oak tree, Michael, Veronica, and Maria said their goodbyes. With moist eyes, they hugged and kissed and promised to come back. Dave, Becky and Clara huddled together on one side while on the other side, Jean-Marc held Shadow the cat, and Jennifer squeezed Tori's hand. They stared, holding on to each other.

When Michael looked into Jennifer's eyes, the young girl's sadness vanished. She seemed transfixed with love and understanding. The tear that came to her eye expressed indefinable joy and pride.

The three immortals waved, ascending along a wide shaft of blue light, then disappeared from sight into the morning sky.

And in the light of day, the untrained eye did not see the spacecraft move slowly from behind the moon and set a course for a distant star, but Jennifer followed it a long time, knowing that some day, she would accompany her father on the long journey to her grandfather's home world.

Archangel Checkmate

Vijaya Schartz

In the cold shadows of space,
a Nefarious Lord awakens,
seeking revenge against the Earthling
who scattered his remains
at the edge of the universe.
Michael, who has since become
a full-fledged Archangel
on his father's home world,
must return to Earth to protect his
planet and his teen-age daughter
from Reptilian enslavement
and extinction.
But the way home is fraught
with dangers,
some more insidious than others,
and nothing prepared Michael
for the kind of trial
he must now face...

Order today
the next adventures of
Michael Tanner

Archangel Checkmate

From Blue Planet books
Using this coupon
Write your comments about
Archangel Crusader
On the last page

ORDER FORM

* * *

Books also make thoughtful gifts!

TOTAL

**Ashes For the
Elephant God** _____copies at $17.95 $________

_____E-books at $10.00 $________

**Archangel
Crusader** _____copies at $18.95 $________

_____E-books at $10.00 $________

**Archangel
Checkmate** _____copies at $19.95 $________

_____E-books at $10.00 $________

Shipping and handling:
$2.00 per book - $1.00 per pdf diskette $________

TOTAL ENCLOSED…$________

Mail this form with your check or money order to:
Blue Planet Books
4619 W. McRae Way
Glendale, AZ 85308

NAME _________________________________

Address_________________________________

__________________ Ste or Apt #_______________

City________________ State______ Zip_________

Dear Reader:

I hope you enjoyed **Archangel Crusader**. *If you did, please take a few minutes to share your thoughts with me. Your comments are appreciated. You may tear out this page and mail it to my attention at Blue Planet Books, or send me a direct e-mail.*

Sincerely,
Vijaya Schartz

____

____

____

____

____

____

If you would like to be notified when future novels from the same author are published, please fill out the form below:

NAME ____

Address ____

City ___________________ State _______ Zip ________________

Mail to: BLUE PLANET BOOKS INC.
                4619 W. McRae Way
                Glendale, AZ 85308

Or e-mail the author directly:
                vijaya@vijayaschartz.com